MY SINFUL LONGING

BOOK THREE IN THE SINFUL MEN SERIES

LAUREN BLAKELY

ABOUT

A sexy, emotional, suspenseful romance novel from #1 New York Times Bestselling author Lauren Blakely...

Some women are just off-limits.

But that doesn't stop me from wanting Elle Mariano. She's clever, big-hearted and the sexiest woman I've ever met.

The thing is, she's fighting the demons of her past and do I ever know how hard those are to battle.

So I try my best to be her shoulder to lean on. Until the night we combust. And one night turns into hot, dirty days, and secret trysts.

If it all sounds too good to be true, it is. Because once I learn the secret she's keeping from me, my entire family's future turns riskier than I ever imagined.

Especially since the bastards who tried to tear my family apart years ago are tailing both of us now. Our every move...

AUTHOR'S NOTE

The events at the start of *My Sinful Longing* take place concurrently with the events at the end of *My Sinful Desire*. The overlapping timeline will give you a more detailed view into how the events transpired, all while taking you on a new couple's romantic journey. Enjoy!

MY SINFUL LONGING

By Lauren Blakely

To be the first to find out when all of my upcoming books go live click here!

PRO TIP: Add lauren@laurenblakely.com to your contacts before signing up to make sure the emails go to your inbox!

Did you know this book is also available in audio and paperback on all major retailers? Go to my website for links!

This is an emotional, suspenseful series, with high-stakes action and consequences. For content warnings go to my web site.

HIS PROLOGUE

I don't claim to be an expert on anything, but life has taught me one hard and fast truth: the moments that change you may take you by surprise.

All the big moments in my life started out as average, ordinary days. Days where I ate my cereal, drank my coffee, and left home. But by the time day turned to night, the earth under my feet had shifted seismically. My place in the world had shattered, my outlook had boomeranged.

I'd counted two days like that so far in my life—the day my father was killed, and the day I decided to get sober.

Little did I know a year ago when I walked into the community center in a beaten-down neighborhood, ready to walk the walk and talk the talk, that that day would be another one of those moments.

One I never forgot.

Because it *was* the start of a new story, the kind that goes like this: *So, there was this woman . . .*

When I walked into her office to introduce myself, I figured I'd say hello, let her know who I was, tell her I believed in the center's mission. I would be polite, professional, and then I'd be on my way.

I didn't believe in love at first sight. I didn't believe in much of anything but family, hard work, and to never bet against the house in Vegas. But when I saw Elle Mariano, her hair pinned up to reveal sparrows inked across her neck, standing at the window watering a tiny succulent plant in a pink terra-cotta pot, I was caught.

Hook, line, and sinker.

It wasn't love.

But it was something powerful nonetheless.

It was instant longing.

She spun around, smiled, and spoke first. "Oh, hey. You must be our newest donor. I'm Elle, and this is Louis Armstrong," she said, introducing me to herself and the plant.

That.

The woman named her plant.

And I was a goner. She was gorgeous, warm, and so damn easy to talk to. All of that was obvious in those first three seconds.

Seismically obvious.

My lips curved into a grin as I answered her. "Colin Sloan, donor and volunteer. Nice to meet you and Louis. What a wonderful world indeed," I said.

She set down the green watering tin, some vintage metal thing that looked like she'd picked it up on Etsy. Walking over to me, she extended a hand, and we shook.

The smile she flashed next—it reeled me in.

Trouble was, I knew better than to mix business with pleasure. And she—well, she had her own reasons to draw all sorts of lines, as I'd learn much later.

That didn't stop me from wanting her though. Nothing

could, not even the friendship we developed over the next year.

That was how it went with the moments that changed your life.

You were powerless to stop them.

It was what you did *next* that mattered.

But with Elle, I wouldn't have stopped anything.

Not even how that friendship would upend my neat, organized life, rocketing it into another moment that would change my life forever.

HER PROLOGUE

Friend.

It's one of those words that's designed to make you happy.

Like chocolate and soft blankets and long, lazy afternoons in the sun.

Friendship is one of the greatest things in life. I was lucky to have lots of good friends, from my sister to the women on my roller derby team to the people I worked with. I was lucky, too, to count my family among that number. My mom. Even my son at times was like a friend.

But . . .

There's always a *but.*

Every now and then, that word can be a double-edged sword. Sharp and dangerous.

Like when there's a guy you maybe, possibly, might want to be more than friends with.

But in the immortal words of social networking, *it's complicated.*

The day I met Colin Sloan a year ago, the afternoon sun streaming through the window as I watered one of my "crooners," I had an inkling that he might not be like any other donor to the community center.

And I didn't think he'd be like any other volunteer either.

It wasn't his tattoos, though I do love me some ink.

It wasn't his stubble either, but oh yeah, the kind of scruff he rocked was a fave of mine.

It was his eyes.

They gave everything away.

His deep, soulful brown eyes showed me his heart. They revealed him. Those eyes told me instantly that we were a lot alike. He'd been to hell and back. And damn, if I didn't know the route to that place too. I'd traveled it without a map. Could find my way in the dark whether I wanted to or not.

His eyes locked with mine, and we sparked. I felt a sizzle that was more than physical. It was a connection. An understanding. And a longing too.

From that first day, I sensed we had the potential to become so much more. My heart dreamed of *more*.

But in my head, I knew we'd be better off as friends. Because I couldn't risk a relationship. Not after what happened last time. Even though Colin and I never said it out loud, even though we never made an agreement, I knew we had to be friends and only friends.

And that was what we were for the next year, until the night everything changed.

But the physical wasn't what made us so complicated.

The physical was easy. The problem was everything else.

It was all the people I never saw coming.

And the choices I'd have to make.

PROLOGUE

Marcus

Present Day

I'd done it.

I'd told them.

The words I'd practiced for months had made landfall mere seconds ago.

My name is Marcus. I was born seventeen years ago at the Stella McLaren Federal Women's Correctional Center. My mother is Dora Prince. I'm your brother. And my father is Luke Carlton.

Now, as I stood on the street with Colin and Ryan, my half-brothers, adrenaline surged through me.

Excitement too, and that was a brand-new feeling. One I hadn't expected in this moment in front of Ryan's home, where I'd tracked them down. In fact, it hadn't occurred to me that I would feel so . . . jazzed.

Unburdened? Yes.

Relieved? God, yes.

But thrilled? That wasn't in my practice tool kit, and Lord knew I'd practiced. I'd absolutely practiced what to say. You didn't walk up to the family you'd never known, reveal who you were, and say *ta-da* without a ton of rehearsal.

Now I was waiting for their reaction. I didn't know what to expect, but I hadn't done this for their response. I'd done it for me. Because I'd needed to.

And the person who'd helped me most to get to this place was Elle.

I was so damn glad I'd walked into her office a few weeks ago. Without her, I'd never have found the guts.

1

ELLE

A few weeks ago

Resist.

That was what I told myself every time I'd seen Colin Sloan in the last year.

On the basketball court. At picnics. During events. In the tutoring rooms. At the vending machines. Everywhere.

That was what I told myself *today* when I spotted him turning the corner in the hallway at the community center.

Looking all broody and sexy and ridiculously charming as he walked toward me. That grin, that smile, all kinds of crooked charm. I could live off the high that smile gave me.

He was as tempting as he'd been the day he strode in here a year ago, having just plunked down a big donation to the center, and introduced himself to me. The donor who also volunteered. That was a rare combination and a whole lot of heart.

Colin smiled as I tucked the mountains of folders tighter under my arm. So much paperwork to finish before the benefit this weekend. But I would never complain, because one of the city's leading philanthropists was hosting a huge fundraiser for the center. I'd fill out paperwork all night and day if I had to.

"Need a forklift for those?"

"Do you have one?"

He hooked his thumb in the direction of the parking lot. "Absolutely. Want me to bring it in now?"

"Oh sure. Let me just go open the back door," I said, deadpan.

"Excellent. I'll put on my hard hat." He took a beat. "I'd ask if you need help, but I feel like you'd roll your eyes and say no."

I rolled my eyes, slowing my pace as I reached him. He'd offered to help me carry my papers a few times, but I'd always declined. Do it yourself—that was my motto. "Don't you worry about me and my papers. I consider them bicep curls." I demonstrated with the folders, curling them like weights. "And triceps too."

"No need for a gym membership, then," he said, rubbing his palms together. "And on that note, I have exciting news for you."

"You had the net fixed on the basketball court?" I asked.

"Please. That was done last week."

"I know," I said with a smile. "And I am damn grateful."

"This is bigger." He drew in a deep breath, as if prepping to say something important. "Did you know there's a new flavor of potato chips at Trader Joe's? I know you and Alex are big fans."

"My kiddo and I do indeed worship at the altar of potato chips. But I'm going to need more details. What is this new flavor?" My fourteen-year-old son and I were dedicated connoisseurs, lovers of the strangest flavors. Lime, avocado, pepper—bring them on.

"Pickle," he declared.

I arched a skeptical brow. "I don't believe you."

"I'll prove it."

I pretended to hunt behind him, looking to one side, then the other. "Got a bag of chips there behind your back?"

He pointed to the doors, and presumably beyond to the parking lot. "No, but I have access to a car, and the GPS that'll take us to the store. I can show you in an hour, o ye of little faith," he said, a playful tone in his voice.

I was off in an hour. I looked at my watch, considering his offer of a chip mission. That fit with our world order—friendship. "I could go, but I need to stop by the library after work. A book I reserved is in, and I've been dying to read it," I said.

"Let me guess. Dragons, shape-shifters, swords, and battles?"

I pretended to be offended. "Way to pigeonhole me."

"Nah, you just have good taste. By the way, did you try that one I mentioned?" he asked.

"Yes, I started it, and it kept me up late on Sunday night. Too late. So thanks a lot for making me yawn through a board meeting on Monday."

He shrugged, a cocky glint in his eyes. "I'd say I'm sorry, but one should never apologize for recommending good books."

I laughed and tapped his shoulder with my free hand. Because, well, because it was there. "Words to live by." I eyed the stack of papers in my arm. "I need to chat with my donations manager. See you in an hour."

"Perfect," he said. "And I'll give you a ride home."

"How did you know I didn't bring my car today?" My mom had needed to borrow mine, so I snagged a ride from a friend. I'd planned to take the bus back, but I'd happily ride with Colin.

Colin shrugged. "Lucky guess. Or maybe I was just hopeful." He gestured to the basketball courts. "Now, stop trying to distract me from my shift. I have basketball games to coach."

Laughing, I shook my head. "Who was distracting who? Mr. Potato Chip Tempter."

He winked. "Potato chips. Swords. Battles. Books. See you in an hour."

He took off, and a few times during the meeting, I snuck glances at the basketball courts. Watched as he tugged off his shirt, tossed it on the bench, and shot hoops with the teenage boys.

Those boys needed a place like this center.

And they needed a man like Colin to look up to. Someone who cared, someone who'd changed his life for the better, like the tattoos on his body alluded to. Ink I admired for so many reasons.

But me?

No. I didn't need a man. Didn't want a man. Men had brought nothing but trouble into my life. Men were off-limits.

I'd put Colin in the friend camp for a good reason. I'd needed a friend. He'd become one. A terrific friend.

Fine, sometimes I thought about what it would be like to be more than friends with the man.

But those were only thoughts. I didn't act on them.

When the meeting ended early, I returned to my office to find one of the boys waiting for me.

Marcus, with his dark eyes, curious heart, and soft-spoken voice. "Hey, Marcus. What's going on?" I asked.

He cleared his throat. "Do you have a second?"

"Of course. I'm always up for talking to you," I said with

a smile as I walked into my office with the teenager close behind.

Marcus had started coming around the center a few months ago when he'd graduated from high school and moved out of his family's house. He'd been a quiet one at first, but lately he'd been opening up more. He'd been raised by his father and stepmother—his biological mother was out of the picture.

Once inside, he scratched his jaw, looking around. "So, listen, it's about my mom. My biological mom."

Shutting the door, I sat, motioning for him to join me. This didn't seem like the start of an ordinary conversation. "Sure. What's happening there?"

"I don't know if I've told you this before, but she has other children," he said, taking a deep breath.

Definitely not a regular chat. "I didn't know that," I said evenly. "Do you know them?" I waited for him, trying to read his expression.

"No, but I want to."

"And why's that?"

I wasn't sure he was going to answer.

That was okay. One thing I'd learned with this job was that patience was more than a virtue.

It was a necessity.

2

MARCUS

I heaved a sigh, dragging a hand through my hair.

How could I begin to explain why I wanted to talk to my siblings?

Because I'd felt like a part of me was missing for some time? Because I'd felt like something inside me was absent? Not empty, just borrowed.

On loan from someone else.

Someone, or many someones, and I wanted to know who they were once and for all.

But how did I just say all that *out loud*?

That having a parent in prison sure as hell made me feel like something was off.

That I'd never truly felt like a part of the family with my dad, my stepmom, and their kids.

I'd always felt like something was missing.

And I finally knew what it was—this huge other part of me.

The other halves. The four unknown halves in the form of the Sloans. We shared blood, but would that be enough?

Would they even want to hear from me?

I had no idea, but now that I was nearly eighteen, I felt compelled to get to know them.

I couldn't share my desire with my father for so many reasons.

I didn't even really know how to share it with Elle. So I didn't quite reply. Instead, I repeated myself. "I want to." Then I gestured to one of her plants, sidestepping the issue entirely. "Ella looks thirsty," I said.

"She's going to cry herself a river soon," Elle said, a little wry.

Frowning, I sat there, not knowing what she meant.

"It's a song. One of Ella's most famous ones," she explained. Then, with a piercing look, she said, "Please tell me you know the plant is named for Ella Fitzgerald."

"I know that much. But her music? C'mon. You know I don't know those oldies from another century," I said, smirking.

She dropped her head in her hand. "Kids today. You're killing me." When she raised her face, I asked her about Ella and Louis.

We chatted about music instead, and maybe that was what I needed. Just someone to listen.

When I rose to leave her office, I made sure that Colin wasn't around. And I promised myself that soon I'd tell her more.

3

ELLE

After I saw Marcus, I gathered my purse and my phone, sent a couple of texts, and met Colin in the parking lot. Once outside, I narrowed in on my Colin mission—the book and the chips.

He waited at his Audi, wearing aviator shades and a grin the size of the Hoover Dam. What was it about aviator shades? They just made a man look . . . devastatingly sexy.

Be good.

Be strong.

You can do this.

Those were the mantras I'd practice before we spent time together.

They'd served me well.

And they did now when I walked up to him, eyed his wheels sharply, and said with all kinds of sass, "That is not your forklift."

"True, but we can pretend it is if that makes you feel better."

"If we're playing pretend, can it be a tractor?"

He laughed, shoved a hand through his hair, and

wandered around to the passenger side. "Your John Deere chariot awaits."

"Why, thank you," I said, sliding into his car.

As he returned to the driver's seat and got in, I tugged on the seat belt. For a second, it stuck, doing that annoying thing seat belts do. Colin leaned in. "My tractor belt is pesky sometimes." He reached for it and gave a few strong tugs, his arm wickedly close to my chest.

My breath hitched as he pulled, and I repeated more mantras.

A second later, he'd loosened it, then he clicked the belt in place and shot me a look out of the corner of his eye. "I should warn you, this bad boy doesn't go over twenty. We'll have to take the back roads."

"Can we play chicken, though, if we run into anyone we know?" I asked.

Laughing, he nodded as he started the engine. "Of course we can play chicken."

And of course we did nothing of the sort. He turned on the radio, asking if I wanted pop, old standards, sports talk, or news.

I opted for news, and as we listened, we chatted about the events of the day, tossing ideas back and forth regarding an environmental story.

A few minutes later, we arrived at the library and popped inside. I grabbed my book from the reserve desk, noticing a zombie tale earmarked for another patron.

"I have an idea," I whispered, and ushered Colin along with me as I made my way to the horror section, hunting for more zombie books for my teenage son, who loved all things undead. I stopped in my tracks when I spotted a row of them.

Colin stopped right behind me. Nearer than I expected. So near I could feel his breath. The library was quiet, as it should be, and an unexpected wave of goosebumps swept over my arms. I reached out for the books, grabbing one.

"In the mood for something scary?" he asked.

"Not for me. For Alex," I whispered.

"Ah, bet he'll love *that one*." He pointed to a book, and that move put his arm even closer to me. He reached past me and tapped the book till it fell out in his hand.

"I bet he will too," I said, trying to focus on the conversation, but with Colin in my space, I caught a hint of his soap, and it occurred to me that he'd showered after coaching basketball.

My mouth watered as my brain inconveniently assembled a series of filthy images of Colin showering.

Not helpful. So not helpful.

Zombies. I'd focus on zombies. Brains. Guts. Gore.

That'd have to do the trick.

But my mind was on a dirty loop. My head swam with enticing thoughts.

"By the way, that benefit this weekend," he said offhand. "Any chance I can convince you to save a dance for me?"

My breath escaped my lungs, and now the images flitting through my mind were of bodies swaying, hands on shoulders and waists, and the delirious possibility that came from dancing.

I'd been the queen of high school dances once upon a time.

I ought to stay far away from dances now.

But I'd be at the benefit that weekend anyway, since the event was a fundraiser for the center.

What harm would one dance do to my resolve?

None.

That was the answer.

A dance was a dance was a dance.

"You're on the dance card," I said, but as soon as those

words came out, I realized I wanted more than a dance. I wanted *time*. "Let's hang out there."

"Yes, let's *hang out*." It sounded tongue-in-cheek, maybe a little flirty. I didn't try to correct him. It didn't need correcting.

Maybe a dance would get him out of my system. Maybe hanging out would too. I turned slightly, meeting his gaze. He was still inches from me. As if he didn't want to move either. I certainly didn't. The heat radiating from him was tempting.

So tempting I had to stop thinking of dances and focus instead on pickle potato chips.

"Let's get those chips," I said, my voice a little wobbly.

Then we left, stopped at Trader Joe's, and picked up a bag of pickle chips.

When I reached my house, I left dances and hanging out behind and focused on the number one priority in my life—being a mom.

Alex lounged on the couch, playing a game on his phone.

"Hey you! Did you just get home?"

"A few minutes ago. The bus dropped me off," he said, setting his phone down.

"Good day at gamer camp?"

"The best."

"I snagged this for you," I said showing him the zombie book Colin had picked for him.

"You rock," he said, and *that brief exchange*—his words— was all I'd ever need. There had been a time when I wasn't sure I'd ever hear them again.

* * *

Later that night, when I was the only one awake, I dipped my hand into the bag of chips, turning the pages in my new book, reading about battles and munching on chips till well past midnight.

Afterward, I thought of Colin under the covers.

He's a friend, he's a friend, he's a friend.

That was how I would see him this weekend, too, at the event. I didn't have room in my complicated life for anything more.

I'd shut the door on *more*, and I had no intentions of opening it again. All the troubles that came with men would stay on the other side, thank you very much.

4

COLIN

The Night of the Community Center Beethoven Concert Benefit
. . .

The sparrows were a treasure map, weaving a path from her right shoulder blade, along her sexy, elegant neck, then curving into her hair. Rich chestnut hair I longed to have my hands in.

Preferably tonight.

Because . . . well, why the hell not? We'd spent the last year building this friendship. Maybe it was finally time to see what else we could be.

After all, Elle was in a good mood as we wandered through the crowd in The Venetian Ballroom, *hanging out*, as we'd agreed to do. No surprise about the mood—the haul tonight for the center had been terrific so far, and now Elle was waiting on the final number.

Looked like it might be coming any second, since Sophie click-clacked her way across the floor, her eyes fixed on Elle. When the woman who'd organized the fundraiser reached us, she said, "I have amazing news."

"Tell me," Elle said, nearly bouncing on her toes.

"This is how much we raised tonight." Sophie slipped Elle a piece of paper. With trembling fingers, Elle flipped open the folded piece, then gasped, covering her mouth with her hand. Her eyes welled with tears, and my heart thumped, hammering hard against my chest. I was so damn happy for her.

Elle threw her arms around Sophie. "You did this. You made it possible," Elle said, her voice breaking.

Sophie shook her head deferentially. "Oh, sweetie. You did. You run an amazing center. You're doing incredible things. People simply want to help."

A lone tear streaked down Elle's cheek as she broke the embrace. "Nothing is simple about what you do. Thank you. We can do so much with this."

Sophie grabbed Elle's hands, squeezing them. "You'll do good." Then she turned to me. "And thank you for being a part of making this possible."

"It's my pleasure," I said, thrilled that my venture capital firm had contributed to tonight's fundraising.

"And now I need to go mingle," Sophie added.

"Go, mingle," I said, then whispered, "And say hi to Ryan for me."

She laughed it off. "Say hi to your brother yourself."

Sophie headed off, perhaps to find my brother after all, since they were an item. But I wasn't thinking of the two of them when I returned my focus to the woman with me.

I was only thinking of *my friend.*

Maybe tonight we'd become more.

Especially since she launched herself at me, wrapping her arms around me now in a triumphant hug, exhaling big sighs of relief.

"Whoa," I said, not expecting the force of her embrace.

"Sorry. I'm just so happy."

"No apologies necessary," I said, clasping her tighter. I was not going to let her go.

She laughed, a buoyant sound, like bells. "I can't believe this happened," she said, breathless. "It feels like a dream."

"I didn't doubt it for a second. We're all behind you," I said, stealing a quick inhalation of the vanilla-honey scent of her hair.

She broke the embrace, but not the contact. She parked her hands on my shoulders, her fingers curling into my suit jacket. Her hazel eyes shone with happiness and the hint of more joyful tears. "I know, and I'm so grateful. But you just don't know till it happens if you're going to raise enough money, and I've been working on this project for two years. Two solid years to finally get the funds to expand the center. It needs it so badly. I felt like I'd been holding my breath for the last month, hoping we'd hit our number. I have so many plans."

"And now you can take a breath because you made it happen," I said, beaming. She'd been driven in her mission to rebuild the broken-down community center.

She wiped her fingertip under her eye, erasing the evidence of that tear. "Colin," she whispered, as if we had a secret, "we have to celebrate tonight."

I could think of a few ways.

Unknotting that hair.

Roping my fingers through it.

Kissing her neck till she fell apart in my arms.

"Are you angling for a little poker?" I asked, since I wasn't going to assume we shared the same idea of what constituted a celebration. No need to make an ass of me, thank you very much.

"Yes," she said, her eyes glinting.

And so it was poker.

I wasn't sure why I'd thought it would be something more.

Wait. That wasn't true. I always wanted something more. And tonight—tonight I was going to let her know. Damn straight.

It had been a year after all, and the woman was as happy as a thousand clams. What better time? Besides, I knew how to read people, and we had a vibe, a connection, a flirtation.

No time like the present to see what might come of it.

"Do you want to play? After the event?" she added in a conspiratorial tone. By no means was Elle a high roller—the baby tables, as she called them, were her idea of a good time. But she was a Vegas girl at heart and loved to gamble now and then. "I don't have much time before I need to get home, but we can finagle a few hands."

I scoffed. "What kind of question is that? Do you take me for a man who doesn't want to celebrate with you?" I was a man who knew how to sniff out an opportunity. I wasn't letting this chance, cloaked in this giddy exuberance of hers, slip away.

"Not at all. You look like a man who wants to lay down some bets," she said with a sexy arch of her eyebrow.

Did I ever want to take a chance. "The chips are on me."

"In that case, let's make big bets," she said in a flirty voice. God, I loved that tone. I ate it up.

"The biggest," I added, then gestured to the exit. "I'm ready when you are, big spender."

She tipped her head to the stage. "After the concert. I can't skip out early on an event for the center I run."

"Okay, we'll be good a little while longer." I raised a hand to brush a loose strand of that chestnut hair over her ear, watching her shiver as I touched her.

Yup. Another sign.

Tonight was it.

We returned to our seats, where she gathered up the silky material of her dress, adjusting it as she crossed her legs. "By the way," she whispered, "I want to hear more about your new tattoo."

I grinned. I'd mentioned earlier in the night that I'd acquired fresh ink, and Elle, being a tattoo aficionado too, wanted details on the new one on my hip.

"I'll tell you when we play poker."

"I can't wait."

I couldn't either.

As the opening notes of a Beethoven Concerto floated through the ballroom at The Venetian, I settled in beside the woman I'd wanted for the last year, since the first day I'd met her.

I hoped I was getting lucky tonight.

And I didn't mean in the bedroom, although I wouldn't say no to that either.

I'd settle for a kiss.

I longed for one.

5

ELLE

His hip.

I was dying to see the new tattoo on his hip. I couldn't stop wondering what it looked like.

Because . . . *his body.*

His gorgeous inked body was my kryptonite.

Except that barely covered the half of it.

He was my kryptonite.

This man I shouldn't want.

Men were dangerous. Relationships were trouble. And love didn't just break your heart. It abused it, stomped on it, wrecking it beyond recognition.

But that didn't stop my wandering thoughts. As the music played, my mind kept returning to what Colin had told me earlier about his new ink. Did this tattoo match my favorite one on him? The one I'd seen when he took off his shirt to play basketball? The simple black lotus design on his right pec—the fine lines and details, the interlocking leaves of the lotus flower. I loved the meaning of it for him —change. Life changes. Rolling with them. Embracing change was as sexy to me as a six-pack. Hell, it was hotter.

As I pictured his ink, a ribbon of heat unfurled in my chest, tracing a dangerous path from my breasts to my belly and down, down, down.

Warming me up.

Turning me on.

What the hell? I was turned on by a tattoo?

But I knew better.

It wasn't the ink.

It was the man.

Our friendship. His heart. His humor. The easy way we talked to each other. The teasing.

Everything with him was so easy.

But easy was deceptive. I knew that too well.

I closed my eyes, tried to focus on the music. Surely Beethoven never had these problems. Wanting what he couldn't have.

And I couldn't have Colin.

I'd made promises. I'd made choices. I had my own demons to face, and I was facing them by abstaining from men.

That was the problem. The *big* problem. Being with anyone would break those promises. So Colin was a line I couldn't cross. A risk I couldn't take.

With a string of not just bad, but horrific relationships in my wake, I was determined to stay the single-and-loving-it course. The one I'd finally set myself on after years of tsunami-strength trouble.

So tonight would be poker, and only poker.

He rustled in the seat next to me, inching closer as the music crested. His sexy scent drifted under my nose. He smelled so good. Like sex in an elevator.

That was not helpful, brain.

"Do you like the music?" he whispered, his lips so close to my skin. Goosebumps rose on my flesh as I blinked open my eyes.

I nodded, trying desperately to let the music guide my thoughts to a sweeter, purer shore. To let the music take me away from these primal, base notions washing over me from the dirty waves in my head.

I sneaked a peek at him, taking in the face I knew well. Strong cheekbones. Lightly stubbled jawline. Dark hair, nearly black. It looked so damn soft. Brown eyes, like chocolate. A body built by rock climbing, hiking, white-water rafting, and Ironman Triathlons.

"Yes, I like the music," I said, trying to center myself.

And music would be my strength tonight, just as it had been over the years.

I'd leaned on Billie, Ella, Louis, Frank. I'd depended on all the crooners. They'd been my great escape during the darkest times of my life.

Music was my rock. It made me strong.

Tonight, I'd need it.

I channeled all my resistance from Beethoven as the concert ended and we said our goodbyes to other guests, then made our way to the tables.

Poker—that wasn't something I needed to resist.

Poker was just plain fun.

* * *

But poker with a man you wanted?

Harder than getting a full house.

Or maybe it was harder than winning a single damn hand. Because I was losing. But Colin was ahead. He slid some green chips forward, raising the bet. A couple played next to us—a woman with curly hair and a man with a newsboy cap and graying goatee. He sighed heavily, but met Colin's bet, sliding chips in too. The woman by his side wiggled on her stool, then cooed appreciatively. "Go get 'em, honey."

I folded, then glanced at Colin. "You must have a good hand."

His eyes danced. "Or maybe I'm feeling lucky."

"Are you now?" I asked, a little sassy. Maybe because I was still on borrowed time. A few more minutes, and then I'd have to go.

As he showed his cards, the dealer gave an approving nod, indicating he'd won.

"Man, you're on some kind of a streak," the guy with the cap said, shaking his head in admiration.

Colin simply smiled. "It's a good night."

The man looked to me. "You must be his lucky charm."

I laughed, shaking my head. "Hardly."

"Oh, c'mon, sweetie," the woman said in a voice thick with gravel. She was probably a heavy smoker. "Don't deny it. A man's sweetie pie always brings good luck."

I flinched for a second at those words.

Sweetie pie.

Did we give off that vibe? I glanced at Colin, who grinned at me like we had a secret. He wiggled a brow. "Yeah, sweetie pie," he said to me, all smooth honey in his tone.

There was something in his voice. Something that said he liked the sound of that nickname.

And I liked the sound of it on his tongue.

Far too much.

6

COLIN

As far as openings go, it wasn't my first choice. But the thing about openings was you didn't get to choose them. You did, however, need to seize them if you wanted to take advantage of every opportunity.

When my eyes met Elle's, I read her in an instant.

Hers said she liked what that term suggested. That we were together. And that was all I needed.

I took my chance, sliding an arm around her waist at the poker table. Hoping she wouldn't mind. Hoping she'd like it.

"Sweetie pie," I said, all flirty and playful.

But there was nothing flirty about the way she responded. Nothing playful.

There was *only* sensuality.

Only desire.

It was electric and instant.

It came in the hitch of her breath.

In the tremble of her body.

In the flutter of her lashes.

Holy fuck.

We weren't playing around.

She was on the edge.

Elle was into this just like I was.

All the answers came in a rush. They came in the way she responded to my hand curling around her, my arm touching her back, my body sliding closer.

"On that note, I think I'd better quit while I'm ahead." I nodded to the chips, then to the couple. "They're yours. A gift."

"Whoa, thank you," the man said, and before they could shake my hand or say anything more, I whisked Elle away, my arm still around her, stealing her into a quiet corner of the casino.

With my arm still around her waist, I tucked a finger under her chin, our gazes meeting. "Hey."

"Hey," she said, so breathy, so sexy.

I ran my thumb over her jawline. "Did you feel that back there?" I asked, because there was no point in being anything but honest.

Her eyes darkened, and she swallowed roughly, then whispered, "Yes."

"Me too," I said as I touched her face. I was buzzed with desire, desperate to connect with her. "Elle. You have to know . . ."

I stopped when she shuddered, whispering my name. "Colin."

But I wanted to continue. Had to tell her. "How much I want to kiss you."

"Oh God," she gasped, then closed her eyes, swaying toward me. When she opened her eyes, she licked her lips. "I want you to, but . . ."

It was like a crashing sound.

But.

That was all.

That was enough.

When a woman said *but*, you stopped.

Plain and simple.

I let go of her face and dropped my hand from her hip. "Are you okay?"

She drew a deep breath, her eyes forlorn. "Yes. I'm just not ready."

My heart sank.

But those were words I understood all too well. "I get it. I absolutely get it."

And I did. More than I wanted to. But I had to. If she wasn't ready, she wasn't ready.

From inside her clutch purse, an alarm sounded on her phone. Grabbing the device hastily, she stared at it, her tone heavy. "I have to go. My mom has a shift at eleven. I told her I'd be home by ten thirty."

"Then let's go," I said, doing my best to restore the friendly vibe and to erase the *let's get naked* one. "Lyft or cab?"

She cleared her throat, seemed to push out a laugh, then said, "Lyft. Always the bargain hunter."

I laughed too, good-naturedly. "Besides cabs aren't what they used to be," I said, and as soon as those words came out, my heart clutched. My father used to be a taxi driver, long ago.

Long before the world changed and taxis became an endangered species.

And there I was, thinking about my dad and taxis and how the world had shifted.

But something else had shifted tonight in my world.

The acknowledgment from Elle.

That she felt this thing between us.

She might not be able to act on it.

But she felt it.

And that gave me hope.

I didn't want to give up.

I walked her to the portico, pressed my lips to her cheek, and gave her a chaste goodbye kiss that I hoped would linger in her mind the whole way home.

7

ELLE

I gave myself the car ride to remember how Colin was so close to me.

To recall his scent, his words, his eyes.

I closed mine, replaying our almost kiss as the driver cruised along the streets to my building.

I'd nearly given in. I'd desperately wanted to be consumed by his lips, his heat, his desire.

But if I did, I'd be lost.

So I allowed myself another minute of meandering, then I folded up the memory and the dizzying sensations that went along with it, tucked it in a drawer in my mind, and put it away.

I reached my house and went inside, leaving that part of the night behind me.

My mother's head was bent over the kitchen counter, her fingers swiping in a wild blur across her phone screen. "Gotcha, flesh-eater!"

Home. I was home. This was my place. My safe haven. "Saving the world, Mom?" I asked as I closed the front door.

"Somebody has to fend off the infected," she said with a final slide before she looked up and closed the game.

I laughed. "I thought you were giving it up. You said it was giving you gamer's thumb or something."

My mother shook her head, her bouncy ponytail swinging with her. "I tried. Oh Lord, you know I tried. But your son . . . he challenged me. I couldn't back down."

I cracked up at her competitive ways. This woman loved going toe to toe in games. "You're going to need to work on the newest versions of *State of Decay* next. Alex and his buddies are moving on in the post-apocalyptic gaming world," I said, dropping my keys on the counter and giving my mom a peck on the cheek. She wore green scrubs with Snoopys and Woodstocks on them. "How was he tonight?"

"Fine. Just fine. I plied him with pizza and schooled him with my survival skills."

"No easier way to the heart of a fourteen-year-old boy, is there?" While there was plenty of truth in that statement, for my son, video games weren't just the snack-food-and-candy path to winning his teenage heart—they were essential to his emotional survival. They were the difference between him talking and not talking. Between speech and a complete breakdown. The main reason I signed him up for the summer gamer camp.

Some parents might worry that their kids played too many video games, and while I set limits, I also knew what they meant for him. Because the time before he'd played? That was the end of the world. Black, empty, cold. A true pit of despair. In those dark days, I'd have given anything—a lung, a kidney, a limb—for him to talk to me. He'd shut down after his father died, completely withered, barely able to utter a word except for the essentials—*yes, no, I don't know.*

Understandable, given what he'd witnessed in our home on that night two years ago.

But eventually, somehow games, zombies, and post-apocalyptic stories became a portal for him. I never would have predicted it, but on the days after school when Alex would come by the center, he was drawn to the gaming room, and to the raucous energy of the boys shouting at the screen. After a year of being so traumatized by what he saw he'd gone nearly mute, video games reconnected the voice inside him to the rest of the world. They'd unlocked the part of him that he'd kept quiet, and how I loved to hear him shouting with his friends.

God bless the living dead.

Zombies had rescued my son from the near-catatonic state that the death of his father had sent him into.

My mother tucked the phone into her purse and gathered up her keys. "How was the benefit? Did you meet your goal?" She held up her hand and twisted her index finger around her middle finger. "I had 'em crossed all night for you."

"We did. It was amazing," I said, bursting with excitement once more as I gave a recap of the night. Well, the pre–almost kiss portion of the night.

Mom beamed, then pumped a fist in the air and did a victory dance in the kitchen. "I knew it, I knew it, I knew it!"

The woman had amazing energy.

Barely fifty, she poured her heart and soul into her two grown daughters, her grandkids, her job as a nurse, and even her new boyfriend. She'd put herself through nursing school when my younger sister and I were toddlers, struggling to make ends meet as a young single mom. She'd wanted different things for her daughters, and she'd achieved that with Camille, who'd wisely waited till she was out of college and married before she and her wife decided to have kids.

Not me.

The bun unknowingly went in the oven on the night of high school graduation, when the condom broke with Sam, the guy who became my on-again, off-again boyfriend, then eventually my husband, then nearly my ex-husband, since I'd been separated from him the last year of his life while he was on-again and off-again in all sorts of ways. On drugs. Off drugs. In rehab. Out of rehab. Like a merry-go-round that gave me whiplash and nothing else but heartache.

"I am so proud of you, baby," my mom said, walking around the counter and clasping me in a big hug. "You worked so hard for this, and those kids need you. You have done so much for them."

My throat hitched. "I'm lucky to work with them."

The kids. The teens. That was another reminder. My focus was on the next generation. Not on me. Not on my needs. I had to keep my blinders on and concentrate on helping the kids who needed me, not sowing any wild oats.

My mom hummed, staring at me quizzically. "You seem different. Are you okay? Did you meet a nice man tonight?"

She was a bloodhound. She could sense anything.

Probably the shift in my mood. Or maybe she was reading my mind.

I laughed her off, hoping to throw her off the scent. "Yes, Mom. I put the moves on all sorts of men tonight at the fundraiser. I was like Tinder, swiping back and forth. Now, get to work." I shooed her to the door. "You're going to be late for your shift. You have fifteen minutes to get to the hospital."

My mom fixed me with a stare. "I want details of your Tinder quest."

I scoffed. "Mom. There are no details. I was joking."

Mostly.

Her gaze said *This conversation isn't over, missy,* and I rolled my eyes. "I love you, but you need to skedaddle. Thank you again."

"Anytime," she said, and walked out. But in two seconds, she propped the door back open and held up a finger. "And 'anytime' means if you want a booty call with these guys, you know where to find me. Because I've got some flesh-eaters to destroy with my grandson."

"I'm not having any booty calls, but thank you for the generous offer," I said, then shut and locked the door and walked down the hall to check on my son.

Alex was sound asleep, curled up under the covers, air conditioning rattling loudly in his pigsty bedroom. His dark hair was a wild mess and would be sticking up in all directions in the morning. I bent down and dropped a quick kiss on his forehead.

"Night, sleepy boy," I said, then left his room and returned to the living room, where I sank down on the couch.

And wished.

Wished my life were different.

Wished I'd made smarter choices once upon a time.

Wished I hadn't stayed so long with a man who'd been a mistake.

My throat hitched.

And another stupid lump lodged.

I was such a fool.

I'd been so caught up.

I had to be better now. Smarter now. I had to protect myself and my son.

My past gnawed at me and vexed me. Nagged and

twisted away at my heart. But my mind tripped back in time again to that almost kiss.

I played it again.

And again.

And, holy hell, once more.

This was a problem.

Maybe a distraction would stop the memories of tonight from sneaking up on me. Leaning forward, I grabbed the game controller from the coffee table and turned on the TV. Lowering the volume so as not to wake my son, I proceeded to blast through a town of the infected, quickly clearing several blocks of zombies as night fell in video-game land. When a flesh-eater appeared out of nowhere, I panicked.

"You need to run away."

Pausing the game, I leaned my head back and looked up at Alex, my heart expanding in my chest, growing two sizes bigger. My boy. "I do?"

With his rumpled hair, basketball shorts, and gray T-shirt, he walked around the couch and parked himself next to me. "Yeah, you don't have to fight the super zombies every time. If you successfully run away from them, you can level up your agility skills."

"My agility skills suck," I admitted with a smile, loving every second of our chats, then added, "Why are you up?"

"Had to pee. Is that a crime?"

I deadpanned an answer. "Not that I'm aware of. I'll let you know if that changes though."

Alex laughed and grabbed the controller. "I'll show you how to run away from the zombies," he said, turning the game back on and demonstrating his speed and skill in evading the enemy. "Now, we just need to get back to the safe house."

"So does this count if you're playing for me?"

He nodded. "Of course. I'm like your pinch hitter."

"When we enter the Xbox tournament, can you just fill in for me when I get in a pickle?"

"If there's a tournament and you're holding out on letting me play in it, you're in big trouble," he said as he attacked bad guys on the screen, then yawned ferociously.

"And that means it's back to bed for you, young man."

He huffed, but a yawn broke through again. "Okay, you might be right." He thrust the controller into my hand. "Try not to get killed before you get back to the safe house."

"I'll do my best. See you in the morning, sleepyhead," I said, and I could barely contain a grin. A simple conversation. It was everything.

"See you in the morning," he echoed, and returned to his room.

A few minutes later, I flicked off the game. Late-night encounters like that—random, casual, exceedingly normal —had a way of settling my nerves and calming my heart. Things were back to business as usual with Alex, and I was so damn grateful for that.

I headed to my bathroom and scrubbed off all my makeup, staring at the calligraphy *T* tattooed on my wrist. *T* for my roller derby name. Titanium. Strength. Unbreakable strength. I dried my face and brushed out my hair, but I didn't feel as strong as metal.

I couldn't stop thinking about Colin.

The last time I'd been caught up in a man like this, I'd nearly made myself sick. I'd barely slept. Plagued by insomnia, haunted by memories, by broken vows and fights. By *this time will be different* pleas.

But Colin wasn't like my ex, I tried to remind myself.

Colin Sloan—tall, tatted, tempting, witty, and forthright. The more I got to know him, the more I liked him, and when he touched me tonight . . . it had been a pure rush.

He was different from my ex. He wasn't an asshole. And as a social worker, I knew people could change. Colin had done everything my ex hadn't. He'd kicked his habit and was living a new life. I left the bathroom, and as I flopped down on my bed, shoving a hand through my hair, I wondered if I could have a little something.

I wasn't ready for a relationship. I'd taken ten thousand chances with the father of my child, and we'd nearly destroyed our son. All those chances had ripped my life to shreds, and I'd finally put the pieces back together in the last year.

But what if Colin and I were ready to spend more time together?

Away from the center.

As friends.

That wouldn't be a broken promise, would it?

Surely there was nothing wrong with that—with a normal friendship.

I'd maintain my boundaries. Only friendship. Nothing more. That wouldn't destroy life as I knew it.

I picked up my phone and texted Colin.

8

COLIN

Nothing like a late-night workout to get your mind off a woman. I powered through a five-mile run on the treadmill as the clock ticked well past midnight. Pushing myself harder because I was training for the Badass Triathlon in a month, and I was determined to conquer that beast of an event after two failed attempts.

Just another mile.

I zeroed in on my goal, pushing, running, reaching.

When I finished, I slapped the off button, my breath coming fast as I hopped off the treadmill, grateful for always-open gyms.

And for phones. Because mine had a blinking message from Elle.

Don't get excited.

Don't read into it.

It's probably something about the center.

I ignored it as I hit the weights.

I lifted, then as I took a drink of water, I finally opened the text.

Elle: Hi. So, this might sound crazy. But what if we really did hang out? Would that be a terrible idea? Just hang out. Because I really like spending time with you.

Colin: I like spending time with you too.

Elle: You do?

Colin: Yes, in case that wasn't readily apparent.

Elle: I just like to hear it.

Colin: Then I'll say it again. I like spending time with you. And if you're not ready, you're not ready. No pressure.

Elle: Thank you. I appreciate that so much as a friend. And I appreciate you as a friend.

Colin: Think you'd appreciate zip-lining?

Elle: Whoa. Hold my feet to the fire.

Colin: Well, you do roller-skate.

Elle: Yes, but skating is not one hundred feet above the ground.

Colin: Then, friend, we are zip-lining.

It wasn't exactly how I'd seen the night going, but maybe this was the true opening.

After we made plans for Tuesday night, I ended the chat

and headed home, munching on carrots when I entered my kitchen.

Carrots and club soda.

Chuckling to myself, I shook my head. Man, my life had changed.

Years ago, I would have been devouring a beautiful bottle of Patrón, like I'd done after my dad died when I was thirteen. Then at age twenty-three, I partied too hard one night, decided to still compete hungover in a triathlon the next day, and wound up collapsing, breaking my tibia, and nearly losing my job.

Wake-up call indeed.

My rock bottom, and I quit after that.

Wasn't easy.

There had been moments in those early days of sobriety when I'd have given my left arm for another glass and my right for a handful of pills. Now, with eight years clean—no slips, no relapses, no *just one drinks*—I felt steady and calm. I'd made it through the hell of withdrawal, I'd had the support of friends and family in getting sober, and I relied on a solid network of like-minded men in my recovery support group. Every day, I aimed to live according to a new way of thinking—a sober way—and I honestly wasn't tempted anymore when I walked past tequila on the shelf or saw a drink being served at a bar.

Nearly every night, I talked to my dad before bed, asking him to watch over me, to keep me on the wagon, to make sure I didn't fall into the wrong crowd again.

I liked to think he played a part.

But then I liked to think he'd played a part in anything good in my life.

And I needed to atone for the wrong choices I'd made. I was doing that by living clean.

Here I was eighteen years later, still hoping I could do right by him.

And by myself too. I intended to do that by competing in the triathlon at the end of the summer. I hadn't attempted it since my epic fail eight years ago. But it was my personal quest to finish it this time. Whether I came in first or last didn't matter. Finishing sober was all I wanted.

A tribute to my dad.

And to myself.

And if I could finish it, maybe I could somehow see this thing through with Elle.

Figure out how to be friends, only friends, with the woman I longed for.

9

ELLE

Billie Holiday sang of standing alone, without a dream in her heart.

My ringtone. Her version of *"Blue Moon."*

One of my comfort songs.

Bleary-eyed and still groggy, I fumbled for my phone on the nightstand.

Squinting, I spied the edge of the red number on my clock radio—eight thirty in the morning.

On a Sunday.

It was too early for anyone to be calling with good news.

An all too familiar burst of panic blasted through me when I saw "unknown number" on the screen. When Sam had called from his many stints in rehab, the number had always shown up as unknown. The times he'd rung me up while out partying, plastered and begging me to take him back, he would block his number.

Logically, I knew that Sam wasn't calling me from the grave. But a rabid fear pulsed through me nonetheless. I swiped my finger across the screen, sitting up in bed and doing my best to clear the sound of sleep from my voice in case it was a client or one of the kids I counseled at the center. They all had my number.

"Hello?"

"Hey. It's Marcus." His tone was nervous.

I sat up straight. If he was calling me this early, it had to be serious. I flashed back on our conversation from the other day. Did he want to talk more about his mom and the family he didn't know?

But then, he might also be trying to get into the center to play hoops.

"Hey there. Are you trying to get into the center? We don't open until ten on Sundays. One of the volunteers should be there then," I offered.

"No, actually. I'm not," he said, speaking tentatively, the vocal equivalent of shuffling his feet. "I'm sorry to bug you so early. I've been thinking about what we've been talking about, and I'm finally ready to do something."

This was serious. I wanted to give him my full attention. "Okay. Tell me more. You mentioned wanting to know your other siblings."

"Yeah, I do," he said, and I had a feeling he was going to say a whole lot more today than he had when he'd come to my office earlier in the week.

I was ready, and I wanted to help.

10

MARCUS

I paced in the park.

I didn't like to make calls at my apartment.

Maybe that came from never wanting to make calls in front of my dad, back when I'd lived at home.

It was my habit, and it was a hard one to break.

So I scanned the grounds, making sure I had privacy.

I cleared my throat, drawing up the courage to tell her more. To say what I hadn't said the other day. Because there were things I hadn't told her. Hadn't told anyone. And they were weighing on me, heavier every day, for so many reasons. *Here goes nothing.* "I just feel like I spent my whole life not knowing anything about my family and where I came from, and now I do," I said, biting off the truth. "And my dad didn't want me to find them, but they're here in Vegas, and I'm not living at home anymore. So this is my choice. I need to do this."

I stopped in place, digging my heels into the ground.

Metaphorically.

But it felt necessary.

Elle answered immediately. "Then you should do it.

Something is compelling you to connect with them, and you need to listen. Family is a powerful pull and a potent bond, and you've never had a chance to get to know them."

Yes. That. Exactly. Who were they? What were they like? Were they like me? Sometimes I didn't feel connected to my father at all, or my half-sisters a lot of the time. But they were so much younger than I was. Would I connect more with the Sloans? But there was another issue. A scarier one.

Just get it out. Just say it.

"But what if they don't want to meet me?" I asked in a flurry. I could hear the tumultuousness in my voice. One moment I felt courageous, the next I was hampered by fear.

This sucked.

"Look, Marcus. I'm not going to sugarcoat this for you. They might have zero interest in getting to know you. They might not care. They might be so busy with their lives that they can't be bothered. But this is something *you* want. You are trying to take a big step, wanting to connect with siblings you've never known, and that is brave."

Brave.

Did I feel brave?

I wasn't sure.

Somedays I felt like my life should have been on daytime TV.

Supposedly, my mom liked those things.

I was the long-lost half-brother . . . appearing out of nowhere . . . showing up on the doorstep of my older brothers.

"My life is a soap opera," I muttered.

Elle's response was swift, confident, and everything I needed to hear. "No. It's not a soap. It's your life. And real life is full of more drama and danger in the world than we often are willing to admit. And we have to make our way through," she said, and her tone calmed my nerves. "Let's talk next steps. What are you going to do?"

Details. Plans. I could focus on that. I paced again, sharing my idea about Ryan, about how I'd start with him. He was the one who'd visited my mom a lot in prison. "My dad once mentioned that one of them was closest to my mom, so I think I'll start with him. Plus, he has a dog, so he's out and about a lot in his neighborhood."

"Marcus," she said, sounding like a teacher who'd caught a student with a cheat sheet. "How do you know that?"

Shit.

"Marcus, have you been following them around?" she asked, now a judge, and I deserved that tone.

"Maybe," I said, under my breath. "But only because I was curious. Because I wanted to know what they're doing. I wanted to know how to approach them."

She sighed, gentling her tone. "That's not a good idea. It can freak people out. You need to be direct. If you want to meet them, you need to man up and go over there."

"I know. I'm just . . ." How could I say what I really felt?

"You're scared," she supplied, speaking softly.

"Yes," I said in the barest voice.

"Remember what we talked about?"

I could hear the way she'd said it, what she'd tried to teach us at the center. "*Rise above,*" I repeated, echoing her mantra.

"Yes. Rise above. You can be so much. If your goal is to meet the family you've never known, I'm behind you. But you have to stop following them. Do not let fear guide you. Rise above it."

I drew a deep breath. "Okay. I'm going to do it. I'm going to head over to this guy's house."

We ended the call, and I steeled myself, ready. I could do this.

I talked to myself the whole way over, practicing my script. As I drove, as I waited at lights, as I turned corners.

When I parked.

But no one was home.

And I didn't know if that was for the best. Maybe it was. Maybe I wasn't ready for this crazy new step in my life. After all, what would I tell my stepmom? Angie had been good to me. Didn't she deserve to know at some point? I'd have to tell her down the road.

For now, I called Elle and gave her the report, and she said it might take a few tries before someone was home.

But I had to keep going.

"It's a risk worth taking," she said, and I let those words sink in, grateful that she was behind me in this — the toughest thing I'd ever done in my life.

11

COLIN

The basketball arced through the air, swirling once, then twice, around the rim and dropping with a whoosh into the basket.

"No way!" Rex stared at the ball in amazement as it bounced on the concrete of the court Tuesday afternoon.

I held my arms out wide as I stood on the free-throw line. *I told you so.* "Angle. It's all angle."

"You have got to be kidding me!" the boy said, his big eyes rounder than ever. He grabbed the ball and held it as if he were weighing it.

I wiped the beads of sweat from my brow. "Nope. Not kidding at all. You'll have a greater chance at landing a free throw if you have your arms at this angle," I said, demonstrating a wider placement of my arms.

Rex made a quick adjustment then threw the ball himself, watching as it sailed into the net. "Holy hell," the teen said as the ball bounced on the court.

Rex's younger brother, Tyler, watching from the sidelines, looked less impressed.

Rex marched over to me and slapped my palm. "I still

don't believe you, but a deal is a deal is a deal. You get to tutor me now in business math."

I beamed. For the last year, I'd been coaching the rec league and tutoring the teens at the center in business math as part of my personal decision to devote more time to service. I'd lost out on a big deal a year ago, and had felt the first inklings of the familiar urge to bury my frustrations in liquor. Rather than give in, I'd refocused my energies, pouring my time into others. That had helped me fight the good fight and stay on the straight and narrow.

"It's all math, man. Everything is math," I said, grabbing the ball from the ground and dribbling it in place. "You will use math in every area of your life. Chance of hitting a free throw from one-third of the way up the court? Math. Chance of landing a slam dunk? Math. How much money do I need to pay my bills? Math. Is it worth missing class to sleep in? Comes down to math."

"What he's saying is—math is everything," Tyler said.

"What? You're on his team now?" Rex joked.

"Listen to Tyler. He knows what he's talking about," I said. A few years younger, Rex's brother dabbled in basketball, but his asthma slowed him down.

"And this is the stuff you do for a living?" Rex asked.

I took aim at the net. The ball soared. "Every day. I evaluate risk. Study balance sheets. Look at profit and loss statements. And take a gamble as to whether some new technology for phones or TVs or gaming or whatever is going to change the world." The ball slinked neatly through the basket. I tossed it to Rex, who took his shot.

"How much green did you bring home last year?" Rex asked.

I laughed, shaking my head as the younger man landed a shot.

"You're not going to tell me?"

"No. I'm not going to tell you. But I will say this: my portfolio of companies had a twenty-four percent return, and that's well ahead of the stock market, and it's also ahead of the twenty percent benchmark for a venture capital firm, so there you go."

Rex's eyes practically turned into dollar signs. "Nice!"

"That money goes back into the portfolio. So we can invest in more companies," I explained, dribbling the ball. Rex was eighteen and headed to community college. He didn't know what he wanted to major in, and I was hoping he'd lean toward business. He just needed a push to see the value in the long-term.

"But that's your goal, right?"

"It is. Find the diamond in the rough. Bet big on it before anyone else does. Grow it and watch it turn into a money tree."

Rex waved his arms enthusiastically. "Oh man, I want a money tree. I want a big fat money tree that grows greenbacks all year round. Ty, let's go grow us a money tree."

"Yeah, right, in the concrete pit at our crappy apartment complex," Tyler said with a snort from his spot on the sidelines.

"Hey! Watch it. We'll move up someday." Rex turned back to me and pointed his thumb at Tyler. "I gotta look out for him. Mom's working too many jobs again."

"That's why she makes sure you're here instead of wandering the streets," I said, passing the ball to Rex. "And if you study business, you'll have a hell of a lot better shot at growing a money tree than you would by chasing after some get-rich-quick scheme. Invest, nurture, grow, make more. That's what I do. That's my job. That's my passion." I held out my arm, showing the tattoo there. *Nothing ventured. Nothing gained.*

Rex tucked the ball beneath his arm and walked closer to see.

"Hey, Rex. I'm hungry," Tyler interjected.

"Give me a second, Ty. I'll make you mac and cheese when we get home. My man Colin is training me to be a venture capitalist. Get over here and join us." Rex turned his attention back to my ink. "So that's your mission at work or something? Nothing ventured, nothing gained?"

"Yeah, but in life too. Means more to me than just work."

"Like what?" Rex asked.

"It means take big chances. It means stay away from drugs," I said, speaking bluntly to the boys as I always did.

Rex sneered. "What do you know about that, Mr. Richie Rich? You probably bathe in Cristal."

"You think I was born rich? You think I was rolling in cash as a kid? Wrong," I said, as if I'd just slammed a buzzer on a game show. "We struggled to make ends meet, and I made a ton of bad choices after my father's death. I was thirteen, and I turned to the wrong crowd and got involved in the wrong things. Painkillers, tequila, and then speed when I was in college. I was a mess. All these," I said, gesturing to my arms covered in ink, "they're my reminders. Eight years clean." I pointed to the art on my body, naming each one. "Lotus, new beginning. Sunburst, truth and bravery. This Chinese character—it's for strength."

Rex raised his chin and peered at an infinity symbol with four interlocking circles on my wrist. "What's that one?"

"My brothers, sister, and me. The four of us. Our unbreakable bond, no matter what."

"That's like us." Rex pointed to his little brother. "I always look out for Tyler. That's why I have this." He pulled up his sleeve to his shoulder. At first, I saw only a few letters of the word *Protect*. My hackles rose. The guy who'd been following Shannon around had some ink on his arm that said *Protect Our Own*—the tattoo of the Royal Sinners.

That reminded me. I needed to show Elle the picture of him. But I'd reset my phone after testing a new fitness app that had downloaded a virus. Needless to say, my venture firm wasn't going to fund that app. I'd just have to snag the photo again from Brent.

To Rex I said, "That better not be what I think it is. That better not be *Protect Our Own*."

Rex laughed deeply, clutching his belly, letting the sound resonate through him. "No. No. No," he said, catching his breath. "No way. No how. Our ink says *Protector*. We got ours together." Rex stepped closer to me and showed me the full wrap of the word around his bicep. Tyler yanked up his shirtsleeve, displaying matching ink.

"I would whip him good if he messed around with that gang." Rex draped an arm around his little brother, then his expression went serious. "I saw some of them a few blocks away the other day."

"Here?" I asked, pointing to the basketball court.

Rex nodded. "Nearby. We made sure they didn't come any closer."

I didn't like the sound of gang members hovering so close to the community center. I wanted the center, the kids, and Elle as safe as could be.

"Who's 'we'? What is *Protector*?" I asked, returning to the ink.

"A group of us who are trying to look out for others," Tyler said, chiming in proudly. He seemed to idolize his older brother.

I arched an eyebrow. "Like the Guardian Angels?"

Rex nodded. "We model ourselves after them. We're all volunteers. We do safety patrols. Walk the streets. Keep an eye out. Elle inspired me to do it. Rise above, as she would say."

"Did someone say my name?"

I turned in the direction of the sexy and sweet voice. Elle wore tight jeans and a little white summery blouse. Her long dark hair spilled down her spine, and she gathered it up, creating a makeshift ponytail, then fanned her face with her free hand.

"We're quoting you, Elle. *Rise above*," Tyler said, raising his fist in the air.

She held up a hand to high-five Tyler, then slapped his older brother's hand too. "Excellent. You boys do me proud."

Rex draped an arm around his brother. "Hey, Elle, did you hear? Colin is trying to turn me into the next venture capitalist."

"That sounds like an excellent pursuit," she said.

"I'm gonna earn twenty-five percent and beat his ass."

"After I tutor you in math, you just might," I said.

The teen turned to Elle. "He twisted my arm. He's going to make me learn my two plus twos for community college. Anyway, it's too hot out here. We're going inside. Catch you later, Mr. Cristal," Rex said with a wink at me.

As he walked away, Elle raised an eyebrow. "Mr. Cristal?"

"Long story. But it has a good ending."

"Maybe tell me tonight?" She tucked her thumbs into the pockets of her jeans. "Turns out I have more time than I thought. Alex is doing a volunteer project after camp as part of his high school's summer community service—reading to some of the younger kids at a local elementary school every day this week. So we can do that crazy scary thing you're forcing me to do."

I laughed. "You're going to love it."

That was my goal. She wasn't ready for romance, but I could damn well make sure she enjoyed the hell out of our time together.

She shuddered. "Are you sure we can't just go for a stroll?"

I shot her a curious stare. "So let me get this straight. You do roller derby, racing around a rink like a speed demon on skates, and you won't do a zip line?" I asked, challenging her.

She narrowed her eyes, parking her hands on her hips. "Not the same. Roller derby is flat. Besides, I've done it for years, I play defense, and it's *indoors*."

"C'mon, Titanium," I urged, goading her with her roller derby name. "You can do it."

"If you insist."

"I do, and I promise we will have fun," I said, since I sensed she needed that. She gave a lot of herself here at the center and with her family. She deserved a night to blow off steam.

She narrowed her eyes and pointed at me. "We better."

"We will."

She nodded to the building. "I should go lock up my office," she said, and those words—*lock up*—flipped the switch on an idea.

I jumped to a new topic. "Hey, would it be okay if I increased my firm's donation to the center?"

She shook her head playfully. "No. God no. Anything but that," she said, waving it off. She rolled her eyes. "Obviously. But why, may I ask?"

"Thought it would be smart to get some additional security for this place while the revitalization is going on,"

I said, gesturing to the courts and main building. "Lots of people coming and going. Construction crews. Just wanted to give a little more for some extra manpower."

"Let's do it. Thank you," she said as we walked off the court.

I pointed to my car parked down the block. "I've got to take Ryan's dog for a quick walk. Meet you at six? You can still be home in time, I presume?"

"Definitely."

"See you soon. I'll grab a shower too."

There was a part of me that was hoping she'd enjoy the image of me in the shower.

Yes, that part.

12

———

ELLE

I stared at the crowds along the Fremont Street canopy seventy-seven feet below.

Deep breath.

I wasn't afraid of heights, but I was afraid of, well, *dying.* Or, more precisely, dying stupidly. Like jumping into a lake and cutting my head on a rock. Or parachuting. Or crashing from a zip line. That kind of death.

Logically, I knew zip-lining wasn't a dangerous activity in the spectrum of dangerous things. But my rapidly beating heart, which seemed to be fighting its way out of my chest, begged to disagree. My skin prickled with nerves —the kind I hadn't felt since I was younger and danced with danger. Now, as an adult, I tried to keep my risks manageable.

You can do this, I told the portion of my brain that had zero interest in skydiving and bungee jumping. *It's just a zip line. It's exceedingly safe and ridiculously fun.*

Plus, Colin waited patiently on the other side, hovering in his seat. The parallel zip lines ran down the length of the covered Fremont Street that was the epicenter of downtown Las Vegas—old Vegas, with the Golden Nugget and slots that still relied on coins rather than tickets. It was Vegas before mega resorts broke ground on the Strip.

Everyone rode the line here on Fremont Street. It was part of the experience. Besides, cruising along a zip line was a perfectly manageable risk. Man-made, controllable. The kind I could handle.

"I'm ready," I said to the attendant. In a rush, so I wouldn't back down, I let go and stepped off the platform, zipping off in my seat harness. I unleashed a roller-coaster shout of excitement. Adrenaline surged through my veins as I soared above the specks of miniature people, and a sense of wild glee engulfed me as I sped faster and faster. I glanced briefly to the left, where Colin sailed above the crowds on his own downhill flight along the canopy.

Screw fear. This was a pure rush as the summer breeze whooshed past me, reminding me of the thrill I felt when roller-skating, the high-speed chase around the rink. The charge that raced through me overpowered my primal worries as I rode past several blocks in the sky.

I flew the final feet to the end of the line.

"How was it?" the guy on the platform asked as he helped unhook me.

I gave him a thumbs-up, my heart still pumping wildly.

Minutes later, I climbed down from the platform and met Colin on the street. He held his arms out, waiting expectantly. "Admit it. You loved it," he said with a gleam in his eyes.

"It was terrifying. But wonderful," I said breathlessly, my pulse pounding in my veins.

"Excellent. Tomorrow morning you'll join me for kayaking at the crack of dawn at Black Canyon," he said.

I shuddered. "Kayaking? Like near the rapids? That comes with a chance of flipping over and cracking your head on a rock? Pretty sure this zip line is all you're getting out of me when it comes to crazy sports," I said, but the truth was I was glad he'd pushed me. I'd never have done it otherwise, and if I was going to give the kids advice about taking risks, it was good for me to take some too.

"No. A lake, woman." Colin nudged me with his shoulder. "It's calm. The chance of flipping over is slim to nil. So low-risk it's beyond low-risk," he said, urging me.

Was I ready to try kayaking?

It wasn't inherently scary. Certainly no more so than roller-skating. But I'd been skating since I was five.

The sports I'd never tried—they scared me. The things I hadn't done—they worried me.

Possibly that was because of Sam too.

My daredevil ex, carefree and cavalier, had loved to ride his motorcycle everywhere. He'd pushed and pushed and pushed for me to join him for a ride once. He wasn't even high. He was sober, but he still ran a light and we'd spun out onto the sidewalk.

Ever since then, I'd had zero interest in anything I didn't know well. Anything new. Anything risky at all.

I had a life to live. A son to look out for. I didn't need to take chances I couldn't control.

But was kayaking one of those?

"I'll think about it," I told Colin, and I would.

"That's all I can ask for." He held up a finger. "When are you free again? Because I have another idea. And I promise it's fun and relaxing."

Alex's community service lasted all week after camp.

And I'd had more fun tonight than I'd had in . . . well, since I couldn't remember.

I said yes.

After all, zip-lining had been exactly what I'd needed. The rush got me out of my own head and away from my worries, my fears.

That was where I enjoyed being.

And I enjoyed being in that place with Colin.

13

COLIN

I'd be lying if I said I didn't want more from Elle.

But I'd be lying too if I said I wasn't enjoying these early evenings together hanging out after work, getting to know each other more.

I supposed I wanted her to see what we could be as friends. Maybe then, when she was ready, she'd know I was the guy to turn to.

The only one.

Patience was all I needed, and I had that.

Along with knowledge. Elle loved gangster movies.

So I knew where to take her Thursday afternoon.

We returned to old downtown, where we wandered through the crowds, soaking in the neon and lights, the exuberance of the summertime atmosphere, and not once did I feel a lick of envy for the twentysomethings bobbing around with long, tall plastic glasses full of liquor in their hands. Nope, I was a happy son of a bitch as we walked through old-time Vegas, then up the steps of the museum that documented the history of the mob.

"I believe you'll get a kick out of this," I said to her.

Her eyes lit up. "I've never been here. Always wanted to go."

"I know," I said, feeling pretty damn proud.

She raised a brow in question. "You do?"

I shrugged, grinning. "You mentioned it once when you were watering Frank," I said.

She stopped on the steps. "And you remembered?"

"I pay attention."

She set a hand on my arm. "You do."

Two simple words. But they sent a charge through me as she wrapped her fingers around my forearm. The combo did me in, and a new wave of desire rushed through me. I locked eyes with her, and for a few seconds, she seemed to lean in, to inch closer.

Were we on the cusp of another almost kiss?

Maybe it would be more than *almost* this time.

It felt like that with the way she stared, how her breath seemed to ghost across her lips.

Shoes clicked on the steps.

"We're closing in thirty minutes," the ticket taker at the entrance said in a monotone, breaking the mood.

And that was that. No kiss, almost or otherwise.

"We'll be speedy," I said, and we walked inside the stone building and strolled first through exhibits on famous "made men," both in the mob and popular culture, perusing photos of some of the most notorious Mafiosi over the last one hundred years, like John Gotti. Next, we checked out an installation of movie posters.

"Is there anything better than a mob movie?" I asked, and Elle nodded in perfect agreement.

"Love them. *Casino.* Epic. *The Departed.* Fantastic. *Road to Perdition.* Chilling."

"*Eight Men Out.* Proof that the mob had its hands in everything. Even fixing the World Series," I said.

"Everything," she said, enunciating each syllable as she echoed my sentiment. We stopped at a huge framed poster of Ray Liotta, Robert De Niro, and Joe Pesci. She pointed. "*Goodfellas*. Best mob movie ever."

"Best closing lines ever too," I added, and we turned to each other, speaking in unison. "*I'm an average nobody. I get to live the rest of my life like a schnook.*"

I raised my hand, and we knocked fists. That sent a charge through me, knocking me back to the lust zone. Hell, maybe this hanging out as friends would be tougher than I thought it'd be.

But maybe not for Elle.

"Isn't it amazing," she said, "how being a regular joe was Ray Liotta's worst nightmare? He dreaded not being a gangster, and somehow you felt for him when it happened. You sympathized with his plight as a regular schnook," she said, her voice rising in excitement.

I gestured to the poster for *The Godfather*. "I don't even know what it is about the mob. They do horrible things and live a life of crime, and yet sometimes we root for them in movies. It makes no logical sense."

"Look!"

She grabbed my arm and tugged me to a series of sepia-tinted photographs of Vegas through the years, highlighting famous moments in the city's history and the role of the mob in each milestone. What would she look like in one of those old-time flapper dresses?

Or out of it . . .

Okay, fine. That was on me.

I could not let my dirty thoughts wander every time she touched me the slightest bit.

Focus, Colin, focus.

"It's just crazy to think how much of this town was built on crime," she said in awe as we stared at a photo of the Flamingo Hotel when it opened in 1946. "'Operated by noted mobster Bugsy Siegel,'" she said, reading the plaque.

I tapped the wall next to an image of the Sands Casino in the '60s, a home base for Frank Sinatra and his Rat Pack that was owned by a New York mob man. "And it spread far and wide. Some of the biggest hotels in the city were owned and operated by this wild combination of Mormon businessmen and the mob, so they could have a legitimate appearance on the outside, and money laundering and street muscle on the inside."

"The whole notion that there is this underbelly of crime everywhere, all around us, blows my mind," she said, pressing her fingertips to her forehead and miming an explosion.

I nodded in agreement. "Handouts, corrupt cops, men on the take, informants, and guys in suits circulating around town every day, weaving in and out of casinos. Looking like me, or like one of my brothers, or just anybody."

She arched an eyebrow. "Is this your way of telling me you're in the mob?"

I affected a wise-guy smirk. "Dollface, it's time you knew the truth. You want to know who I really am?" I pointed to an interactive screen on the far wall that read *Mob Nickname Generator.*

"Ooh, I'm finally gonna learn my gentleman friend's real name." She rubbed her palms together as we reached the screen.

I tapped it, and we chuckled at the rubric the screen asked us to fill in: *name your racket,* with "options like money laundering, casino skimming, and blackmail; *what's your role,* such as capo, soldier, business associate, or corrupt judge; and *what is your mob era,* with choices like Prohibition, the Swinging '60s, and the modern era.

Elle went first, entering her picks, then reading her status report. "Ooh, I'm a mob girlfriend. Men buy me things, and who am I to turn them down? They parade me around town and take me to dinner, and my name is Elle 'Moneybags' Mariano." She snorted. "Ha. I wish."

"My turn," I said, and together we decided I'd be a corrupt politician, and I read the results aloud. "I just take what's offered to me, okay? Nothin' wrong with that. The mob slips me a few things now and then—some cash, a free meal, a bottle of my favorite bootleg whiskey. What's the big deal? I'm Colin 'Scotty' Sloan."

She tapped my chest, and I braced myself. "Colin Scotty Sloan, you are one handsome fella," she said in an over-the-top floozy accent. Her proximity made an instant impression on certain parts of my anatomy.

Maybe I was a bad friend.

But I had to be a good one, because the woman wasn't ready, so all we had was this—playing, flirting in some small fashion.

"I'm gonna take you out for that fancy meal you deserve, Moneybags," I said with a wink. "Show you off as mine."

And a wish.

How I would love to show her off as mine.

"Oh, I like that, Scotty Sloan. I like it very much."

But that wasn't in the cards tonight, and I had to wonder if it ever would be.

Or what it would take to get her there.

When we left, I walked her to her car. "I had a really great time," she said, and her voice was soft, sweet.

But with a hint of resignation.

As if a great time was all she'd ever allow herself.

"Good. You deserve it, you know?" I said, but it was a question, because I wanted her to know. She hadn't told me everything. She hadn't told me much at all about how her son's father died, but I knew he'd battled addiction too. Battled and lost. Part of me wondered if that was in the back of her mind with me.

"I don't know if anyone deserves anything," she said, a little sad now, wistful. "Well, of course you don't deserve to have lost your dad."

"And you don't deserve to have gone through some crazy shit either. Like with your ex."

"But I chose him," she said, her voice tight, strained. "I chose Sam."

"Elle," I said softly. "Don't beat yourself up."

Her voice was tight with rebuke. Self-rebuke. "I made the wrong choice."

So that was it. She was afraid of making more bad choices. "You think I'd be one?" I asked.

"No. But I think I don't know how to make smart choices. So it's not about you, I promise. It's me."

That I understood far too well. Self-doubt. Self-blame. I got where it came from. Choices have consequences. Every single one. I'd made some terrible choices when I was younger, and even though those days were far in the rearview mirror, I understood where she was coming from. "Listen, I get it. I've done things I'm not proud of. I've made the wrong choices too. When my dad was killed, and then my mom went to prison for it, I was lost, so damn lost."

Her eyes edged with sadness. "Of course you were."

"And I turned to liquor for comfort. I was thirteen, and I made some dumb-ass choices."

"You were thirteen, just a kid," she said sympathetically.

I shook my head, a small laugh escaping. "Nope. I'm giving you the straight talk now, Ms. Community Center Director. And the straight talk is this. We all mess up. And

I messed up big time. I fell into the wrong crowd. I had friends who were Royal Sinners," I said, disgust on my tongue. "A guy named Danny Nelson was my best friend at the time, and his older brother TJ was in the gang. He got alcohol for us, and we'd get wasted. Then painkillers. Then speed. And here's the thing. I was friends with those guys before my dad was killed," I said, swallowing past memories.

A familiar pang of guilt washed over me as I remembered those friendships. The wrong crowd. The crowd that had played a part in my father's murder. Maybe not directly, but I wondered again and again if my friendship with guys connected to the gang had led to my mom reaching out to a shooter who was part of the Sinners.

The thought made my gut churn. Made me feel like my blood was tar. Was I responsible? Had I played a role?

I focused on my breathing, on tricks I'd learned through meditation, letting go of those ideas. And I focused on Elle.

But she was focusing on me. "It wasn't your fault."

"And it's not your fault. What you went through with Sam," I said. "It's life. It happened. But it's not your fault."

She gave me a soft smile, then whispered, "Thank you."

I wished she'd forgive herself.

Not because I longed for her.

But because she was a friend.

I lifted a hand, tucked a strand of hair over her ear, and leaned in to wrap her in a hug.

When we separated, she was smiling. "You're a good one, Scotty Sloan."

I hoped so. Hell, did I ever hope so.

14

———

ELLE

Fun.

That was good, plain fun.

That was basically the best night I'd had in ages.

I shook my head in amazement as I slowed my car at a red light on my way to pick up Alex. He'd texted that he'd gone to a friend's house near ours, so I was picking him up there.

"*Fun,*" I said out loud, as if the word was a new concept.

In many ways, it was to me. I hadn't had that sort of evening in . . . well, many years. Sure, I always had a blast doing roller derby, but that was more of a necessary outlet, my own therapy to handle living with an addict. And, yes, my son and I had gobs of fun playing zombie games, going bowling, and challenging each other in Pac-Man at the roller rink after my matches.

But adult fun?

That had been eons ago. Like maybe the Paleolithic period. Getting knocked up as a teenager didn't give you many opportunities for fun.

The last several nights, though, from the game of poker

to the zip line to the museum visit . . . every single second was lovely, and a small part of me already longed for more like it.

I never thought I'd have a bad time with Colin, but I hadn't imagined we'd have such a good one. It made perfect sense that we'd jell, I reasoned, as the light changed and I hit the gas. The two of us had clicked from day one.

We'd chatted easily when we first met, sharing a similar view on the value of community service, the importance of being role models for youth, and the benefit of giving kids a chance to have fun too. But tonight I'd learned we had even more in common, little things like our shared affection for mob movies and our fondness for the history of Las Vegas.

But there was something else too.

That moment by my car.

When he seemed to simply get me.

When he understood my walls.

My boundaries.

Could I forgive myself for having loved an addict? But Sam was more than an addict, and the time with him had been more than destructive.

It had nearly shattered my family.

Forgiveness wasn't the issue.

It was choice.

How to live now.

How to protect the ones I loved.

Because I didn't trust myself.

So I was better off alone.

Yet Colin seemed to sense that. I'd never told him all the details, but he gleaned where I was at, what I allowed, what I didn't allow.

And he didn't judge one way or the other.

Then there were the little moments. The way he tucked

my hair behind my ear, the tender words, the playful touches.

They made me . . . zing.

Like the zip line had.

As I turned onto the next street, my chest tingled at the memories of the last few nights, and of that almost kiss.

The man was direct and patient, and he seemed to embrace that I needed time.

But how much time? How long would he wait? Would I ever be ready?

I didn't know.

Admittedly, a quiet part of me wanted more of him. A part I rarely acknowledged. Try as I might to keep him in the friend zone, being friends with him only made him more appealing. But I had to stay strong.

I pulled into the driveway, cut the engine, and walked to the door. My girlfriend Janine answered, since our kids were buddies. "Hey, girl. You look happy."

I smiled. "I had a nice night with a friend."

She arched a brow. "A male friend?"

I shrugged playfully.

"Details."

I shook my head. "Nothing happened. We're truly just friends."

She leaned in closer. "But you want to be something more. I can see it in your eyes."

"Who has time for that?" I asked, dodging the issue.

"Make time for *that*. If he's a good one. Is he a good one?"

"He's great," I said, but that already felt like too much talk about men, so I shifted to roller derby chatter, discussing the Fishnet Brigade's game plan for our match next Friday. "And I will be on fire, blocking for my Cool Hand Bette," I said, using Janine's skate name.

"Excellent. I'll pick you up and drive?"

"It's a plan."

She leaned in closer. "And you ought to think about plans with the good ones." She leaned back, shooting me a saucy look. "The great ones."

I laughed it off, focusing on Alex as I drove him home. "How was the volunteer reading program?"

"Super cool," he said, then proceeded to tell me about a second-grader he worked with, and the whole time, all I could think was the sound of my son's voice was magic.

It was moonlight.

It was everything good in the world.

And it warmed my heart.

Alex glanced over at me, offering up a smile. "What were you up to? You look like you had a good time."

I blushed. Did I look that way? Was there something obvious to everyone in my expression? "And what is the look of a good time?"

"You're all super smiley."

I laughed at his teenager-y way of putting it. "I hung out with a friend at The Mob Museum."

"Oh cool. I want to go there."

We chatted the rest of the way home and through dinner, and I found myself wondering if fun was such a bad thing.

When it was time for bed, Alex said, "You were in a good mood all night. Maybe you should go to The Mob Museum more often."

Or maybe I should spend more time with Colin.

It wasn't exactly permission, but maybe in a way it was.

I could be a good mom, and maybe have a little more fun. Was that such a bad thing?

Maybe Elle "Moneybags" Mariano did deserve some fun.

I pondered the idea of fun the next day as I worked, and through the night too.

And on Saturday morning when I rose, that piece of me that had longed for more tugged at my heart again. I didn't entirely know what it wanted. I wasn't even in tune with the language it was speaking. But *something* compelled me to go.

As I peeked out the window, the sky had turned the shade of dark blue that comes before the sun rises.

I pulled on shorts, a tank top, and a pair of my white roller-skating socks with the row of red skulls around the knee. I confirmed with my mom that she'd be here soon, since she was hanging out with Alex today.

I checked on my sleeping boy, dropped a kiss on his forehead, and took off to surprise Colin.

This was going to be fun.

15

COLIN

This was a perfect dawn. Calm, quiet, and beautiful.

The craggy canyon rocks loomed larger as I drew closer to the lakeshore. The cool waters were still and serene, reflecting the soft rays of the rising sun that peeked over the horizon.

The near silence surrounding me was like a natural tranquilizer. Only the splash of the paddle with each stroke broke the quiet. I'd already gone for a swim, and tomorrow I'd tackle a morning climb.

Then at the end of the summer, I'd do the swim, bike, and run, plus a rock climb. But that wasn't what made the triathlon so badass.

After you scaled the rock wall, you turned around and did the first three legs in reverse.

I'd be ready. I concentrated on finishing my workout, heading to the shore, focusing on each stroke of the paddle.

One motion at a time.

One day at a time.

Splash.

I raised my eyes to the edge of the lake and blinked. What the hell?

A woman with long brown hair looped into a ponytail and a badass skater-girl outfit waved to me—big, broad, wildly happy waves. She cupped her hands around her mouth. "What do you think? Can I wear this kayaking?"

Striking a playful pose, she gestured to her outfit. She was a sight all right, in her tattered jean shorts, crazy socks, and wifebeater tee, which displayed the ink on her arms. She didn't look outdoorsy at all, but who cared? We'd make it work, if she was willing. I cracked up as a surge of happiness bounded through me. The last thing in the world I'd expected to see this morning was Elle. But the furious beating in my heart as I dragged the kayak ashore had little to do with the exertion and more to do with the utter delight of my unexpected Saturday morning visitor.

I tapped the side of the fiberglass hull. "You can wear anything kayaking. But does this mean you decided to take me up on my offer to hit the lake?"

Her eyes widened, and she drew a deep breath, like she was girding herself.

"Yes."

I punched the air.

"But just for a few minutes. To try it. Is that okay?"

"It's more than okay."

She held up a hand. "Wait. Did I ruin your workout? I can wait till you're done."

I laughed, and my heart soared. "You are not a Kayla, I assure you."

Her brow furrowed. "Who's Kayla?"

"My ex. We went out last year. Before I started at the center. I was training to redo the Badass Triathlon, and she didn't like that I spent so much time working out."

"Does she hate men with great bodies?" Elle deadpanned.

I wanted to thump my chest. To square my shoulders and strut like a peacock. But I *knew* Elle's issues weren't about attraction. She'd made that clear last weekend. Still, what man wouldn't enjoy the *great body* compliment? After all those years of pouring crap into my body, I now chose to do the opposite. To treat my body like a temple.

I was glad she liked it.

"Evidently," I said. "She tried to get me to stop spending so much time training. Stupidly, I listened to her and abandoned my quest to compete."

"That sucks. I know how much you want to do that event. You've been training all summer." She gestured to the water, barking like a drill sergeant. "Get back in there. Now. Stat."

I saluted her. "And I'll give you one hundred push-ups too."

She rubbed her palms together. "Make it five hundred, soldier. Keep working out."

"Glad you like the results."

"I do, and I will be cheering you on when you finish, because you will."

She was so different from Kayla. "Want to hear the most ridiculous part? We split a few weeks later, after I decided not to do the race."

"Because of that?"

I scratched my jaw, reflecting back on those times. "Because of that, no. Because of everything else, yes. We were wrong for each other. We didn't support each other. Didn't get each other." Then I narrowed my eyes. "But don't distract me from your first kayak lesson, missy. All this talk of appreciating my body will not make me forget."

"A girl can try."

She definitely seemed to be up for trying, and that thrilled me.

I pointed to the water. "Try that."

Her expression turned serious as she nodded. Ready.

* * *

She spent maybe fifteen minutes in the water. Most of it near the shore. I showed her the basics, helped her with her life jacket, and then cheered as she paddled a short distance away.

When she got out of the kayak, the grin she wore was magnetic.

I pulled her in for a hug. "You did it. And I bet you love it now. I'll be running into you every morning."

She laughed against my chest. "Don't get ahead of yourself."

That seemed to be my mantra with Elle.

I met her gaze. "Don't worry. I won't."

Her eyes darkened, and she nibbled on the corner of her lips. Then she whispered the sweetest words. "Thank you."

"For what?"

"For making me feel safe."

In that moment, I understood why she'd been so wary of so many things.

Safety wasn't something another person could entirely promise you. But when I could, I would give it to her. "I'm glad you tried it."

"Me too," she said, her voice a little breathy, her body still close to mine. My thoughts spiraled away, and I pictured yanking her against me, kissing her hard and ruthlessly, and taking her home with me.

But I knew that wouldn't happen.

Except there was something in her eyes that wasn't there before.

Another deep breath, then she let go.

"Want to grab some breakfast?" she asked, as if rerouting her thoughts entirely.

And I'd have to do the same, because maybe my wishful thinking was leading me to misread her expression.

"Breakfast and I have been known to get along."

She grinned. "Great. I thought I would take you out to say thank you for getting me out of the house a couple of evenings this week. I did some Yelp research, and there's an organic café on the way back to town that serves steel-cut oats and handpicked blueberries. I'm guessing that's the only thing you put in your body in the morning?"

She knew me too well.

"Don't know where you got the idea that I was some kind of health nut," I said, with a *who, me* to my tone.

"It's a mystery to me too."

The real mystery, though, was why she was here. This wasn't like her. Not the Elle who had defined lines, rules, and boxes.

But maybe there was another side of her she was starting to embrace.

An Elle who'd tried a few new things this week.

I could only hope she'd try more.

16

———

ELLE

We ordered breakfast at Ampersand & Pie, an off-the-beaten-path café with chalkboard menus and wooden chairs painted sky blue. The sun warmed my shoulders on the outside patio, and Ella Fitzgerald crooned softly from the speakers inside the café, filtering out here.

Music. The balm to my soul.

But it wasn't music that had driven me to get out of bed this morning. To show up.

It was Colin, and I was trying to figure out what to do next with all these feelings I had for him.

Like how much I'd wanted him to kiss me on the shore.

How much I wanted to kiss him now.

I had to get my mind off kissing or I'd be a see-through woman, like I was to Janine and Alex the other night.

"So, my mom is with Alex today," I said, talking to keep myself busy.

"Oh yeah?"

"I think they're going bowling."

"This early?"

"Not yet. After lunch, I'm guessing. She's probably there

now. But he wasn't even up when I left. Not sure if you know this about teenage boys, but they have a thing for sleeping in," I said, tapping my watch as I prattled on. "He'll be sound asleep till at least nine."

He gestured for me to come closer, then dropped his voice to a whisper. "I do know that about teenage boys, having once, you know, been one," he said, then shifted gears to the mob voice he'd used the other night. "But it's time to fess up."

"What am I confessing to? Mob crimes? Did you get the dirt on Elle 'Moneybags' Mariano?" I asked, keeping up the playful mood.

He laughed. "I've got all the deets on you." He reached for his coffee, took a drink, and turned more serious. "But I was hoping you'd fess up about why you showed up this morning. It was quite a surprise to see you at the shore."

I tensed. I couldn't dance around anything today. "Not a bad one, I hope?"

"Never a bad one. But tell me. What made you want to go kayaking this morning?"

I reached for a napkin on the table, needing a distraction. Was I going to say this?

I was still trying to figure it out. "I'm not entirely sure."

He shot me a lopsided grin. "Fair enough. I'm glad you did though. But what made you nervous in the first place? You can swim, right? Wait. Don't tell me. Elle Mariano can't swim and my next project is to teach her how to dog-paddle?"

I tossed a napkin at him, pinging his shoulder with it. "I can totally swim!"

I just didn't like to anymore. I didn't like to take chances.

"So, what is it?" he asked, tilting his head, waiting. Simply waiting. Giving me time to answer, as well as to study his handsome face. Dark scruff lined his jaw—that sexy, allover stubble. How would it feel against me?

As good as it felt when he looked at me? His brown eyes were the shade of espresso, and they focused intently on me. I'd made a career out of listening to others, but I suspected I could learn from him, because this man made me feel as if he was hearing every single word.

This felt less like fun and more like talking. But it turned out that's what I wanted. I wanted the talking. I wanted the connection. Not just about movies and the mob, but other things—the things that had brought us together in the first place. Talking about life. Was this why I'd felt the urge to find him this morning? To talk more, as we had on Thursday? About deeper topics?

To seek a connection?

Maybe it was, so I womaned up. "Sam took me on his bike once, and we crashed. Spun out on the sidewalk. It was horrifying. I was banged up all over, bruises and cuts, and all I could think was there but for the grace of God," I said, recounting. "I've been cautious since then."

"Wow. That's terrible." He reached for his mug and lifted it. "And understandable why you felt that way. Why you'd be cautious." He sipped his coffee, taking his time, like he was considering what to say next. "But you liked zip-lining?"

I smiled. "I did."

"So what about roller derby?" he asked in a gentle voice.

"Ah," I said, holding up my index finger to make my point. "The seeming contradiction. But see, I've always skated, and it's indoors. And I like to be active, so skating seems like a more reasonable risk. But that's also why I'm a blocker, not a jammer."

He raised an eyebrow in question.

"Blocker is defense. Not as many injuries. It's the safer position."

"I see." He nodded slowly. "But this morning, you came out here, ready to take a chance. Fair to say?"

That was the question, wasn't it? And would I take the chance?

I stared at him, licked my lips, and thought about risks. Rewards. Chances. "I think I just wanted to surprise you. That was all I was thinking."

"Lucky me. But I also think maybe you do like to take chances, but in a safer way."

I noodled on that for a few seconds. Maybe more. "You might be right. I did feel safe on the zip line. And I felt safe kayaking with you."

"Good. That's key. You should always feel safe. We can go again if you want."

I flashed back on my fifteen minutes in the water, and how he'd walked me through all the basics. He hadn't pushed like Sam. He hadn't insisted. He'd respected my boundaries, while offering a hand. "I would go again with you. But no car racing, bungee jumping, or rock climbing."

He laughed, holding up his hands in surrender. "Bungee jumping is fun. I've done it several times, but I don't go regularly. Rock climbing though? You can't keep me away from that sport."

"Isn't rock climbing how you broke your tibia? How did that happen?" I asked, since he'd mentioned it in passing.

He rubbed a hand over the back of his neck. "Ah, remember what I said the other night about bad choices?"

"Sure."

"That was another one of mine. When I tried to do the triathlon the first time, I had the bright idea to do it hungover."

"Ouch."

"Ouch indeed. I fell, landed wrong, broke my leg, passed out, and wound up in the hospital. Fun times."

My heart squeezed for him. "Was that what did it? What made you stop using?"

He nodded fiercely. "Yep. Nothing like your family showing up and learning you've been doing drugs since you were thirteen."

Instinctively, I reached for his hand, clasping it tightly. "That was brave."

He cocked a brow as he squeezed back. "Yeah?"

"So brave. Change is the most courageous thing of all."

"I'm glad you tried kayaking, then."

But I needed to do more than try a sport that wasn't scary at all.

I needed to say the hard things.

The reason.

It had been sequestered inside me for the last two years. But I wanted to say it. He'd been so earnest. So open.

I'd never told him all the details. And now, as we were opening up to each other, the time seemed right. I felt ready. I let go of his hand. "He died in my arms," I said, giving voice to the worst night of my life, saying the hardest thing.

His jaw dropped. "Oh, Elle. I'm so sorry. I knew he OD'd, but didn't know the details."

I steeled myself to tell the story. "We weren't together. We hadn't been for a long time. But he showed up at my house, smashed, sick as a dog, white as a sheet. He stumbled inside, and I started to call my mom, since she's a nurse. But then he just started convulsing." The cruel memory flickered in my mind—Sam's eyes bugging out, his breath coming in spurts, his chest seizing up. I'd called 911 immediately, then crouched on the floor, holding him, desperately waiting for the ambulance to show up. It was too late. The medics pronounced him dead on the scene. "Alex saw the whole thing."

Pain sliced through me, and I winced at the memories.

Colin stood, moved around the table, and wrapped an arm around me. "That's such a terrible thing for him to see. I didn't watch my dad die, but I saw his body a few hours later when my mom found him. I'll never forget the image. It must have been so hard for Alex."

"It was. He didn't talk for a year. Only the basics. He couldn't speak. It was awful," I said. My voice broke, and a tear slipped down my cheek. "In some ways, I thought for a while there that I was going to lose Alex too. He was so far gone, I was afraid I'd never be able to reach him."

Colin swiped away the tears that had begun to fall faster.

"Colin," I said, sniffling, my voice thin as air. "That's why I'm scared."

"I get it. I do. I completely get it." His tone was a caress. "I was so scared when I lost my dad. I turned to the wrong things for a long time, and if it hadn't been for my brothers, my sister, and my grandparents, I don't know if I would have found my way out either. I'm glad Alex has at least come out the other side. I know with you as his mom, he's going to make it through just fine."

He smiled gently at me, and my heart thundered. With possibility.

I looked down, reached for his hand, threaded my fingers through his, and squeezed lightly. His touch was like turning on a light switch in a basement. It flickered briefly then started to light up the dark inside me.

"Maybe some days you'll want to kayak and some days you won't, and whatever you want is fine by me," he said. It made me hopeful.

Because . . .

"I feel safe with you," I said softly, circling back to what he'd said.

"Good." One word, that was all that was needed.

And now I wanted a little more. I could do this. I could manage a sliver of desire without my life crashing.

He was Colin. He was in recovery.

"I think I'm ready for something," I added.

"Tell me what you're ready for," he said, his voice rough with longing.

"To kiss you."

His grin was dirty and vulnerable at the same time. And it hooked into me.

It made my chest tingle and my skin sizzle.

And I waited, on the cusp of chances.

Nervous, but not at all.

Because once I closed my eyes and he dipped his mouth to mine, everything felt right.

Correction: everything felt electric.

Because holy hell.

Colin Sloan could kiss.

His lips were soft and confident. His touch was tender and possessive. His lips brushed mine in an exploration, and my head went hazy. My body turned hot.

And I lost all interest in breakfast.

In worries.

In talking.

I wanted to kiss and kiss and kiss.

I kissed him back, letting him know how much I liked it.

Only it felt like need.

I needed his lips, needed his tongue. I deepened the kiss, my tongue tangling with his, our lips exploring. He responded instantly to my pace, his hand cupping my cheek, his thumb stroking my jaw, as his lips claimed mine.

He kissed me like he'd been holding on to this kiss for ages.

Like he'd been holding back forever.

Like I was the only one he wanted to kiss.

It was that way for me—he was the one I wanted.

And I didn't want to end it.

I wanted more.

But the creak of the screen door broke the trance.

We pulled apart, breathless. I was sure my desire was written in my eyes.

The waitress didn't blink. She simply smiled and set down our food.

And then I took the biggest chance of all. "Actually, can we get that to go?"

17

COLIN

We reached my house minutes later, her car pulling in behind mine.

I half expected her to change her mind.

To say she'd been rash.

To backpedal.

But as soon as I got out of my car, she slammed her door shut and grinned. "I'm hungry."

"I've got your breakfast right here," I said, holding up the containers as we walked to the door.

"Not for that."

I drew a satisfying breath. "I had a feeling."

"You should. You should definitely have a good feeling about this," she said, frisky and sexy.

As I turned the key in the lock, I looked at her, all eager and ready. "I want to make you feel things you've never felt before."

Her skin shimmered with the flush of desire. "Like what?"

"Like pure desire. Because I'm obsessed with your pleasure. Every ounce of it, every inch of it, every second of it."

I ran my hand down her arm, leaving a trail of goosebumps in my wake.

"Colin," she said, as if she was trying to resist me. Trying futilely. "You say these things . . ." She trailed off as she seemed to collect her thoughts. "You say these things that make it so hard to resist you."

I opened the door, shooting her a grin. "Good. Don't resist me."

"I'm not."

Once inside, I set down the food, grateful that Shannon and Brent had swung by earlier to take Johnny Cash for the day. I didn't have to worry about letting him out. I focused on Elle, only on Elle. I held her face and kissed her deeply again.

She murmured as I explored her mouth, her lips, her neck.

Dear God, her neck was divine.

I broke the kiss and swept some hair off her neck. "These sparrows need attention right now."

"They definitely do."

We made our way to the couch.

I brushed my thumb over her top lip, tracing a soft line, and she parted her mouth, closing her eyes. But I didn't kiss her. I had something else planned. I moved my mouth to her ear and whispered, "I bet your neck is insanely sensitive."

She shivered, then moaned. "Want to find out?"

"I absolutely do."

I adjusted her so I was behind her, then pressed a hot kiss to her neck.

She gasped.

Perfect. Fucking perfect.

But she'd made it clear earlier what she liked, and I was all about giving the woman what she wanted.

"Just one second." I stood as she watched me. Reaching down to the hem of my T-shirt, I tugged it off.

"Oh God," she said on a heavy breath as she stared at my chest. "You are gorgeous."

She'd seen me shirtless before, but never like this. Never before I was about to have her. From the edge of her seat, she stared unabashedly, with hunger in her hazel eyes. The way she watched me sent bolts of lust through me.

I returned to the couch, sitting next to her, my every nerve ending firing for this woman. What I felt for her was physical and so much more. Her passion for her work, her drive to make a difference, her heart that gave and gave and gave—all of it had spurred on my feelings. But then *this*—her body, her desire that she was finally admitting—drove me wild.

"So, tell me something," I said, moving closer, dropping my hand behind her to touch her lower back, then tracing a line up her spine with my fingertips. She arched into me.

"Yes?"

I bent my head closer to her ear and whispered hotly, "Did you wear your hair up today for me?"

She exhaled deeply. "Yes."

I dragged my index finger up the back of her neck, loving that one word. *Yes.* "Because you know I have a thing for your sparrows."

"Do I know that?" She sounded breathless, and I rewarded that sound with a sweep of my lips across her throat.

"You do," I said rough, commanding. "You know exactly how much I want you. And I want you so damn much, Elle."

I needed to say these words. I'd been holding them inside for so many months. They had to be set free.

And as I kissed the gorgeous column of her neck, I repeated them. "So much."

"Same here. I want you so much," she said, and I could hear the fevered desperation in her tone. I was going to reward that wanting, as she tugged off her shirt, wearing only a bra.

Gorgeous.

Lowering my mouth to her shoulder and working my way over, I licked the line of birds to the edge of her hair. She shuddered. I smothered her neck in kisses. Up, down, across. Over her shoulder blades, and down and back up her spine.

Every kiss unleashed another moan from her, a sexy gasp, a needy sigh. Noises that were only a prelude of what I wanted to hear from her today.

18

ELLE

No one had ever made me feel like this. Like I was high on touch. Like I was dizzy from a kiss. I wanted him so badly, and not just physically. I wanted more of him, but my emotions had to be cordoned off. I'd already let so many of them escape, and I didn't know where emotions, dangerous, deadly things, would take me.

But I wanted to let go for this one day.

Let go of everything but the way he made me feel so alive.

"Close your eyes," he told me firmly, and I let them drift closed, giving in to the other senses. Giving in to touch, as he dipped his mouth closer to my skin, his lips fluttering over me once more. Giving in to sensation, as my hair spilled from its tie onto my neck when he undid my ponytail.

"Oh God," I gasped as his hands dove into my hair.

What was he doing? No one had ever touched me like this. Finding a spot on me and worshipping it.

And I'd never realized I'd wanted that till now, as he zeroed in on a part of my body that cried out for him.

With every kiss, I melted.

With every touch, I ached.

He read my responses as if it were his top-secret assignment to know every inch of me, and now he'd learned my neck was the gateway to my pleasure.

He'd unlocked the code to all my desires, and he was using it masterfully.

He threaded his talented fingers through my hair, gripping it, and I moved with him, moaned for him, as if I were notes he played on a cello. He was the musician; I was the instrument. He played and played and played, and my body sang for him, a song of pure desire. Of heat. Of want.

He twisted my hair once around his hand, pulling it to the side, and I tilted my head that way, giving him more room to devour my neck with kisses, like he was starved for me. He lavished pleasure all over, leaving me drenched in sensation from soft, fluttery whispers along my neck and territorial kisses that claimed me as his, all mixed with the whiskery rub of his stubble. His ever-present scruff was trimmed but long enough to brush against my skin with every kiss, bringing the intoxicating blend of soft and hard, of tender and rough.

He snaked an arm over my shoulders, grazing my breasts as he traveled down my belly, his fingertips dancing along my waist.

"You like what I do to you." It wasn't a question.

"So much," I said, as he flicked the tip of his tongue across my shoulder. When he kissed me like this, and he touched me like that, I wanted to give myself to him fully. But that was risky, so risky. A voice in the back of my head told me to stop thinking, just feel.

That was what today was for. And I wanted to relish it.

It had been a year in the making.

His hand reached the crest of my hip, and he traced the top of my panties through the fabric of my shorts.

"Touch me," I whispered.

He smiled against me, wickedly. "I will. But first, show me how much you like giving in. Show me how wet you are."

How much I liked it? Try craved it like air.

I unbuttoned my shorts and pushed them down, showing him my panties.

"Elle." He groaned huskily, moving his hand between my legs, touching my thighs. "Look at you, Elle. Look at how wet you get. For me." His fingers glided up the soft flesh of my thighs, and I parted my legs for him. Grazing the wet panel, he whispered, "I want to feel you on my cock. I want this sweet wetness all over me. Tell me how much you want me inside you right now. Tell me."

My body was a storm of lust as I said, "Yes, I want that. I want you so much."

He rose, shucked off his shorts, then his boxers, and my mouth went dry as I stared at his erection—hard, heavy, and so many glorious inches that I longed to take deep inside me. Bending to reach for his wallet on the table, he found a condom inside.

I pulled off my bra, then skimmed off my panties and socks, and I lay down on the couch.

But he would have none of that.

He sat and pulled me up. "Ride me," he commanded.

I gasped. I was nothing but cells and atoms, electrons and protons, smashing and colliding into lust and desire. I straddled him as he kissed me.

His lips were on my shoulders, my neck, my throat. His hands grabbed my breasts. His fingers raced down my arms. His erection bobbed against me as he tore open the packet.

As he rolled it on, I spotted the new ink on his hip. A simple black phoenix, akin to a stencil design. It matched the lotus, like he'd said. Matched it in its symbolism.

"For new beginnings," I whispered softly, tracing it with my fingertip. It mesmerized me, the art and lines, the placement on his body, but I shook off my reaction because I didn't want to think of beginnings. I wanted to think only of ending this epic ache in my body.

"Yes, for new beginnings," he said as his fingers grasped my hips, and I lowered myself onto his shaft.

I moaned decadently as I took him in, inch by inch, savoring the way he filled me. "I almost forgot . . ." I said as I started to move on him.

"Forgot what?" he asked, thrusting up into me.

I clenched around him. "How to feel good."

He groaned, jerking me down harder. "Does this feel good?"

"It's incredible, Colin. It's . . . intense," I said on an exhale.

The intensity thrummed in my bones, sizzling across my skin as he thrust up into me.

Then, because he was a fast learner, because he'd picked up in seconds all the shortcuts to my pleasure, he looped his fingers in my hair and pulled hard, exposing my throat to him. It was like an electric burst of ecstasy.

"This is better than my fantasies," he said, layering kisses onto my skin. "You get so wet, and I love how it feels to slide into you over and over."

"Tell me how it makes you feel," I said, losing touch with reality as he talked to me, his dirty words sending me onto another plane. The way he spoke to me was such an insane turn-on, and I was already aroused beyond my own comprehension. He kissed the hollow of my throat and drove deep into me.

"It's extraordinary. Being inside you is extraordinary. I want to feel you come on me." He slid a finger between my legs, brushing it lightly against me. He stroked me, and I moaned, a sound that contained all the pleasure in the universe. He'd flipped that switch, pushing me from chasing an orgasm to falling apart in his arms. I shuddered, pleasure wracking my cells, racing through me to flood every inch of my being.

I shouted his name. And with that, he thrust up into me like a mad man on a frenzied ride, desperate to follow me to the other side. He fucked me as aftershocks rippled through me, the sensation spreading to my fingers and toes.

As my moans subsided, I opened my eyes, watching him, loving the way he looked when he came. Nothing was sexier, nothing was hotter than watching the man I wanted lose control.

All for me.

Somehow I was his undoing.

And it turned out he was mine.

He fucked me into his own release, his eyes squeezed shut and his face contorted in pleasure. He grunted and groaned my name before biting my collarbone as he came.

"We can't stop," I whispered, voicing the most dangerous words. Words I shouldn't say. But my body had the reins, making decisions for me, seeking more bliss.

"We can't, and we shouldn't," he murmured, layering soft kisses on my neck.

Soon, when we came down from our high and my senses attuned to the world around me again, my stomach rumbled.

I was hungry for breakfast.

"Glad we got it to go," I said.

"Me too."

19

COLIN

That night

Colin: That thing you want me to do to you . . .

Elle: You'll need to be more specific. I want you to do a lot of things to me.

Colin: My bad. The thing where I make you come hard. Many times.

Elle: Oh, that thing. That little thing.

Colin: Your orgasms are not little. They're quite epic.

Elle: Give credit where credit's due. YOU.

Colin: *thumps chest* *squares shoulders* *asks when you can come over again so you can come over and over again*

Colin: Wait. I meant to say, can I take you out first and then make you come again? Ideally, countless times on my face?

Elle: I'm sorry, what did you say? I was suffering from an intense bout of text message–induced lust.

Colin: I have just the cure for that.

Elle: You are the cure for all my lust.

Colin: Excellent. Let's keep it that way.

Elle: I want to. My mom offered her services tomorrow night, so let me get back to you on a time. Actually, she offered her services anytime I want to get serviced by you!

Colin: You better not get serviced by anyone but me.

Elle: Um. It's more than service, Colin.

Colin: So much more.

Elle: Want to meet for dinner after my roller derby practice tomorrow? Alex will be at a friend's house, and then my mom can get him.

Colin: Dinner and then you.

Elle: Or me and then dinner.

Colin: I like this new side of you.

Elle: The voracious side?

Colin: Yes, and the one where you let me service it.

Elle: I like it too.

20

COLIN

We ate dinner on Sunday at a Thai restaurant on the second floor of a hotel on the Strip. Over pumpkin curry and drunken noodles, we talked about our siblings. She told me stories of things she and her sister did as kids – pranking each other and then sassing each other, she'd said. "Camille and I had tongues of fire, and we could unleash the insults."

I shared tales of the four of us, how my brothers and I pretended to do ballet jumps when Shannon was practicing for dance recitals and then how she'd write us fake notes from girls at school. Elle and I laughed at the silliness of our younger selves as we devoured the meal and the good conversation.

As we left, we headed for the stairwell instead of the crowded elevator.

Ah, stairwells. The perfect location for a little something.

She slid her body close to mine, rubbing her sexy frame against me, making contact with my erection. She arched an eyebrow and gazed south. "Hello there."

"Greetings to you too."

She pressed harder against my dick and started circling her hips in the empty stairwell. Then she dropped her hand to my jeans, grabbing me through the denim as she palmed the outline of my cock. "I guess you liked dinner," she said.

I jerked her even closer. "And now I want dessert."

Her eyes blazed with mischief as I spun her around and backed her against the wall. Cupping her face with my hands, I gazed at her. I drank in her absolute beauty, savoring the way she looked up at me. Her lusty expression, her parted lips, her racing breath.

I lifted my thumb to her mouth, brushing it against her lips. I half wanted to ask what we were doing. Half wanted to ask for clarity. I had a sense she wasn't ready for that though.

But I suspected she was ready for this. I stroked her bottom lip softly with the pad of my thumb, then asked, "Know what I want to do right now?"

"Tell me."

"I want to spread you out, worship your sexy body, and take my time licking and kissing and sucking you all over. I want to taste every inch of your skin before I bury my face between your legs," I said, dropping my hand to her jeans and cupping her. She moaned as I felt how hot she was through her clothes.

"I have to be home in less than an hour." She sounded so damn desperate and hungry and horny that I was dying to strip her jeans to her ankles, kneel before her, and taste her heat. But I was patient. I was going to have her when I had time to feast.

"Not now," I whispered. "But when I do, it'll be like this." I angled her head slightly, then flicked my tongue gently over her mouth. She gasped, shuddering as I lightly brushed my lips over hers, as if I were tasting her sweetness. She trembled in my arms as I showed her precisely how I intended to lavish attention on her, how I'd kiss and suck and then devour her. God, I wanted her. I wanted her so badly. On my mouth, flooding my tongue, all over my lips, drenching my chin. I kissed her like that. Like a man consumed. My hands clutched her cheeks, my lips fused to hers, and my mind raced with images, sensations, and fantasies about how she'd taste with her legs wrapped around my neck, writhing and bucking as she grabbed my hair and came hard on my tongue.

I couldn't take it anymore. In a mad fury, I unzipped her jeans and dipped my hand inside her panties. Oh hell. This was wetness. This was lush, delicious heat. I stroked her, and in seconds my fingers were coated.

"Look at you," I said, breaking the kiss. "Look at how wet you are." I pulled my hand out of her panties and brought my fingers to my mouth. My eyes rolled shut as I tasted her. She tasted like sex and lust. I opened my eyes to find her staring at me hungrily, jaw agape.

The stairwell was dark and echoey, and every sound, every moan bounced on the heavy walls as I stroked her.

"Take me someplace. Anyplace. Now. Please," she said, gripping my shoulders as I rubbed her clit, a hard little diamond—swollen, wet, and begging for my touch.

"Now?"

"Yes," she said, but her body said she wanted it here.

And I didn't want to deny her.

I slipped a finger inside her heat, thrilling at the instant reaction it elicited from her. She clasped a hand over her mouth, capturing her own moan. Her knees buckled, and I used my free hand to steady her. Gripping her hip, I moved my mouth to her ear. "Fuck my hand," I told her.

She rolled her hips, riding my fingers as I thrust inside her.

My dick was so hard it was practically staging a mutiny. I ached to sink in and spend the whole night inside her.

But I wanted her pleasure more. Her release. Her bliss. And I knew how to find it. I knew the way around her body because I'd never wanted anyone with this kind of raging intensity. I crooked my finger, hitting that magic spot that sent her flying. She curled her fingernails into my shoulders, digging in, holding on, as her mouth formed a perfect O. I sealed my lips to hers, swallowing her cries of pleasure as she came hard on my fingers in the stairwell.

* * *

The clock was ticking.

But I knew this city. Knew all the private spots.

Knew them from my days of causing trouble.

I drove her to one on the edge of a park, dark and quiet.

We scurried into the back seat of my car. I pulled down her jeans to her knees, put her on all fours, and unzipped my pants. I tapped her knees.

"Spread wider."

She obliged, widening her position, as I rolled on a condom.

She bent her back and lifted her ass, and I smacked it once with my palm. "Couldn't resist," I said playfully. "Too tempting."

"Don't resist."

"Never," I said, and then like we were in high school, like we couldn't wait, like we had a secret, I slid inside her in the back of the car.

"Oh fuck, Elle," I said on a groan, as I savored that intense moment when I was first inside the woman I craved. I picked up the pace. "Need to get you home soon, so I'm going to have to pull out all the stops."

"Yes, please. Fuck me harder."

Lust sizzled down my spine. I loved learning that Elle was rough and carnal in the bedroom. Outside she was strong, serious, focused.

In bed, she was intense, dirty, and hungry.

Perfect for me.

Setting a fevered rhythm, I stroked into her. She moaned with each thrust, panting as I filled her. "You tasted so damn good on my fingers," I said huskily. "I can't wait to have you. When I do, I'm going to show you exactly why you came so many times alone at night thinking of me."

"I did, Colin. I do," she said, swiveling her hips as I pumped into her, admitting how much she'd been wanting me too. "I thought about fucking your face all the time."

Oh hell. Those words were like a straight shot of lust through my bloodstream. They set me on fire. They flipped switches all over. I groaned deeply.

Her body answered with an epic shudder, a wild tightening against my dick, which was so damn hard inside her. Her slick walls gripped me as I slammed in and out of her, pulling back so only the tip was in her.

"You're close, aren't you?"

"So close."

I paused momentarily, then whispered in a low, dirty growl in her ear, "Say it. Say it when you come. Say you're going to come so fucking hard," I said to her. Her body trembled, and everything in her reaction told me she was there, finding her way to a second coming. "Say it," I commanded, as I fucked her.

"I'm going to come so fucking hard," she said, her voice falling to pieces as she came on me. She cried out in ecstasy as I fucked her furiously, my balls tightening as my own orgasm tore through my body.

I wanted to collapse onto her, to wrap my arms around her and just exist in this sated, blissful state. Instead, I looped my hands around her sexy waist, holding her close as we collapsed onto the seat. I brushed my lips against her collarbone, and she shivered then flashed me a small smile.

"What are we doing?"

The million-dollar question. I hadn't wanted to push. I didn't want to define this.

"What do you want this to be?" I asked.

"I don't know. All I know is I don't want to stop."

"I don't want to stop either," I said.

Whether that meant we were a thing or a no-strings thing was anyone's guess.

Until she spoke. "But I think I'd like to see you more."

I grinned. So wide I could feel it in my heart, especially when we made plans for later in the week.

21

COLIN

The face was eerily familiar.

I nearly stopped in my tracks as I rounded the corner on my way to the game room at the community center a few days later. *That guy.* Walking toward me. I had noticed him shooting hoops a few times. I'd seen him in a math tutorial a couple of months ago.

But I'd also seen him in a photo on Brent's phone.

My eyes widened as I studied the guy heading in my direction. That was the dude who'd been stalking my twin sister. Brent had taken a picture of him outside Shannon's home one afternoon more than a month ago.

What the hell?

The hair on my neck stood on end. A primal instinct to protect my flesh and blood kicked in. I wanted answers. Wanted to know why the hell a teen at the community center had been parked outside Shan's house . . . more than once. The guy had dark eyes, dark hair, and ink covering his right arm. He wore jeans. His boots clunked on the linoleum floor.

I hadn't yet gotten Brent to resend the image so I could

forward it to Elle. Now the guy was here, and I was going to cut out the middleman.

"Hey," I said to get his attention.

The guy stopped short and peered around, like he was making sure who I was talking to. He pointed at himself and mouthed, *Me?*

"Yeah. You," I said, tilting my head. One part of me wanted to demand an answer. But the other part, the rational, logical, adult portion, told me not to jump to conclusions.

Give him the benefit of the doubt.

"What's your name?"

"Marcus," the guy answered, shifting on the balls of his feet.

I motioned him to the side of the hallway, next to the bulletin board layered with announcements for center activities: a poetry class, the free lunch schedule, basketball leagues.

Marcus joined me. I scrubbed a hand across my chin, then dived into business, meeting him square in the eyes. "This might sound weird. But I'm pretty sure you were hanging around outside my sister's house a few times. Shannon Sloan. What's up with that?"

He answered immediately. "It's not weird." Marcus pulled up his right shirtsleeve. I flinched, but quickly relaxed when I saw the ink. It matched Rex's arm. *Protector.* "I do safety patrols with the Protectors," Marcus added. "If you saw me somewhere, that was probably why. We go to a lot of neighborhoods."

I blinked. "Really?"

Marcus nodded. "Yup. We do. And I do."

A smile broke out across my face. Color me impressed. "Rex was telling me about the Protectors. Like the Guardian Angels."

"That's where we got our inspiration from. Rex and I do patrols together sometimes. By the way, it's nice to meet you officially." He extended a hand. Something that looked like happiness flashed in Marcus's eyes as we shook. I wasn't sure what to make of it.

"Sorry, I should have given you my name. Colin Sloan. I volunteer here. Good to meet you too. Truth be told, I was worried you were part of the Royal Sinners. We thought you might be when I saw you outside Shan's house. That you were targeting my sister for something."

Marcus held up both his hands, a sign he had nothing to hide. "No. God no. I want nothing to do with them. I was just checking things out. We've been scoping out a bunch of neighborhoods, even nicer ones. Just to make sure."

"Make sure of what?"

"That the streets are safe. No matter what." Marcus tapped his arm. "Always."

"That's awesome. Keep it up, man," I said. I couldn't wait to tell Shannon and Brent that there was nothing to fear, and that this kid was doing a good thing for the community. I knocked fists with the young man. I started to walk down the hall, when Marcus called out to me.

"Hey."

I turned around. Marcus swallowed then cleared his throat, as if he was about to say something difficult. He was quiet, and I waited, giving him time. I didn't want to pressure him.

"I sat in on one of your math sessions a few months ago. When I first checked out the center," he said, and that wasn't what I expected him to say.

But I was glad to hear it.

"That's good. What did you think?"

Marcus nodded several times and ran a hand over his

chin, a gesture that I often did. Well, it wasn't unique to me. Lots of people did that. Still, I felt as if I was looking in a mirror for a second, seeing my younger self reflected back at me. "Yeah. Learned some stuff about P and L statements. I'm going to college in the fall."

"Good for you. No better decision in the world than to go to college. I'm glad. Let me know if you need any more help. Math is kind of my forte. I'd be happy to work with you if you need anything."

Marcus smiled briefly. "I will. Thanks. That means a lot to me," he said, and his voice sounded like the very definition of the word *hopeful*. Odd, considering we were talking about math. For a moment, Marcus seemed like he was about to say something more—he had that look again, like he was on the cusp of something, almost like he'd been practicing something he wanted to say. But then he cut himself off. "I gotta run."

"Take it easy," I said, and turned the other way.

I had an appointment with Rex to work on advanced algebra, thanks to the bet I'd won on the court the other day. As I headed to the homework room, my phone buzzed in my back pocket. My heart beat faster in the hope that it would be Elle, confirming a time for tomorrow evening. Then I nearly smacked myself for being so damn eager to see her.

Take it easy. Play it cool.

But fuck it. I'd been waiting a year, and we were becoming something.

Only her name wasn't the one on my screen.

It was my brother Michael.

Michael: Detective wants to meet again tonight re: some new info. Ryan has some details. He's going to call you a little later when he's in a better cell zone. I told the detective he could come to your place, and I'm going to be there to talk to him with you.

I heaved a sigh.

Typical Michael. Even though the detective liked to meet with us alone to discuss the reopened investigation, Michael would have his way. I suspected this was his means of making up for something that had never been his fault. He'd blamed himself for the trouble I'd gotten into in high school, especially because of the company I had kept as a young teen.

Now, he was likely trying to protect me, where he felt he hadn't before.

He was wrong. But he was also stubborn.

I fired off a return text.

Colin: Working with the kids now. Should be done in an hour or so and hope to catch Ryan then. Did he give you the details?

As I walked into the game room, a reply arrived.

Michael: The call kept breaking up. Something about that pattern. Sounds like it's a hell of a lot more than a few names and addresses.

The pattern again. That damn pattern Ryan had told me about. When I'd first learned whose names were in it, TJ and Kenny Nelson, I couldn't believe that I'd known both men many years ago. Now they somehow held clues to my father's murder.

22

ELLE

A construction crew jackhammered outside my closed window, smashing the broken sections of the basketball courts in preparation for smoothing them over with a fresh concrete surface. A pair of new security guards patrolled the block, courtesy of Colin. The sight of them brought a smile to my face—the man had moved quickly to make sure the center was safe during this time of transition.

As I surveyed the signs of change, I chatted on the phone with some of the center's biggest donors, making my round of calls to thank them for their contributions.

I dialed another number and spoke briefly with Charlie, a benefactor in San Francisco who'd attended the Beethoven concert event more than a week ago. "We couldn't have done it without you. We're already starting the work, and I'm thrilled to say it's going well so far," I said as I gazed out the window. "I'm watching them rebuilding the basketball courts right now. And the boys spend a lot of time there, so your contribution is being put to good use immediately."

"It is a pleasure and an honor to help such a worthy cause."

"If you're in Vegas again, I do hope you'll stop by the center to see our work."

"I come to Vegas often. Once a week now, it seems, and I will take you up on that. And, please, you can count on me to be a regular contributor. Giving to the center allows me to right some wrongs from my past."

"It does?" I asked, curious as to what he meant.

He sighed with a note of regret, but his voice seemed hopeful too as he answered me. "I made some mistakes when I was younger. I held on to a debt longer than I should have. This is my amends."

"I'm a big fan of making changes," I said, smiling as we talked about redemption and all its possibilities. Sam had never truly embraced the concept of making amends, though I desperately wished he had. Even during his rehab stints, he'd never tried to apologize for his past sins and omissions. His sober behavior was remarkably similar to his behavior when he'd been high—yet another reason I'd never trusted his recovery. It had never stuck, and he'd never truly changed.

Colin was the opposite.

He gave of his time. He opened his heart. He'd learned from the past. What would it be like if I were to truly give in? To let go of all my rules? To break my promises to my son?

Because I'd promised it'd be only him and me.

I'd promised I wouldn't get involved with someone else while he lived with me.

And I had to protect him first.

After the call ended, someone rapped on my door, so I swept aside my musings about Colin and making amends.

I rose and opened it, delighted to see Marcus on the other side. But my smile fell quickly—his face was white as snow.

"I need to talk to you. Badly." His voice shook.

Worry coursed through me, a prickly flurry of nerves as I shut the door. "Of course, come in. What's going on?"

He sank onto my couch and dropped his head in his hands, running his fingers roughly through his hair. My heart lurched toward him.

"I need to talk. About some heavy shit. And you can't tell anyone," he said, raising his face.

"Are you going to tell me something I'd *need* to tell someone else?" I looked him in the eye, making it clear that I'd keep his confidences if they didn't cross certain lines. "Because if you tell me you're going to hurt yourself or someone else, there's no confidentiality."

"No. God, no," he said with a brief laugh, but it was a joyless sound. "I just need this to be between us."

While I wasn't technically Marcus's social worker, I'd been trained as one. And as the center director, I strove to abide by proper guidelines. That meant I'd keep whatever we discussed between the two of us.

"My family, who I've been trying to meet? My brothers? My sister?" he said, as if he needed to remind me.

"Yes."

He sighed deeply. "You know one of them."

I cocked my head, trying to figure out who on earth it could be. "I do?"

He nodded and gulped. "You do. He's a volunteer here, and I knew that when I first came here to play hoops. He's the reason I started coming around the center. To see what my family was like. To get a sense of them before I met them."

The world froze. Everything and everyone became a statue as I swayed, absorbing his news.

"Colin Sloan is one of my brothers."

I clasped a hand to my mouth. Then it was my turn to sink down, as I fell into my chair and tried to rearrange my shock so I could lend my support to Marcus.

"My dad never wanted me to meet them," Marcus said. "He always told me I was safer staying away from them. So I respected his wishes while I lived under his roof. I'm worried he's going to be pissed when he finds out, but I don't care. I have to do this. I need to go back and try again. Especially since I just talked to Colin in the hall."

"Does he know?" I asked, my voice papery.

Marcus shook his head. "No. Not yet. But he seems like a good guy, and I want to do this right." He talked more about his parents and the twisted tale of how his dad met his mom, and how his dad felt about her. When he was done, he took the biggest inhalation in the world and relaxed into the couch, spreading his arms across the back of it. "You're the only person I've told about this. God, it feels good to finally say their names. To finally be able to talk to someone and share all the details."

He was unburdened, buoyed with relief. Meanwhile, I'd taken on the weight of one of the biggest secrets I could ever imagine keeping from someone I cared for.

Deeply.

Holy smokes. The realization crash-landed into me that Colin wasn't just the man I was having fun with. He was more to me than that. And even if I couldn't have it, I realized I wanted more than these nights with him.

This wasn't the plan. This wasn't supposed to happen. He was supposed to be my shot at fun.

Which made this new situation that much harder. Because I'd just spent the last hour in a strange state of suspended animation as I counseled a boy on how to reconnect with the family of the man I was involved with.

Never in my life had I wanted to clone myself like I did now. Never had I so badly needed there to be two of me at once.

23

––––––

COLIN

I closed the math app on my laptop, pleased with the progress that Rex had made. After winning the basketball court bet, I had expected some resistance, but he'd taken quickly to the business math we worked on, and had decided to sign up for a math placement test at the community college in just a few days.

As a reward for all his hard work, Rex now attacked a fleet of zombies as he played video games with Tyler and Elle's son, Alex.

Alex pointed, practically stabbing the screen. "Get that one. Do it now!" he shouted at Rex.

My heart lurched for a second, and it had nothing to do with zombies. I felt a pang of sadness for Alex, understanding him in a new way. I'd lost a father too.

We'd responded in different ways. I'd turned to drugs. He'd turned inward.

But somehow we'd both found our way to the other side.

What was the other side for Elle though?

Would she ever allow herself to be on it? I understood

her need to protect her son, but I feared she'd never truly let herself be happy again.

"Rex, look out! There's another one. You have to book it to the safe house!" The warning came from Rex's little brother. Rex narrowed his eyes in fierce concentration, jamming his thumb hard on the controller, firing away at a zombie and blasting him to smithereens.

"Oh yeah! You did it! Man. You don't suck as much as I thought," Alex said to Rex, then punched him on the shoulder.

Rex craned his neck to catch my attention. "Hey, man! Got any tips for us on this game?"

"You know anything about video games?" Alex asked as I stuffed my laptop into my messenger bag.

"Video games are in my wheelhouse."

Alex's eyes lit up, eager. "Can I have a tip? I want to up my game."

Do something cool for Elle's kid? That was a no-brainer—I liked working with the boys, and I liked that I could be a positive influence rather than a bad one. "Here's your tip. It's all strategy. You just devise a strategy and follow it. But don't be afraid to pivot if things change, and then to pivot again," I said, letting my own advice register. Because as I pondered these words, I realized they might apply to my approach with Elle.

My strategy had been to take my time, to practice patience, to hold back on emotions.

The approach had worked, to a point. Each encounter we'd had was hotter than the last, and each moment together seemed to show us how good a time we could have. The question was, when would it be time to let her know what I felt for her? I sensed she felt it too, and maybe she needed the same thing again—someone to make her feel safe before she took a chance.

As the boys returned to the game, I tapped the back of the couch and told them I'd see them later in the week. On the way out, I walked past the vending machine. The Diet Cherry Coke had been restocked. A rarity. I plugged some quarters in and snagged a cold one, then stopped by Elle's office to say a quick goodbye.

She loved Diet Cherry Coke in the afternoon. A pick-me-up. Yes, it was a small thing. But wasn't it the little gestures in life that often mattered the most?

The door was shut. I knocked and heard some rustling and the squeak of a chair. There was no answer. I waited ten seconds before I knocked once more.

"I'm busy now." Her voice was tinny from behind the walls.

I set the can on the floor and left, sending her a text that the soda was from me.

A few minutes later, as I drove home, my phone rang with a call from an international number. I swiped over the screen immediately, eager for the information Ryan had.

"How's Johnny Cash?"

I laughed deeply. Only my dog-loving brother would focus on the four-legged beast first. "I'm on my way home to take care of him now. He is a prince among canines. I took him to the dog park the other night, and all the lady dogs ran up to him," I said into the speakerphone as I slowed at a red light.

"They can't help themselves around him. You can use him as a wingman if you think he can help you land a woman. Wait. What's the latest with that woman from the benefit?"

I tapped the steering wheel and blew out a long stream of air. "Like I said before you left, it's complicated. Speaking of complicated, you know that kid who was following Shan? I've got great news for you." I told my brother what I'd learned an hour ago about the Protectors. "So it's all good. We don't need to worry about him," I said, pressing the gas as the light changed. "Now, why don't you tell me why the hell you're calling from Germany at midnight your time when you should be focusing on your woman?"

"Don't you worry. I am focusing on my woman, but you will not believe what she found out the other night."

"Lay it on me."

"Sophie was jet-lagged and couldn't sleep. So she was working on deciphering the rest of the pattern, the sewing pattern that Mom gave me before she went to prison."

I clenched my jaw. "I still can't believe she asked you to do that, asked you to keep that dog jacket pattern like a trophy, knowing that you believed in her and held out hope she'd be found innocent and freed one day."

"Yeah, Sophie cracking the code that it wasn't really a sewing pattern at all, but Mom's dirty breadcrumb trail back to her crime was what it took to open my eyes to the truth," Ryan said.

"So, the first row of the pattern revealed the addresses of Stefano, the shooter, and the two alleged accomplices—the broker and the getaway driver—in Dad's murder. What else did Sophie find out? What were the rest of the lines?" I asked.

"It's a list of more addresses. They had missing numbers and symbols, but she worked on it and she figured out all of them. She gave it to John, and when he put it together with the leads he's been looking into, he believes the pattern reveals a hell of a lot more than just those two guys. You better be sitting down," Ryan said, his voice heavy and intense.

I slowed the car, pulled over, and cut the engine. "Talk to me. What is it?"

Ryan heaved a sigh, then told me the newest wrinkle.

I was damn glad I'd pulled over. My head fell back against the headrest, the shock of Ryan's new revelation echoing in my bones.

When I reached my home and leashed up my brother's dog, my phone buzzed once more. Elle had messaged me at last. But when I read her note, frustration seared me to a crisp.

Elle: I'm so sorry. I have to cancel tomorrow. Something came up.

24

COLIN

Johnny Cash trotted perfectly by my side as Michael pulled up in his black BMW, a mountain bike on the roof. I slowed my pace and met Michael as he stepped out of his car. My brother must have come straight from the office—he wore his usual striped button-down, tie, and dark pants. When he reached me, he whipped off his sunglasses, his cool blue gaze sharp as ever. "Did you talk to Ryan? You ready for the detective?"

I pushed my palm down as if to say *Let's take it easy.* "It's just a talk. I've got nothing to hide."

Michael clapped me on the back. "I know that, man. I was just asking. Just making sure."

I brushed off Michael's hand. "I get it. But the point is I'm neither worried, nor surprised about anything related to our mother," I said, though that wasn't entirely true. I'd been shocked by the news Ryan had shared about her, but only for the first few minutes. At this point I was accustomed to hearing that she was a less than stellar citizen.

What had me so prickly was Elle's cancellation of our

plans tomorrow with zero explanation. Nothing. Not a word. That confused the hell out of me, especially because I had no right to ask her what was up. We weren't a thing yet. She'd made no promises, and I had no reason to feel slighted.

Except . . . she'd been giving off some serious vibes the last night we were together.

Maybe that had been wishful thinking on my part. Maybe I'd been reading too much into one small, sweet little moment. And maybe I'd read too much into the "see you more" line.

Time to wise up and accept what she would give, instead of angling for something I couldn't have.

Best to focus on my present, and that involved a detective, who parked his Nissan LEAF at the curb in front of my house. I nudged Michael, then dropped my voice. "I never would have pegged the detective as the owner of an electric car."

Michael laughed. "Doesn't he know he's required to drive a sedan? Four doors, dark blue, unmarked. Just like in the movies."

John walked over to the two of us, took off his shades, and said hello. Johnny Cash barked at the man. I tugged on the dog's leash, giving him a quick correction. "It's okay, Johnny Cash. If you're nice to him, the detective won't throw us in the pokey," I said.

John rubbed the dog's head. "Nice name for a dog. And I don't have any plans to throw you in the pokey." He paused, then added, "At least not today." John shifted his gaze to Michael. "Good to see you again too, Mr. Sloan."

Michael nodded. "I know you were planning on talking to Colin, but I see no reason why I can't be here."

John nodded and shot him a closed-mouth smile. "Not

a problem. Happy to chat with both of you about the latest. Do you want to talk inside? Or chat on the porch?"

My street was quiet now, so I opted for the porch.

John dived right into the heart of his visit.

25

JOHN

It had been a helluva week. Working around the clock. Gathering info. Talking to witnesses.

"Here's the deal." I took a piece of paper from my pocket then spread open a copy of the sewing pattern on my lap. The dog lifted his snout to sniff it. "We knew from Sophie's first attempts that this pattern contained more than just a few names. Now that she's figured out all the addresses in it, we were able to track them to who lived in those houses at the time of the murder. We believe this was a drug dealing route," I told them.

"Surprise, surprise," Michael said. "Inmate 347-921 was a drug dealer, in addition to being a murderer. What next? She ran a child pornography ring? Oh, wait. She probably operates an underground sex slave business from prison." Michael shoved a hand through his hair. "Every time it's something else with her."

That was part and parcel of my job, delivering news no one wanted to hear. A pang of sympathy played inside me. "Sorry to be the bearer of more bad news," I said, then moved on to the facts. "We believe these men were at the top of the pattern not only because of their potential involvement in the murder, but because of their role in the drug ring, and we think below them is the list of people Dora was selling to regularly. Presumably, she hid her route in the pattern so no one in her family would know what she was doing. We'd previously thought Stefano was her dealer, but it seems he was a step up. He was her supplier and provided the drugs she sold. That's why she owed him money—for the drugs she'd procured from him." I turned to Colin, hoping he could shed some light. God, I hoped he could. "But we don't believe Stefano was the one who recruited her into the ring. Do you know anything about how she got involved? Can you remember anything?"

Michael raised a hand and cut in before his brother could say a word. "Why are you asking him?"

"Because of the friends he had when he was younger," I said, answering in a cool, even tone. That's how it needed to be. We needed to traffic in facts in order to crack this. "That's why I'm here talking to him."

"I'll answer it," Colin said firmly, taking the reins. "The answer is no. I have no clue how she got involved in dealing drugs. I had no idea she was selling, but it doesn't surprise me, because she was a fucked-up, desperate woman. But if you're asking for details about the drug business the Royal Sinners were in, I'll tell you anything I know. I've been up-front with you from day one, Detective. When I was thirteen, I hung with the wrong crowd. I was friends with the wrong people, and yes, I was friends with the brother of one of the men whose address was in the pattern. TJ Nelson's brother Danny. He was fifteen and I was thirteen, and when Ryan told me TJ's name was in that pattern, I was shocked—and frankly embarrassed that I was ever friends with his brother. We did stupid shit.

Egged houses, TP'd them. That was as far as we went. But we knew what the older guys were doing because we heard them talk."

"What did you hear?" I asked, a kernel of hope rising inside me. This whole case had popped up again because of what Bianca Rosa—Stefano's girlfriend at the time—had overheard. You never knew where information ignited, and what it would lead to. I had to chase those leads to see where they'd take me.

"They were always talking about territory. They claimed 'hoods' for fencing their stolen goods, and when they moved deeper into drugs, they claimed sections of neighborhoods for selling those too," Colin said, outlining what had gone down. "They marked everything that was theirs with gang logos, insignia, personal graffiti. They'd have a field day on Facebook today with the way they tagged stuff."

I nodded, since all of this added up. "The gang culture, oddly enough, loves social media. They post pictures of themselves online, on Instagram and Facebook, holding wads of bills from their drug sales or showing off electronics they stole."

"That's what it was all about then, too, in an old-school way."

I scratched my chin, sliding into the next question, a mission-critical one. "What do you know about TJ Nelson?"

"He's the guy you think brokered Stefano's hits, right?" Michael chimed in.

He was right—after my sister uncovered the code in the pattern, and Ryan delivered some fresh details on potential names, I'd had enough info to pinpoint the suspected accomplices, thanks in part also to the initial intel from Stefano's long-ago girlfriend.

The men in question were a pair of cousins, TJ and Kenny Nelson. And I believed they'd helped Jerry Stefano pull off the murder. When Stefano went to prison, he never gave up their names. But once I'd started working the case now, new evidence pointed to their roles—TJ as the broker and Kenny as the getaway driver.

"We think that's a strong possibility. We want to know more about him, and how big his role was," I said.

"Big? Like he was a mastermind of the whole thing?" Colin asked, arching a brow.

But I had to keep certain details close to the vest, including that one. "There are a number of possibilities we're looking into. Tell me what you know about him."

I'd like to say I'd been waiting patiently to learn more about TJ Nelson, but that'd be a lie. I was as eager as a kid at an ice-cream truck in the summertime to learn all I could about that man.

That man who I suspected had committed terrifying crimes.

26

COLIN

I sighed deeply, rewinding to my days as a thirteen-year-old, picturing TJ Nelson, the towering older brother with the short mohawk, gold earring, and menacing smile. His arms were made of steel, and he had a head for strategy. He was always plotting. "What I remember overhearing was TJ talking about who was handling what in the Royal Sinners. He was very focused on which guys were responsible for which areas. The territories, they called them," I said. "And they also talked about the protection of them."

"Of the territories?" John asked, his voice tight and clipped, a shift from his previous tone, as if he was holding something in.

"Yes. I didn't have any of the details, but that's some of what I overheard when he was around. Who handled the fences. Who picked up the drugs. That sort of thing." I held up my hands like an innocent man, telling the whole truth. "I had no clue my mom was selling, dealing, or using. But given what you figured out with that pattern, maybe that's what she was doing talking to them. Maybe she was negotiating her territory for selling."

"Seems she got a prime one," John said. "Any idea why she would?"

"No idea. Except that she was desperate, and maybe she had some strings to pull, because she was willing to do whatever she had to do to get what she wanted. That's what I know to be true about her. Maybe she and Stefano were working together," I said, because that seemed plausible to me.

Michael jumped back in. "What's going on with the Royal Sinners these days, Detective? I follow the news—I've been reading up on them, seeing more and more stories about them rising in power. More crimes, more problems, more trouble. More organized, too, than their rival gangs. I keep hearing 'Don't mess with the Sinners.'"

A somber look flitted into the detective's eyes. "You're hearing right. They're a top priority for Metro, and my men are working hard on gang activity enforcement and prevention. We've got an anonymous tip line for concerned citizens to report suspected gang activity, an anti-gang initiative, and strong public education. We're doing everything we can on the enforcement front. Last week, we had a few more arrests of Royal Sinners members for grand theft auto, and some from rival gangs for burglary."

"Glad to hear it's being taken seriously. Some of my other clients have also been asking about it and increasing their security services based on what they've been reading in the news," Michael said. "They want to protect themselves, and to know the authorities are working hard on it too."

"I assure you, we are. And you can let your clients know that you've talked to Metro and that we're committed to this," he added. "We're doing everything we can to dismantle the gangs, member by member."

My brain latched onto that last word, making me wonder if my old friend Danny had gone down the path of his brother into the Sinners.

"Hey, what happened to Danny? We didn't stay friends."

"Danny Nelson is dead," John said matter-of-factly, and my blood froze. "Shot three times in a drive-by shooting a few years ago. Retaliation from another gang over a murder. One we think TJ was involved in. Both TJ Nelson and Kenny Nelson seem to be on the run. They're wanted for other crimes over the years."

My whole body turned to ice. "Wow," I said heavily, grappling with the shocking news. "Danny died before he was thirty."

"Gangs are a young man's business," John said. "You don't find many old men in street gangs. The young men usually die or wind up in prison by the time they hit thirty. Like Danny Nelson. Like Jerry Stefano."

"What about TJ and Kenny Nelson? They must be in their forties. What's their secret to a long life as gang men?"

"I'd like to know. Because they're the exception to the rule," John said, then thanked us for our time and left.

27

MARCUS

The bell above the door jingled. I looked up from my math book as a guy in jeans and a black T-shirt entered the convenience store where I worked.

I nodded a hello then returned to the page in front of me, as my mind replayed the day. Talking to Elle had unburdened me, and I was more fired up than ever about my plans. College, living on my own, getting to know my unknown family—I'd wanted all of that for so long, and I was close to having it. Living with my dad had been stifling for so many reasons. Sometimes I missed seeing my step-mom, Angie, and my little sisters now that I was no longer at home with them, but Angie kept in touch, checking in about my college prep. I was glad to be on my own, and I was on a path to becoming an assistant manager here at the store. That was helping make ends meet, along with my savings from other little jobs over the years.

As I worked through some equations, the guy grabbed a bag of chips and sauntered over to the counter. He was about my age, maybe a year older. He had a goatee, light eyes, and a black-and-blue fingernail on his right hand, as if he'd slammed it in a car door.

He tossed the bag on the counter, as if it were a prize he'd won at the fair. *Okay.* "I'll take this tasty bag of barbecue chips, *please*," he said, stretching out the last word.

"Sure," I said, scanning the bag. "That'll be a dollar and two cents."

The guy jammed his hands into his pockets, riffling around. He pulled out a flip phone and set it on the counter, eyeing it dismissively. "Someday I'll get an iPhone." Stuffing his hand into his pocket again, he produced a wadded-up bill, then spread it open. "Shit. I only have a one."

"That's cool. I got it," I said, reaching into the change tin to grab two pennies. It was just easier to cover for him.

"You are the man," the guy said with a too-wide grin as he pointed his index fingers at me like guns.

Yeah, I wasn't too wild about the gesture, but he'd be out of my life any second. "No problem."

The guy glanced at my textbook and stabbed his finger against it. "You learning algebra or something like that?"

I nodded, not bothering to explain that I was well beyond ninth grade math at this point. "Studying for a test."

"College?" the guy asked, as if he'd never heard of it before.

"That's the goal."

"Man, that shit looks hard. I can't even imagine."

I smiled faintly. I wasn't worried. I wanted the challenge. Wanted to meet it and exceed it.

The guy ripped open the bag with a loud pop and stuffed a chip in his mouth, crunching loudly, like he was showing off how well his teeth worked. "My goal is to never need college," he said, then cocked his head like he was studying me. "See you later," he finally said, then walked to the door and stopped to add, "*Marcus.*"

A chill swept through me as the bell jingled and the guy left.

How the hell did he know my name?

I glanced down at my work shirt and laughed at myself. My name tag was on. "Duh," I said, relieved, then grabbed my phone when it buzzed with a text from Angie.

Angie: How's the studying going? I would offer to quiz you but I'm pretty sure you want to pass.

I replied right away, her note resetting my mood.

Marcus: Pass? C'mon! How about ace it?

Angie: That's what I meant!

Setting the phone down, I returned to my textbook, putting the odd moment with the guy behind me. But something uneasy still ran through me from the encounter.

It just felt . . . off.

28

COLIN

My bike pounded against the bumpy trail, vibrations thrumming in my bones. I leaned into the curve, relentlessly focusing on the single track beneath the wheel and the 180-degree turn ahead of me on the descent.

Whipping past the switchback, I stomped the pedals, chasing speed, chasing adrenaline, and finding it on the hills of Red Rock Canyon with my mountain bike. Dirt churned up beneath me as I tackled the toughest trail, leaving the latest twists and turns in the never ending saga of our mother in a swirl of dust.

When I reached the bottom, my heart hammered mercilessly, but I'd beaten my brother.

Michael had determination on his side, but I possessed that too, along with a more potent dose of fearlessness. Sometimes fearlessness meant you were faster on a down-hill. Tonight, with the sun sinking low on the horizon, the time on the bike was therapy—it was necessary to shed the frustrations I felt over Elle, but also the guilt I still harbored over my mistakes as a kid. Riding a rocky down-hill required extreme concentration, and the rattle and hum of the wheels on the ground had forced everything else from my brain, narrowing my focus to only the bike and the trail—and besting my brother.

Michael rolled up next to me, stopping his bike.

"Streak's still intact," I said, my breath coming fast as I wheeled to the water fountain at the base of the hill. "I continue to reign supreme on two wheels."

"Watch it. You're lucky I still ride with you," Michael teased, as he unsnapped his helmet.

After a drink of water, I let the therapy continue, this time with words. Because I wasn't done. The silt on the riverbed of the past had been well and truly stirred up tonight. "Michael," I said, stripping away the macho bravado. "I still feel like shit for being friends with those guys."

My brother got off his bike, resting his palm on the seat. "You're not responsible. Your friendship played no role in the murder."

"But what if I hadn't been friends with Danny? What if I'd never known them? Would things be different?" I asked, letting the question hang in the air.

Michael dropped a hand on my shoulder. "Forget the what-ifs. Focus on the real. And that's this: Mom didn't find Stefano through you," he said, his voice firm and clear. "She found Stefano on her own. She found those others on her own. Hell, for all we know, she might have found them through her lover. The one thing I know for certain is she didn't find them through you being buddies with TJ's little bro when you were thirteen. That is not how it happened. But even if it had, for the sake of argument, let me ask you this. Who planned a murder?"

"She did," I said softly.

"Who hired Stefano?"

"She did." My voice picked up volume.

"And who saw the murder of our dad through?"

"She did." My tone was strong and certain now.

"Exactly," Michael said, bending to the water fountain and gulping up a stream. As he rose, he wiped the back of his hand across his mouth.

"But I've made the same mistakes she made," I said quietly, guilt stitched into my voice, into my goddamn heart and soul. Most days, I didn't beat myself up. But some days, I was consumed with the emotion.

Michael raised a finger and pointed it at me. "You didn't do what she did. You made mistakes that are fucking forgivable. You made mistakes that hurt yourself. You made mistakes that a human being makes. You did not kill a man. You are not like her."

I pressed my thumb and forefinger against the bridge of my nose and exhaled, visualizing letting go of all this guilt.

Soon, soon, I had to say goodbye to it.

"Speaking of what-ifs, have you ever heard from your what-if girl?" I asked as we loaded our bikes on the roof rack a few minutes later.

Michael shook his head. "Not lately. That's why she's a what-if girl."

As we left, I asked myself if I'd be happy letting Elle become a what-if girl.

29

ELLE

Big dots of primary-colored lights swirled in a speed race across the slick hardwood floors, as the music of The B-52's pulsed throughout the rink.

"All right, my crazy skaters, I want to see how excited you get when you go to the looooooove shack!" The directive came from my sister, Camille. Mic at her mouth, she worked up the crowds at the Skyway Roller Rink.

A flurry of teens, sprinkled with a few moms and the regular crew of older skaters who still rocked out nearly every night, motored around the oval, picking up the pace to the popular skating tune. An appropriate number for the conversation I needed to have with my little sister, considering Colin and I were having a "Love Shack" kind of relationship.

The getaway kind. The sneak-off-and-get-together kind.

Did I need to cut things off with him? I wasn't sure if the news about Marcus meant I should end things with Colin. But I flinched at the mere thought of ending the sweetest thing I'd had in ages—our wonderful . . . what was it? A tryst? An affair? I didn't know what to call it.

"That's right!" Camille shouted. "Skate like there's glitter on the highway!"

As I waited for the upbeat song to end, Marcus's confession echoed in my mind. There was no way I could tell Colin about his brother. That would be wrong. It wasn't my place. But I felt awful knowing this news was barreling toward him and that any day now he'd learn he had a long-lost brother.

There was something so very soapy about it, as if I could be reading the crib notes to a storyline on *The Young and The Restless.*

The character of the mother becomes pregnant before the murder of her husband. The mother hides her pregnancy during what turns out to be a speedy trial. She goes to jail six months pregnant. No one in her family knows about the baby in her belly. The only one the wiser—besides the medical staff at the correctional facility—is her lover on the outside. The lover whose hands were clean of the crime.

I shuddered as my sister encouraged the crowd to "Bang, bang, bang on the door."

Then the half-brother is born in prison and handed over to his father, who moves far, far away from Las Vegas with his baby son. He's not required to tell a soul. There are no prison rules, nor federal ones, requiring a parent to disclose to half-siblings that they have a new little brother.

The father meets a new woman in San Diego, falls in love with her, fathers more children, and returns to Vegas a few years later with his oddly blended family.

I started to replay the rest of the story, when the song ended and Camille introduced an MC Hammer tune then set down her mic. She nodded to the little gate at the edge of her DJ booth. I rose and followed her to the skate racks as she began straightening pairs of rental skates. I joined in, knowing the routine well from having helped out before.

"So, what's the story? Time to spill," Camille said in her no-nonsense tone as she tucked some laces into a pair of skates.

"The problem is, I can't even tell you what the problem is," I said, frustration thick in my voice as I adjusted the wheels on another pair.

Camille arched an eyebrow and stared at me with her deep brown eyes. "What's that supposed to mean?"

"Just what I said. I'm sworn to secrecy."

"Well, unswear yourself, girl, so I can help out," Camille said, nudging me with an elbow. "Or do I need to tickle it out of you, like when we were kids?"

I stepped away and held up my hands in surrender. "Not the tickle! Anything but the tickle."

"Fine. I won't torture you like that. But tell me what's on your mind. I have ten minutes of MC Hammer and Vanilla Ice queued up before I need to get back there, and I want to help you," she said as she worked her way down a row. Camille's dark hair was twisted into a looped-over ponytail, and she wore jeans and a T-shirt. She'd been managing this rink since after college.

I sighed and tried to figure out how to begin to ask for the advice I couldn't even truly ask for. "So, there's this guy . . ."

"Ah, the plot thickens."

"And I like him."

"Ooh. It's even thicker."

"*A lot.* But I don't know if it can be serious."

"Because of you or him?"

I stopped unknotting a gnarled lace to consider the question. Did Colin want to be serious with me? He'd seemed to. But he never pushed me. He understood my boundaries. The trouble was, I didn't fully understand what to do with this new rush of feelings. Especially now that I was privy to the Marcus news. "Because of a bunch of things. Especially because I learned something about him and his family that he doesn't know."

"Oh, now the plot is molasses thick," Camille said, her eyes glittery with excitement at the prospect of a juicy tale.

"And I can't divulge what I know because of confidentiality guidelines as a social worker, and it's kind of a big thing, so I just have to wait and see if this other person will divulge it to him. And I just feel like a mess in here," I said, grabbing my belly. "I'm all twisted and turned, and I feel like I'm lying to him, but I'm not. I just can't tell him. It's not my secret to tell."

Camille's expression turned serious, and she stepped away from the row of skates. She parked her hands on my shoulders. "You can't solve every problem. If this is something you can't do anything about, you need to try not to let it eat away at you. You worry too much, and you take on the weight of everything. And I get it. You've had some tough shit to deal with yourself."

"But do I keep seeing him while knowing this secret and not being able to say it?"

"Do you want to see him?"

I nodded. Easiest question of the night.

"If your hands are tied, your hands are tied. You can't untie them, just like you couldn't make Sam a better dad," she said, reminding me of how hard I'd tried to fix the things beyond fixing. "Lord knows if you're having a nice time with this new guy, you deserve it. Let go of the things you can't control." Camille snapped her fingers. "That reminds me of a song. Lace up!"

I grabbed a pair of skates, tied them quickly, and rolled

over to the rink, eagerly anticipating my sister's musical choice for my life.

Camille returned to her perch at the mic. "Boys and girls, men and women of all ages. I need to take a break from Vanilla Ice because every now and then we must heed the advice of the one and only Ice Queen, Elsa."

I cracked up over my sister's choice. Only Camille could find inspiration in the insanely popular Disney song that blared through the rink. Maybe the verses of "Let It Go" weren't entirely on point where my problem was concerned, but the chorus and the final few lines gave me something else I needed.

A reminder that this battle wasn't mine to pick and choose. It wasn't mine to fight or not fight. All I could do was stand on the sidelines and let the storm rage on.

Whatever was brewing in Colin's life wasn't my storm. It would rage on its own power, whether or not I saw the man again.

* * *

Later that Wednesday night, Alex grabbed a composition notebook as we passed the school supplies aisle at Target, and showed it to me. "For planning."

"Always good to plan for school." The start of Alex's freshman year was just weeks away.

He shook his head. "No, this is for *State of Decay*. I came up with a new strategy today, and I want to write it down and test it out step-by-step," he said, his voice rising in excitement as I continued to push the cart. "That guy at the center, Colin, told me to."

I stopped immediately and tilted my head. "He did?" I asked, intrigued to hear his name in this context. True, the two of them had talked before. But still, I was damn curious what they had chatted about.

"He said you just devise a strategy and follow it," he said, sweeping one hand across the other and pointing forward, like a general launching into battle. "But don't be afraid to change if it's not working."

As he dropped the notebook into our cart of groceries, I had my answer. Funny that it came from Colin through my son.

Time for me to change my approach.

30

COLIN

From the twenty-ninth floor of my office building, the icons of the Strip looked like Monopoly hotels. Up here, they became little Lego structures with playful shapes and Lilliputian charm—the pyramid of the Luxor, the miniature Eiffel Tower, the roller-coaster that wrapped around the New York–New York hotel . . .

The view from miles away was akin to how an idea took shape for me. It started small, but as I zoomed in closer, it had the potential to become a glittering star on the skyline. That was what I was looking for today from my team of venture capitalists as they presented the start-ups we were considering funding.

When Larsen, one of the youngest and brightest staffers at Redwood Mountain Ventures, finished his presentation, I leaned forward in my chair, ready with questions.

"What is your risk analysis? Is it worth it?" I asked, wishing I could apply a simple mathematical formula to understanding Elle and her radio silence, like I did with scrappy little start-ups. But as Larsen shared both the potential of the advertising tech firm under consideration as well as the risk, I was reminded once again that even black-and-white business decisions weren't rubber-stamped through mathematical equations.

It was math plus intuition. It was analysis plus gut. In business, I had always relied on my razor-sharp instincts. I'd leaned on them too with Elle. But all of a sudden, they'd stopped working. And I had no clue what to do next.

I was still somewhat lost in my own thoughts when the meeting ended and the other team members left, distracted as I headed back to my office. Once there, my assistant rang. "There's someone here to see you. She has a delivery of flowers."

31

———

ELLE

The big bouquet of orange lilies and purple asters hid my face. Clutching the blue glass vase tightly, I walked into Colin's office, nerves bouncing across my skin.

I had no clue if he was pissed at me.

If he even wanted an in-person delivery.

But this was the least I could do.

I'd never been to his office before, and from my place behind the vase, the first thing I noticed was the burgundy carpet, then a soft beige couch and a shiny oak coffee table arranged in front of his desk. Slowly, like in a game of peekaboo, I moved the vase and revealed my face.

Holy shit.

I nearly dropped the flowers.

The view from the window was stunning, but it had nothing on Colin.

He stood, resting casually against the edge of his desk, wearing the hottest two pieces of a three-piece suit. He didn't have a jacket on—he wore tailored pants, a white shirt, and a vest, and I had to force my lips together so I wouldn't start panting, drooling, or just gaping at him. The sleeves of his shirt were rolled up twice, revealing a hint of the infinity symbol on his forearm.

If ever there were a more perfect image for edgy businessmen than him—Colin, with his dark eyes, sexy scruff, rolled-up sleeves, and that vest that was killing me with hotness—I couldn't imagine it. Nope. The evidence was in front of me, and I had to have him. I had to somehow cordon off the secrets I couldn't reveal from the man I couldn't resist.

Two of me. Plain and simple. Here and now, I declared myself cloned.

I cast my gaze to the bouquet. "They call it a carnival of color," I said, trying to act normal.

He didn't move an inch. His arms were crossed. "It is colorful. What do *you* call it?"

I stepped closer. "A thank you. An in-person thank you for your firm's amazing generosity in supporting the community center."

He walked over to me, took the flowers, and set them on the coffee table. His expression was unreadable, but when he neared me, his eyes softened. "You're welcome," he said as he sat down on his couch.

My chest tightened with nerves. "It's also an apology."

He cocked his head. "For what?"

"For canceling."

He offered a sliver of a smile, perhaps warming up. "You don't have to apologize for that."

"I do though," I insisted. "Because I didn't want to cancel."

"Elle, you don't have to say you're sorry. I don't expect an apology. I don't expect anything." He sounded resigned.

And maybe I'd trained him to expect nothing from me because I felt like I had nothing to give.

And while I couldn't give him the full truth, I could

offer him *my* truth. So I marched to the door and shut it, affording us complete privacy, and returned to him, sitting on the edge of the coffee table in front of him.

"I know you don't expect anything, but I left you hanging, and that's not fair, no matter what this is," I said, gesturing from him to me. "I had a lot of stuff on my mind, and I kind of freaked out, and that's why I was out of touch."

"Elle, it's okay. I get it. I was a little frustrated, but I understand we need to take this slow." He took a beat. "And we don't have to be in touch all the time. I understand being busy."

"I know." My heart softened more. This man. He was so damn understanding. I didn't deserve him. But I could give him something. I could make him feel good.

I reached for his right wrist, tracing the infinity symbol, forcing away the thoughts that threatened to touch down in my head—he'd gotten this ink to symbolize the connection between him and his siblings. The four of them. But there were more than four.

I stroked the lines on his wrist. He hissed in a breath as I made contact with his skin. I raised my chin and met his eyes. "You look so beautiful," I said in a whisper. "So sexy."

"So do you," he said, his eyes blazing.

I glanced at my attire—a summery skirt and a sleeveless top. Hardly my hottest outfit. I let go of his wrist and leaned closer to him, dropping my hands to his thighs, so strong and firm under my touch.

I swallowed nervously, then tried even harder to tell the man what he meant to me. "You are so good to me. In every way."

He leaned closer, sliding a hand along my leg. "It's easy being good to you."

"But right now, I'd like to be good to you."

He arched a curious brow. "How so?"

I moved to the edge of the table. "I want to be good to you with my mouth."

He groaned. "Elle Mariano, you're a dirty girl."

I pulled back, met his gaze, and smiled wickedly. "Yes. I'm feeling good and dirty, so let me suck your cock."

His breath came out in a rush. "Yes. Yes. And yes."

"I'll lock the door."

"Brilliant idea."

I laughed and practically vaulted over the chair and table to flip the latch on the door.

Returning to him, I dropped to my knees. Palmed him through his pants. A burst of sparks ignited in my belly as I stroked his erection, loving that he was already rock hard, that all it took was this momentary closeness, the heat of suggestion, and a few words to ratchet him up.

In a flash, I unzipped his pants, pushing them open so I could see his newest ink. My breath caught as I gazed at the phoenix tattoo on his hip. I ran my thumb over it then lowered my lips to flick my tongue across it. I raised my face.

His eyes were blazing. "Take me in your mouth," he rasped out.

He watched me draw his cock into my mouth, groaning as I did.

"I definitely accept your apology now," he said with a light laugh then threaded his fingers into my hair, pushing it all over to one side.

Smiling, I flicked my tongue along the hard length of him as I sucked.

"You can cancel on me anytime," he said.

I grinned even with my mouth full, then my smile vanished as he groaned louder and gripped my hair with both hands. There was no time for smiling or laughing with his cock all the way in my mouth. All I cared about was making him feel good, because he'd only ever made me feel amazing. Beautiful. Craved.

I wanted him to feel the same. I drew him in deep, sucking hard. Friction, lots of friction, and speed, and his groans told me he liked it this way. I loved it too—on my knees, in his office, with the stunning view of Las Vegas splashed behind us.

"Suck me harder," he urged in a heated whisper, and I couldn't resist. I loved that he was vocal and direct. That he told me exactly what he liked. I moved faster, cupping his balls in one hand, playing with them as I licked, sucked, and aimed to steal every last breath from his lungs with a blow job that would blow his mind.

"Ah," he said on a moan. "Like that. Just like that."

I knew what he meant, so I moved my hands faster across his balls, gently tugging as I showed him how incredibly much I loved his cock. Heat blasted through me like a rocket. I was so turned on from blowing him. Wetness pooled between my legs, and I ached. My sex pulsed with need. I could practically come like this, and I rocked my pelvis as he fucked my mouth. My hips moved back and forth because I wanted to be riding him so badly. But I wanted this more—all of him between my lips.

"Yeah, that's perfect. So fucking deep," he said, as his fingers gripped my skull and he kept my head firmly in place.

Faster and harder, more frenzied than ever, I sucked him, imagining him as king of this town, presiding over partnerships, striking deals and making decisions, but here, for these few moments in his office, I controlled all of this man's pleasure. With my mouth. With my tongue. With my lips.

With my ravenous appetite for him. With my bottomless desire to touch him, to taste him, to feel him.

Because of him.

Because of all I felt for Colin Sloan.

He groaned louder and rocked up into my mouth. A quick, hard thrust. Then another. He was starting to lose control, going so deep I nearly gagged.

But I didn't, because I needed his pleasure desperately. Had to give it to him. Had to take him deep.

Had to show him how much he meant to me.

He shuddered, grasped my head as if holding on for life, and grunted. There were no words left to say. Only feelings. Only pleasure. Only release. I swallowed every last drop of him then licked his length up and down before letting go and meeting his eyes.

I stripped away all my fear, all my anxiety, and asked him for one more thing. It was hard, but it was also remarkably easy.

"Can I come over tonight?"

32

COLIN

There was only one answer.

Still, I wanted to know something. Pulling her up on my lap, I adjusted her skirt so she straddled me. "You said you kind of freaked out. Why did you freak out?"

She gulped, pushing her hair—slightly messy from my hands—away from her cheek. Then she looked me in the eyes. "Because I like you."

Oh hell. There it was. My heart hitched a ride on a hot-air balloon, sailing up to the sky. I was hopeless around her. "I like you too," I said, looping my arms around her and planting a quick kiss on those wickedly talented lips. "Does that scare you?"

"To like you? Or that you like me too?" she asked.

I smiled. "Both."

She nodded. "Both scare me."

"Just be honest with me. That's all we have, Elle," I said, cupping her cheek, keeping her gaze on me. "That's all I ask of you. I respect your boundaries and your wishes. All I want is the truth."

She closed her eyes. Her face looked pained, and she

sighed, but when she opened her eyes, she nodded. "So much."

Yup. I was a goner. But I was also a realist. "It's the same for me. You are in my heart and my head. But I respect that you don't know if you can get involved. I respect your fear. I know you need time. So, listen—no strings, no promises, nothing more. But if you cancel, don't say something came up. Say 'I have to see my sister,' or 'I'm too tired,' or 'I need to work late,' or 'I don't want to see you again.' Or 'I met a guy with a bigger cock, and—'"

She grabbed my hand and squeezed. "Just go ahead and strike that excuse. Because you know that will never happen."

I wiggled my eyebrows. "Good. It's my secret weapon."

"You can use that weapon against me anytime."

I gave a quick thrust up, showing I was always armed around her. "Another option would be 'I'm going to surprise you at your office tomorrow with flowers and the blow job of a lifetime.'"

She cracked up, then her expression shifted, and she gave me a soft smile. "If it was good, it's because I like you so much."

Thump. Thump. But I didn't tell her my heart was jackhammering for her. Instead, I said, "It was great, because I am crazy for you."

She didn't say it back, but her smile was genuine and warm. And when she reached for my hand, threading her fingers through mine and squeezing, I was sure that was her way of telling me we were in this together. As much as we could be. She leaned against me, sighing happily, then whispered my name.

Yup. This would do. This would definitely do.

I ran my hands up her back, softly stroking her,

savoring the quiet moment as we showed each other that we were becoming more.

The moment ended when she said softly, "Alex told me you gave him some video-game pointers at the center."

"Yeah. I was there after a tutoring session, and he was playing with Rex and Tyler. Is that okay?"

"Of course. He insisted on getting a new notebook last night to write down his new strategies for the game, courtesy of your advice. Thank you for sharing that little tip with him. Very analytical," she said, and I nodded.

"Sure. I'm well-versed enough that I have a few tricks. I can share them with him anytime."

She smiled. "Really?"

"Yeah, let me gather some thoughts, and I'll send them to you later."

"You can send them to him directly, if you don't mind. I'll text you his number."

I grinned. Progress. This was a big step forward. "Absolutely."

She leaned forward and dropped a kiss on my nose. "Thank you," she said softly. Then, in an even quieter voice, she said, "You are my hero."

That's all I want to be.

But aloud I said, "I'm glad I can help."

"Isn't there anything I can do for you? Help you find the next Snapchat to fund?" she asked, teasing.

"I'm always on the hunt for the next thing."

"Or should I just get to work on topping the blow job of a lifetime?" She winked. "Now that you've set the bar so high for me."

"Yes. That. Do that. And you set the bar yourself with this fantastic mouth," I said, running my fingertip across her lips. "But you know what I also want?" I dipped a hand under her skirt and stroked her damp panties. Ah, there was nothing I loved more than the evidence of her desire.

She moved gently against my hand. "What do you want?"

"I want to taste you tonight," I growled as I slid a finger inside her underwear, feeling her slick flesh.

She leaned her head back and groaned. "I believe I'd like that more than pickle potato chips."

33

ELLE

Let this day end now. I stared at the clock on my wall, willing it to tick faster.

But the tortoise speed of the second hand was a cruel joke. Colin was all I thought about as I finished up some paperwork about the status of the center's programs.

I'd be seeing him tonight.

We were connecting on a new level.

We'd navigated a road bump, and that gave me faith that we could handle whatever troubles came next.

At least, that's what I told myself.

That's what I wanted—for us to manage the news barreling down on him the way we'd moved through today's hurdle.

But I knew it wouldn't likely be the same.

My stomach churned as I thought about Marcus and Colin and the way their lives were on a collision course toward the truth—a truth that would shock one of them, and perhaps unburden the other.

And there was little I could do for Colin on this front,

other than wait and hope. And be there for him during any fallout.

So I handled what I could handle.

My work.

My projects.

My phone calls.

And my schedule for tonight.

I called my mom. "Hey, world's coolest mom."

I could hear her roll her eyes from across the city, and I deserved an eye roll.

"Hello, daughter who is obviously about to hit me up for a favor."

"Who, me?" I asked, laughing.

"Yes. You. And if the question is can I get you the Barbie Malibu Dream House, the answer is no."

"Just like it was when I was a kid," I said, adding a pout.

"I was so mean to you."

I smiled. She was the opposite of mean. "Any chance you can hang out with Alex tonight so I can maybe possibly see a guy?"

"Ooh! Tell me more," she said. "And then I'll say yes."

"I like him, and that's all you're getting out of me," I said, but she already knew the basics, since I'd told her about Colin, and I was glad of that, glad I could confide in her.

"Fine, twist my arm. I'm feeling like a night of arcade games, the Chinese buffet, and a sleepover is perfect for my grandson and me," she said.

"It does sound perfect," I said, twirling absently in my chair. "Hey, Mom?"

"Yes?"

"Thank you for doing this. For spending time with him."

"It's only my favorite thing to do."

"I know, but I appreciate it. And *you*. And I love you."

"And I love you."

I was lucky, truly lucky, to have a mom like mine. She was here for me, as a mom and a friend.

After I said goodbye, I pushed back from my desk, only to see Marcus rapping on my door. His face was etched with worry, and he fiddled with a leather band on his wrist. "Do you have a second?"

"Of course."

He stepped into my office, and I shut the door.

"Is this about . . ." I asked, letting my voice trail off in question.

"Yeah. You didn't tell him, did you?" Marcus asked, terror in his brown eyes. For a brief moment before I answered, I studied his eyes. They were dark brown, like Colin's. Another secret I had to bear—a small one that was folded into the big one. But still, I now knew they shared a family resemblance. That gnawing in my chest resurfaced, and I tried valiantly to swat it away. I clenched my fists and refocused away from Marcus's eyes and back to his question.

"Of course I didn't say anything. I told you I wouldn't, and I meant it. Now, tell me what I can do for you."

"Sorry. I didn't mean anything by it. I know you wouldn't tell him. I'm just . . ."

"You're nervous," I supplied, as I placed a hand on his shoulder. He was shaking. "Hey, it's going to be okay. Talk to me."

34

MARCUS

A possibility nagged at me.

One I stupidly hadn't thought about before, but now it was like a warning light, beeping in front of me.

"What if they don't believe me?" I blurted out. "I'll just be showing up out of the blue and saying, 'Hey, I'm your little brother. I was born in the pokey. We don't even have the same dad, but isn't it cool?'" I swung my elbows back and forth in mockery of a too-happy person. "I mean, my mom never told them. My dad never did. I don't think they have a clue."

Elle took a beat, like she was processing this, but she seemed to know right away how to handle this new wrinkle I'd found. "Show them your birth certificate. You have one, right?"

"Yeah, I have a copy of it," I said, my gaze drifting to my feet, because that piece of paper was a cruel reminder of where I came from. It said I wasn't like everyone else. I wasn't like many people at all. "Says right there in black and white that I was born behind bars."

Elle's eyes were sympathetic. "There's no shame in

where you came from. We all came from different places. So don't let a few words on your birth certificate affect how you see yourself."

But they'd colored who I was for as long as I'd known the truth of my birth. And maybe that's part of what had held me back from talking to the Sloans. The weight I carried with me. "I just feel like I'm blindsiding them," I muttered.

"You're just telling them the truth, but you need to be smart about it. And be prepared, because it is hard. Maybe that's why no one was home the other time you went there. Maybe the universe knew you needed to have all the evidence before you went."

She was right, and truth be told, the Sloans carried their own weights. I had to remember that. And I had to act soon. "I need to do it soon. The detective called about the reopened investigation. He wants to talk to me. I don't want to talk to him though."

She drew a worried breath, held up both hands, and backed away. "You shouldn't tell me more on that. I can talk to you about the family stuff, but anything involving the case, I need to stay out of."

The last thing I wanted was for Elle to be in trouble. I'd hate for anything to happen to her. I flashed a small smile. "I won't. But thanks again. I think I'm going to rip off the Band-Aid. Do it tomorrow."

She offered a fist for knocking. "Good luck. You're brave."

"Thanks," I said, a knot of emotion tightening in my throat as I quickly added, "Because of you."

It was true.

She was the first person who'd listened, when for so long no one wanted to.

35

COLIN

A female Elvis impersonator with drooping breasts dangling out of her jumpsuit mugged for the camera on the street below. She draped her arms around two guys with sunburns and foot-long plastic drink glasses. With their free hands, both men mimed grabbing a breast. The Elvis outfit was made *modest* by pasties on her nipples.

The woman laughed, and so did the guys. Until one stopped laughing, started hacking, and promptly heaved into the nearby garbage can.

"And that's all, folks, in today's five p.m. Parade of What We Might Have Been," said Kevin, my friend and mentor from my recovery group. The two of us stood on the elevated walkway at the corner of Bally's, surveying the madness and mayhem of an early happy hour on the Strip. This was one of the many faces of Vegas—the city embodied glitz and glamour in its classy hotels, sex and sin in its nightclubs, beauty and class in the fountains of the Bellagio, but also the seedy and grungy in the late-afternoon crowds weaving up and down the sidewalks, drunk as skunks.

I held up my iced coffee and toasted. "Here's to my best friend. Coffee," I said, since caffeine was the one "vice" I allowed myself to have.

"Hear, hear. May it never ever be banned," Kevin said, swallowing the last of his drink then returning to the conversation we'd started before She-Elvis had arrived on the scene. "So, the meeting with the detective and talking about the past, did that stir anything up?"

"Not really," I said, quickly glancing at my watch, calculating how much longer until I saw Elle.

Kevin shot me a steely stare. "Really?"

Busted.

I forced my mind away from the anticipation of tonight, and back in time to my conversation yesterday with Michael at the base of the mountain after we'd met with John. I sighed, dragged my free hand through my hair, and shrugged. "Guilt. It brought back a lot of guilt."

The other man nodded sagely. "That makes sense. But you need to keep working on letting go of that. Guilt—and I mean the misplaced kind—can eat you up. When you start to feel that way, the things that you think will take the pain away seem a helluva lot more appealing. Tequila looks a lot prettier the worse you feel."

"Yeah. That's true," I admitted. The moments I'd been most tempted to crack open a bottle were when I felt the shittiest about myself.

"Just be aware that revisiting the past can mess with your head. Keep doing the things that make you feel centered. Your exercise. Your work. Your meetings. All of it. Okay, man?"

My gaze drifted to my arms, to the inked reminders of the man I wanted to be. The strong one, the kind one. The man who didn't live a wrecked kind of life. Strength, love, passion, family, truth—they were my touchstones, my hall-marks, and my guides. "I will."

"Because something this big could knock you off your game. Falling in love. Breaking up. Losing a shit-ton of money. Even good things, like landing a new deal. Hell, just getting news out of the blue. *Anything can be a trigger.* That almost happened to me a few years ago when I fell in love with my wife. You'd think falling in love would be this wonderful thing that would keep me straight. But I very nearly popped pills again because I didn't know if she was feeling the same thing, and I felt so out of control."

Kevin's admission knocked the air out of my lungs. I'd never imagined falling for someone could have those kinds of consequences. "Seriously?"

Kevin nodded. "Love nearly kicked the shit out of me."

"How did you deal with it?"

"I told her how I felt. I was honest with her. I spoke the truth, and she loved that I was open, and the rest is history."

His words struck a chord. I'd delivered a world of plea-sure to Elle, I'd proven I was a reliable, steady guy, I'd shown her I was patient.

But I'd only skirted the thorny ground of feelings.

Saying *I like you so much*, saying *I'm crazy for you* barely covered it.

There was one last thing to do.

Open my heart.

* * *

Of course I had some business to attend to first. After the meeting with Kevin, I swung by the Luxe for a brief chat with my sister, so we could catch up on how her shows were doing at Edge, her husband's club.

"Customers are loving my dancers," Shannon said, gesturing to the stage where her dancers performed her choreography. The club was quiet now. It would open in an hour.

"No surprise. You're a rock star," I said, then filled her in on some of the expansion plans I'd been working on for Shay Productions as the shows rolled out across Brent's clubs.

As we finished, Brent strolled into Edge with Mindy, his long-time best friend.

"You still fraternizing with this guy?" I asked, teasing.

"Only so I can give him a hard time about everything," Mindy said, then Shannon gave the petite blonde a hug.

I smiled, glad that my sister got along so well with her husband's good friend. Mindy was practically family. She'd been at my grandparent's house a few times now that Brent and Shannon were together.

"By the way," Mindy said, "I'm glad to hear those guys at the community center were looking out for Shannon. The Protectors are the good ones."

"That's what we like hearing," Brent said.

"I couldn't agree more," Shannon echoed.

And on that all-is-well note, I took off.

I hit the trails for a forty-five-minute pre-date trail run. I pushed myself extra hard with a punishing uphill route in the early evening heat. But I'd needed it, because Kevin was right. The challenging workout had helped settle my mind and heart, dislodging some of yesterday's latent guilt and also strengthening my resolve to share my feelings with Elle.

Now, I stood under hot jets of water, rinsing away the remnants of the sweaty workout. I turned off the shower, dried off, and wrapped a towel around my waist so I could get ready for my date—*at my house*. The best kind of date.

As I finished brushing my teeth, my phone rang, so I tossed the toothbrush in the cup holder and grabbed the phone from my bed in case it was Elle.

Rex was calling.

"Hey, man, what's up?"

"Okay, here's the deal. I am *almost* ready," Rex said, stretching out the word. "I'm like ninety percent ready. And I just want to kill it on this test. But there's one problem that's making me absolutely batshit crazy."

"Lay it on me," I said, as I opened a drawer to grab a pair of boxers.

Rex rattled off the details, and I walked him through the steps to solving the equation as I pulled on black boxer briefs and hung up my towel.

"Awesome," Rex said, relief and exuberance in his voice. "You are clutch, man. You are so clutch."

I smiled at the compliment. "Need anything else?"

Rex cleared his throat, then said, "*Um.*"

Uh-oh. Rex never hemmed and hawed. The guy was the king of boldness.

"What is it? Just tell me."

Rex sighed. "I hate to ask. But I need a ride tomorrow to the test. My mom is taking the car for a job interview, and Marcus's ride is in the shop—the tires are being rotated. So he can't drive us."

"Us?" I asked curiously. "He's taking the math placement test too?"

"Yeah. He's a math whiz, though, just like you. He's done all the studying on his own, and he's aiming to place into calculus or some shit like that. He's trying to find a ride, but I just figured I'd take the initiative and ask you. I guess I could take an Uber though."

"No, you won't take an Uber," I said with a wide grin. I was so damn grateful to be hearing this—that both boys were eager and ready to learn. "Tell me where to pick you up, and I will gladly be your driver."

Driver.

That word clanged loudly in my brain. My dad had been a limo driver and would have been proud of me—not for driving per se, but for helping the kids who needed it, especially when it came to math. My father had never gone to college, but he'd tried to work on his own skills with numbers during the last year of his life, taking accounting classes at night school. Maybe I had picked up where my father had left off, carrying on his memory as the numbers guy of the crew.

Rex gave me the address, and I wrote it down. "Got it."

The doorbell rang, sending Johnny Cash straight out of an evening snooze and into a brief bark-fest at the door. I headed to the entryway and peered out the peephole.

Even through the tiny window, Elle looked edible.

I glanced down, realizing I'd only managed to put on boxers.

So be it.

I opened the door as I finished my call with Rex. "I'll be there at eight a.m. That work for you?"

"Absolutely. You're the best," Rex was saying as Elle stepped inside my house and mouthed *Wow* as she raked her eyes over my barely-dressed body.

"See you then." I hung up, tossed my phone on the entryway table, and kissed her.

A soft kiss for a mere few seconds.

Then a hard and furious one that had hands wrapped around bodies, and fingers diving into hair, and breath coming fast from both of us. We were a collision of lust and heat. We clawed at each other, grasping, grabbing, needing contact. Fierce and fevered contact.

She giggled, breaking the kiss.

I shot her a curious look, and she pointed downward. Johnny Cash was licking her calf.

"I think he likes my lotion."

"Is it eau de filet mignon?"

"No. It's satsuma orange from The Body Shop."

"Mmm." I pointed to the living room. "Go lie down, Johnny Cash."

The dog obeyed, trotting to the rug in front of the gray couch.

She gestured to my briefs. "Nice boxers," she said, and I followed her gaze. She was staring at my erection, a full tent against the cotton fabric.

I gestured to her. All of her. Her tight skirt, her heels, her blouse. "Nice everything."

"Who are you meeting at eight?" she asked, as I reached for her hand and led her into the house.

"Rex. He needs a ride to his math placement test tomorrow."

She beamed. Her whole expression lit up with the biggest smile I'd seen in ages. "That is so cool of you to do that. I'm so thrilled," she said as she reached for my arm, running her fingers along my skin. "I love it when you help them. It kind of turns me on."

"I'm taking Marcus too. Does it turn you on twice as much that I'm driving two of them?"

She blinked. Once, twice, three times. Her face seemed to freeze, and her smile fell. Her body was a statue.

I frowned, confused at the shift. "Are you okay?" She closed her eyes for a second, squeezed them hard, then pressed her fingers to her temple. "Elle. What's going on?"

She opened her eyes, her brow furrowing like she was in pain. "Sorry. Sometimes I get these headaches. It's nothing." She waved her hand as if to dismiss it. Then she reached for my shoulders, grasped them, and walked me backward to the couch. "You know what really turns me on?"

"Tell me."

"Thinking about you all day," she said as we reached the couch. "I've been hot and bothered since I left you."

She pushed me down on the couch then followed me there, sprawling beside me.

"Did you count down the hours?" I asked as I ran a hand up her bare leg.

She nodded as she settled back against a pillow at the end of the couch, her chestnut hair spilling across it. "It was pure torture."

"Were you wet just thinking of me?"

"Yes. I ached for you," she said, as I glided my fingers across the damp panel of her panties. My cock twitched against my boxers as I touched her. My delicious, wet, sexy Elle. God, I loved how much she wanted it. I loved turning her on. I loved touching her. Pushing her tight little skirt up to her waist, I groaned when I saw her panties—black lace with a tiny bow in the center.

"You need to be naked, right now. Completely naked," I said, tugging off the panties and removing her heels too. The shoes were sexy as hell, but a plan was a plan. I needed her in her birthday suit when I went down on her for the first time. "Nothing on. Nothing but you, naked from head to toe, as I bury my face in this sweetness." I slid a finger through her slick heat as she arched into me, wriggling out of her top at the same time.

She moved to her bra next, freeing her tits. My breath hitched. There she was, down to nothing but her beautiful bare self and the shimmer of desire evident in the flush on her skin. Her eyes, so dark and hungry, told me that she had indeed been one tortured woman all day long.

"I almost feel bad for making you think about me for

nine hours straight," I growled, as I pressed my hands on the insides of her thighs.

Her legs parted, and I groaned as I drank in the sight of her wet pussy. I wanted her more than I'd ever wanted a woman in my life. "But I can't find it in me to feel bad when you're this worked up already."

She ran a hand through her hair and moaned. "I'm dying for you."

Her words stoked the raging fire in me. It crackled and burned with rampant desire as I opened her legs farther, savoring the utterly intoxicating view of this beautiful woman arching her hips toward my mouth.

My dick ached. My erection throbbed against my boxer shorts. My mouth watered as I settled between her legs, hooked them over my shoulders, and at last, at long fucking last, kissed her sweet honey center.

Later, I would tell her how I felt.

Now I would show her.

36

───────

ELLE

It was like a match on tinder, igniting me instantly. I groaned, I moaned, and I cried out his name. I was a live wire, exposed, ready, and waiting. I'd wanted this for so long, had pictured it often, and had fantasized about it so many times with him.

It was a first for us, and if it happened right, it would be a first for me.

I'd never come like this, but this was my ultimate fantasy.

As he swept his tongue across me, I bowed my back, so ready to sing, to shout, and to scream. His lips were soft, his stubble was rough, and his tongue was insistent as he flicked it up and down along my swollen, aching clit. I grabbed his hair as if my hands were a steel grip and I couldn't let go. I wouldn't let go. I rocked into his face. Electricity crackled through me, lighting up all my nerves, sizzling my skin.

I cried out his name, and for a second, he broke contact to look at me—his eyes were heated, full of the same wild longing. That moment was like a thread between us, a tight, neat line that tethered me to him. To share in this desire for another person was the greatest high, the sweetest intoxication, and hell, did we have it. I wanted his mouth as much as he wanted to consume me.

"Tell me what you say when you fuck yourself," he said in a dirty growl. "Talk to me like you did all the times I devoured you in your fantasies."

Another wave of desire crashed through me, and I dug my nails into his scalp. Gladly. I'd gladly tell him. I'd used him so many times—I'd gotten off to him countless nights. I'd come to his image over and over.

"Fuck me with your tongue," I said, panting as I thrust into him.

He moaned as he cupped my ass, pulling me closer. His tongue explored me. His sinfully delicious lips devoured me, and I'd never felt so lavished, so cherished, or so utterly craved. His hot kisses turned me into a wet, writhing collection of sparking nerve endings.

I closed my eyes, sharing with him all the dirty things I'd said in my head as I'd masturbated to him.

Ride your face.

Come so hard.

Want you so much.

His tongue kicked into some kind of overdrive, flicking against me wildly. He let go of his grip on my ass and grabbed my hands, clasping them tight, clutching them as he feasted on me. Hand in hand, this act became all the more intense.

Closer. I felt closer to him than I ever had before as he held me tight, our fingers laced together, while he drank me in. My muscles tightened. The first wave of pleasure crashed over me, and it was happening.

I cried out as the sensations rolled through me, overwhelming me, flooding my brain with nothing but beautiful bliss.

I was losing control, letting go, and giving in to everything I felt for him. "*Coming.*" He gripped my hands so damn tight as he ravaged me. "It's so good with you, so good with you."

Then I screamed, and nothing else existed in the whole damn world except this perfect moment of pleasure, this unparalleled ecstasy with this man who was so unbelievably good to me in every way.

And I knew as I said those words—*so good with you*—that I meant so much more than the physical.

I meant it all, since I was falling so hard for him in every way.

Every terrifying way.

37

COLIN

She sighed happily as her eyes fluttered open, so dreamy and sexy.

"Hi," she whispered as I rose up. "That was . . ."

"You are . . ."

Neither one of us could seem to finish our sentences. She scooted down into the pillows then lifted her hand, tracking the lotus design on my chest. She traveled lower, over my abs to my waist. She pushed down my briefs. I was sitting on my knees, still between her legs. No better place to be.

She ran her tongue across her lips as she freed my cock, then stroked it. Shuddering, a bolt of desire tore through me. I loved how she touched me, from the way she ran her fingers over me to how her breath came fast and heavy as she gripped my cock.

Mostly, though, it was her eyes. The way she gazed at me. She looked at me with so much want, so much desire, and so much more. Like she wanted me in all the same ways I wanted her.

My breathing turned erratic the more she touched me.

The craving inside me multiplied.

She whispered my name. "Colin?"

"Yes?" I answered, as I pushed off my briefs. My voice was soft, but it echoed, the only sound in the quiet house.

"I want to know how it feels without any barriers," she said, wrapping both hands around me now, leading me closer to the promised land.

The prospect of flesh against flesh, skin on skin, electrified me. But a kernel of worry set up camp too, and I remained stock-still as I asked, "Are you sure? Should we?"

"I'm on protection. I wasn't when I was younger. The condom broke. But we don't have to if you're not comfortable."

"No, I want to. I just want to make sure it makes sense for you. For us."

"It does," she said decisively.

"You know your body," I said, running a hand along her thigh. "And your mind. That's so sexy."

"You're pretty sexy too." Roping her arms around my neck, she drew me closer. She spread her legs, wrapping them around my hips as I sank into her. I trembled from the absolutely exquisite feel of her. I hitched her leg up higher, giving myself a better angle.

She raised her face to mine and claimed my lips. She kissed me, and I fucked her, and soon that was all I knew. The deep and primal drive to fill her. The heat flooding my body. Her fingernails running the length of my spine. And her mouth, her decadent, sinful lips fused to mine, kissing me greedily as I took her.

Hard.

Deep.

Rough.

She let go of my mouth and yanked me closer, kissing

my neck, my face, moving her lips to my ear. "I love the way you fuck me," she whispered, her voice fevered.

So fiery. She was so damn fiery and passionate. It drove me wild. "Fucking you is amazing. Do you have any idea why it's so good?"

"Tell me."

"Because it's more than fucking." The words tumbled from my lips. I hadn't planned to tell her now, but I couldn't hold back. I couldn't pretend. We were so much more than just the physical. I pulled back to look at her. Maybe I'd scared her. But her lips were parted, her eyes were wide open, and she gazed back at me, not letting go.

"I know," she whispered, the words like poetry to my ears. Sweet, gorgeous music.

"It's more than what it used to be."

"So much more," she murmured as she moved with me. We were finishing each other's sentences, filling in what the other was saying. We both felt it. There was no other way.

I couldn't get close enough, couldn't have enough of her, couldn't imagine this stopping at just sex. No, this was way more than fucking. It was fucking and falling at the same damn time, and nothing—no drug, no drink, no high-flying parachute dive—had ever felt as good as coming together with the woman I desired madly.

Coming together . . . and falling apart.

38

ELLE

He ran his fingertips over my sparrows, then kissed them. "These are my favorite."

I trembled in his arms, my back to him as he held me. I barely felt like myself. I was some other version of myself in these stolen moments with Colin. And I loved this version. I savored being this woman. Not a mom. Not a social worker. Not a woman with secrets that couldn't be shared. I wore only my bra and panties, and he was clad in his briefs. We'd eaten Chinese takeout while watching the final ten minutes of *Goodfellas*, reciting the closing lines together. Then we'd managed one more quick round, and now the clock was racing closer to the end of the night.

"Why do you like them?"

"Because I love your neck, and these birds are like a homing beacon to me."

"That's why I got them."

"To draw me to your neck?"

I laughed and shook my head. "No. Because in olden days, sailors would follow birds to land. That's how they knew when they were coming close to shore. There's a legend about a sailor who found his way home by spotting sparrows. I loved the idea of finding your way home."

"Why did you decide to get the sparrows?"

"I did it five years ago. Things were really rough with Sam then. It was his third or fourth rehab stint. I lost count. But I needed the reminder that I could find my own way home," I said, glad it was a topic I could freely discuss with Colin.

"I like that idea. I believe that's true. You can find your way home," he said softly, and I craned my neck to look at him. The sun had dropped below the horizon, and night had fallen.

"I believe it too. And sometimes you have to rely on something outside of yourself to do that."

"Who or what did you rely on?"

"My mom, my sister, my son. Basically, my family," I said.

He smiled against me. "I love that you're so close to them. It's the same with my brothers and sister."

Worry thrummed in me. What would happen to that tight-knit foursome when they learned they were five?

Would they stay strong? Would it rock them?

His hand dropped to my hip, traveling across the cherry blossom tree that decorated my side up to my rib cage. "Wait. I was wrong. This one is my favorite," he whispered, dusting a kiss across the blossoms. "It's beautiful and sexy, like you. And it means something. Tell me why you got it."

"It inspires me. It reminds me of what I want, what I value. In Japan it's a symbol for the preciousness of life, and I believe wholly in that. I also like that it represents femininity and beauty."

"Both are perfect." He traveled across my body, landing on the script-y *T* on my wrist. "But this one truly is my favorite. Titanium. You told me you got this after Sam died."

My throat hitched with the memory. "Yes. My reminder to stay strong. *Obviously*, since that's what titanium is." I inched around, facing him, meeting his eyes.

"You needed that after what happened to you. And to Alex," he said, kind and gentle. It was a relief, that he knew what had happened that night two years ago when Sam died in my arms. "You needed the reminder. And you are strong, Elle. I see it every day in you. I see it in how you are."

Emotions swelled in me again, but this time they weren't from the past. They came from the present. My throat tightened again, but I pushed past it, compelled to speak from the heart. I met his gaze, trying to move past my own deep fears. "You're the best man I know," I said, holding his gaze tight. "The kindest, smartest, most thoughtful gentleman I've ever met. The guy who helps the boys at the center. Who drives them to their tests. Who helps them study and inspires them with gaming strategies." His expression was soft, vulnerable, and grateful. I ran a hand over his cheek. "And you're the man who treats me like a queen."

His smile was priceless.

It warmed every inch of my soul.

I hadn't come here tonight expecting to want so much more from him, but I couldn't walk out that door the way I came in. Every second I spent with him, naked or clothed, I became more connected, more linked to this man. This was no longer about sex. It was about *why* the sex between us was so spectacular. Because of how we felt.

Before he could say a word, I pressed on. He'd taken the lead with us, he'd batted first every time. I needed to be the one to take this next step. I looped my hands in his hair and tried to push past the fear. "You make me feel things I've never felt before."

"It's the same for me. I've never felt anything like this," he said, and the look in his eyes was one of pure joy. I wanted to remember it always. I clutched that emotion tighter now, because it was giving me the strength to say the next thing—to tell him I was ready to try.

I parted my lips to speak when my phone buzzed.

"That might be Alex," I said, sitting up and reaching for my purse. "As you'll probably learn, he texts a lot. Which is good. I want him to. But—"

I stopped speaking when I saw my mom was calling. My mom never called when she was with Alex. Worry flooded me, and I answered instantly. "Hey, Mom. Is everything okay?"

"Everything is fine. I just dropped Alex off at home, though, because the hospital called. They're short-staffed tonight, and I have to go to work an hour early to fill in. But he's totally fine by himself. He's not even playing video games. He's reading," my mom said.

I breathed easier, but still stood up and started hunting for my clothes. "Did you have a good time?"

"The best. We always have a great time. I beat him at bowling, but he beat me at some crazy motorcycle game. Anyway, I just wanted to let you know that I wouldn't be there when you got home, but you still are under orders to have a good time."

I found my skirt and pulled it on. "I had an amazing time," I said, locking eyes with Colin, who'd tracked down a pair of gym shorts. He smiled at me as I slid into my shoes.

"Then you need to do it again."

"I do need to do it again," I said, wiggling my eyebrows

at him. "I love you, Mom. I'll see you soon. Are you coming to my match tomorrow night?"

"As soon as my shift ends, I'm there."

I said goodbye and turned to Colin. "I need to go. I know he's old enough to be home alone, but I don't like to leave him on his own too long, especially at night. You know?"

He nodded. "I get it."

I pulled on my tank top, wishing I could have finished what I'd started to say. But maybe this was the universe's way of slowing me down. I had been prone to rash decisions before. Perhaps I needed to meditate more thoughtfully on what to say. Or maybe what I really needed to do was talk to my son. I'd been protecting him, keeping him safe from the kind of hell he'd witnessed with his father. Before I told Colin that I wanted to try with him, I should tell my son what Colin meant to me.

Then perhaps the three of us could hang out after the match.

That sounded like heaven.

Like the life I'd always wanted.

My heart squeezed as I imagined it.

My greatest dreams come true. "Hey," I said softly, taking a step toward a new future. "Would you like to come to the match too? My mom will be there. Alex usually goes. It would be fun to have you there too."

"I'd love to. I'd absolutely love to. Ryan gets back tomorrow, which means he'll be jonesing to see Johnny Cash, and once he picks him up, I can come see you. Are you going to be wearing those crazy hot socks that go to here?" he asked, wiggling his brow as he tapped me above the knee.

I laughed and nodded. "I will."

He adopted an intensely serious face. "So when I come

up and say hi, I need to act like I don't have fantasies of fucking you while you're wearing nothing but those socks?"

A sweet rush of heat spread down my spine. "Yes. Try to pretend you're not thinking that."

"I'll just pretend I'm one of your loyal volunteers at the center coming out to support you."

I leaned in and kissed him. "Pretend for now. Maybe not much longer," I whispered, then turned on my heel to go as he walked me to my car.

That was all I could manage for the moment. I had so much more to say. I felt so much more in my heart.

39

ELLE

My heels clicked on the concrete steps as I walked up the two flights to my apartment. I slid the key into the latch, but there was no give. The door slipped open.

Alex appeared, a *gotcha* look in his brown eyes. He pointed at me. "Now, where were you tonight?"

Heat spread across my cheeks. My mom had picked up Alex before I'd gotten home from work, so he hadn't seen me when I left for my date, but my attire said it all.

"Out," I said sheepishly, slipping past him. He shut the door behind me, letting it close with a loud bang.

"*Out.* Is that his name? You were out with *Out*?"

I laughed as I headed to the kitchen and poured myself a glass of water. I took a long gulp then figured now was as good a time as any. Speaking the truth—at least the start of it—to Colin had been such a refreshing change from holding back. Perhaps telling my son would have a similar effect. Besides, it was the right way to handle this blossoming relationship.

I walked around to the stools at the counter and patted one. "Sit."

"Uh-oh," he said as he plopped down. "Am I in trouble?"

"No." I took the other stool and crossed my legs. Nerves beat a path through my chest, but I glanced down at my tattoo. *Be strong.* "Alex, I made a promise when your father died that I would never put us in that situation again."

He furrowed his brow. "What situation?"

"Me being involved with someone dangerous. Me being involved with someone, period. I don't have a great track record with relationships, and you're the most important person in my life."

"Is this the part where you tell me you met a hot meth head and you have bags of kitty litter in your car?"

I laughed softly and shook my head. "You do know there is no such thing as a hot meth head, right?"

"Yeah. I know. Meth heads are nasty."

I crinkled my nose. "So gross," I said, then returned to the topic. "But I've been seeing someone who's a recovering addict."

"Oh," he said, his voice flat. I didn't know if that meant he didn't care or he was disappointed.

"And he's a really good guy," I added.

He arched a skeptical eyebrow. "Like my dad was a good guy?"

I shook my head vehemently. "No. Good guy like the real deal."

"Okay," he said, his tone easing up. "So what's the issue?"

"I want to know how you feel about that. He's been in recovery for eight years. He's a good, solid, strong man who hasn't relapsed."

He shot me a look like I was nuts. "I don't get it, Mom. What's the problem? He sounds cool."

"He is cool. You know him."

I could see the gears turning in his head. Then they

clicked, and he wagged his finger at me. "No way! You're dating Colin."

I couldn't help but grin. "How did you guess it was him?"

"Duh."

I jutted out my chin. "Duh, what?"

"I can't believe you thought I wouldn't guess him," he said, laughing at me, clutching his belly.

I straightened my spine. "I'm sorry, but did you have radar installed?"

He stared at the ceiling as if he was deep in thought. "Hmm. Let's see. Could it be the way you flirt with him at the center?"

"I don't flirt with him."

"Could it be the fact that he started texting me video-game tips?"

"Oh, excuse me. Did any of them say, 'I like your mom'?"

"No. But get real. What guy does that?" he scoffed.

"A nice guy," I said insistently.

"Exactly. That's my point. He's a good guy. He volunteers. He helps Rex for free. And I've seen the goofy look you get when you're texting."

I was so busted. "Would you prefer that I didn't go out with him?" I asked gently, giving him the out that I felt I needed to. Alex was my top priority, and even though I prayed he'd say no, I'd have to honor his wishes if he said yes. "I want to protect you. And my history of picking men hasn't been the best."

"No," he said with a laugh. "It's fine."

"Do you mind if he comes to the match tomorrow, and maybe we can all hang out and get ice cream or something afterward?" I asked with a cocktail of nerves and hope that I hadn't felt since I myself was a teen asking out a boy. Such a strange feeling, to want my son's approval so badly.

He shrugged happily. "Sure."

"Does it bother you that he's a recovering addict?"

He shook his head. "Mom, he's nothing like Dad. We're cool." His phone rattled, and he grabbed it. "Oh man, James just got a new cheat code."

And that was that. He'd moved on. I'd clung to fears of what our life might be like if I ventured down this path again, but Alex was resilient. He'd taken his punches and gotten back up.

I was the one who'd been living in fear. He'd been living his life.

It was time for me to do the same.

Fully. In every way. Not only as a mom, but as a woman too. A woman who was falling hard for a man.

40

COLIN

"I owe you, man. The Cristal's on me," Rex said, offering his hand to shake as I pulled up to the building at the community college where Rex and Marcus were slated to take the math test. "Wait. I meant the Shirley Temple's on me."

I waved him off. "Get out of here. Happy to do it."

"What are you doing today? You gonna go find the next Google to buy, or go scale the side of a mountain with your Spidey hands?"

"Both," I said. "Work. Some climbing, a run, then a swim."

"You're nuts."

"You should go with me sometime."

"Now you're really crazy," Rex said, laughing. "But I will cheer your badass self on when the day comes."

"Or maybe if you score well, you can intern for me, and we can go rock climbing to celebrate."

He jerked his head back. "Intern like a J-O-B?"

I laughed. "Yes, I pay my interns."

Rex offered a fist for knocking.

"Excellent," I said, then looked into the back seat as Marcus grabbed his backpack. The kid had been quiet the whole ride. Then again, Rex tended to occupy the majority of the conversational space in any room. "Good luck, Marcus."

"Thanks for the ride. I didn't know till Rex told me this morning that you were picking us up."

I furrowed my brow for a moment, wondering why it mattered that I was the one picking them up. But I figured Marcus had more important matters on his mind. "Happy to help. You guys will do great."

Then I went to my office, where Larsen greeted me with a coffee and the sheer excitement of having found a kick-ass start-up.

"Talk to me. Tell me why I want in," I said as we walked down the hall. And later, as I worked on a term sheet for the first round of funding, the day was made perfect by the photo that landed on my phone. An image of Elle's legs from the thighs down in her roller derby socks.

Elle: See you tonight. I can't wait.

I replied from the heart.

Colin: Literally counting down the hours.

41

ELLE

The whistle blared loudly that evening, and Janine took off around the track, hell-bent on scoring more points. I joined in with the other blockers, jostling and jockeying against the Resurrection Girls' efforts to score on the Fishnet Brigade. My quads burned, and my heart beat furiously. My focus narrowed, as it always did during matches, to my mission—protect the jammer and win the game.

On the next lap, I held out a hand for Janine, who gripped it for a few seconds then let go as I sent her shooting faster around the curve. As Janine sped past a Resurrection Girl, an image of Colin popped into my head. I shook it off. I couldn't think about him now. Couldn't think about the fact that he wasn't here. Hadn't shown up. The match would be over in two minutes. My team was ahead. The point Janine just scored from my assist was more padding on the total.

Maybe by the time we finished he'd be here. He'd show, right? He had to.

A brief burst of frustration powered me around the track, my muscles cursing at me. I didn't want to believe that the man I was falling for would fail to show up for me and my kid.

The only thing that would hold him back would be—

Oh God. Oh no. Now? Was it happening now?

My wheels slipped out from under me, and I crashed hard onto the sleek wood.

42

COLIN

A little earlier in the day

As soon as I heard the rumble of Ryan's truck, Johnny Cash whimpered and thumped his tail against my floor. "He's back," I said to the dog, who wagged his tail even harder. "C'mon, boy. Want to go see Ryan?"

The tail became a propeller, moving so fast it could power a motorboat. I opened my front door, and the border collie took off like a shot, tearing across the lawn to greet his master. I joined the two of them on the sidewalk. "Looks like someone missed you."

Ryan stood up and gave me a quick hug. "Thanks for watching him. I appreciate it."

"He's easy. Welcome back. How was it?"

Ryan cocked his head and seemed to consider the question for a few seconds as he petted his dog. "I'm going to ask her to marry me next week."

"Guess you had a great time." I shook my brother's

hand in congratulations and proceeded to pepper him with more questions.

Ryan answered them all then capped it off with a simple truth. "She's the best thing that's ever happened to me."

I parked a hand on Ryan's shoulder and looked him square in the eyes. "She is. And don't ever forget it."

"I won't," he said, then opened the door of his truck for the dog. An engine rattled down the street, as I patted Johnny Cash goodbye.

"He's back," Ryan said in a hiss. "Looks like he knows where we all live. Sophie told me he stopped by my house right before we went to Germany."

I furrowed my brow and was about to ask *Who's back?* When I heard a familiar-sounding "Hey."

"What's the deal?" Ryan said, and I nearly stumbled when I turned and saw who my brother was addressing. "My fiancée told me you stopped by my house the other week. Just man up and tell us what this is about."

Shit. I had told Ryan about Marcus and the Protectors, but I'd had no idea that the kid had stopped by Ryan's house before. What the hell?

"Marcus?" I asked, trying to figure out why he was here, and how he knew where I lived. Was he here to share his math results? But then why had he gone to Ryan's house the other week?

Ryan turned to me. "You know this kid?"

I simply nodded. I tried to form words, but I wasn't even sure what to say. I was used to assessing situations, but this one had me perplexed.

Marcus cut in. "I want to talk to both of you," he said, a touch of nervousness in his voice. "We all have something in common."

"What are you talking about? And why are you here?"

Ryan demanded of Marcus, then to me, he said, "Who is he?"

I was about to say what I knew—*I know him from the center, I drove him to his math test this morning, he's friends with Rex, Elle knows him, he's a member of the Protectors*—but all those words crumbled to dust when Marcus spoke next.

"My name is Marcus. I was born seventeen years ago at the Stella McLaren Federal Women's Correctional Center. My mother is Dora Prince. I'm your brother."

All the sound in the universe was vacuumed up. My heart stopped, my brain short-circuited, and the ground began to sway.

43

COLIN

I was frozen, but I wasn't cold. My breath didn't fit in my chest. My skin was two sizes too small.

"Who—" I started, but got stuck on the question. "Who is your father?" I managed to ask, the words thin and tentative as I tried to make sense of the way north had become south, and how up was now down, and who the hell this kid's dad was. Had our mother been knocked up courtesy of Stefano? That thought churned my stomach. Or did we share the same dad? But if Marcus had been born to Thomas Paige, we would surely have known about his existence, because the prison would have turned the baby over to Thomas Paige's parents to raise—my grandparents.

Which meant . . .

My blood went cold.

"My father is Luke Carlton," Marcus supplied.

The name of my mother's lover.

I was ice.

My mother had not only cheated on my dad, she'd

gotten pregnant from the affair. And that was the least of her crimes.

I didn't speak right away. I tried to process this news, tried to find my voice. When I did, all I could say was the obvious. "So she was pregnant when she went to prison?" I asked, the words tasting like gravel.

"I guess she had to have been," Marcus said. The three of us stood in our places like actors on our marks, no one moving at all.

"Pregnant? She was actually pregnant?" I asked again, as if repeating the facts would assemble them into a neat, orderly package.

But before Marcus could respond, I turned to Ryan. "Can you believe this?" I said to him, holding my hands out wide. I'd barely batted an eye when the detective had told me last that my mother had been dealing drugs.

But this—this was something else entirely. This was the true bombshell.

I had another brother. One who was fourteen years younger. One I'd never known existed.

This was a meteor crashing into my backyard, slamming a crater in the earth. This was me standing over it, trying to figure out what to do with that gaping maw in the ground.

"No. This is insane, even for her," Ryan said, the look in his eyes mirroring mine.

I snapped my gaze back to Marcus, who was rubbing a hand over his chin, a gesture that I often did too. I flinched at that one small shared trait. "I can't believe she was pregnant that whole time when everything went down. Her arrest. The trial. And she hid the pregnancy through all of that?"

"It sounds like it," Marcus said. "We had to keep a lot of

things quiet. My dad didn't want me mentioning it to anyone. Judging from things he told me later, I had the impression that my mom was scared of word getting out that she was pregnant." His early nerves seemed to have evaporated, replaced by something that sounded like relief. He straightened his spine, standing taller. He still wasn't as tall as Ryan or I though. Perhaps the height genes among the Sloan men had come from our father. Somehow this small detail mattered to me—mattered because I'd loved my dad. Because I missed my dad.

"When were you born?"

Marcus gave us his birthday. Three months after our mom went to prison. Which meant she would have been six months pregnant when she was locked up. I tried to remember how she'd looked then, during the trial and her arrest. She wore baggy clothes, if memory served. As a seamstress, she'd have known how to make the right outfits to hide a growing belly. And, none of us had visited her during that first year, grandparents' orders. The thought of her planning a whole deception hit me like a sledgehammer.

"Holy shit."

There were no other words for this situation. Just none. I backed up, reaching for a railing, a tree, something to hold on to.

Nothing was behind me—only sidewalk, yard, and the utter surprise of our foursome becoming a fivesome. I grabbed Ryan's shoulder, and my older brother steadied me as the news started to register as real.

My own mother had methodically hidden her fifth child, keeping him secret as the tsunami now rocked our family.

COLIN

I was one of five, not one of four.

And none of us had a clue.

I started traveling back in time, trying to add up the facts and make some sense of this latest machination of our mother's. "So she was pregnant when she was arrested," I said, thinking out loud, taking a minute to process the absolute fucking weirdness of *that* detail. "And she was clearly pregnant when she was sentenced and went to prison." My brain kicked back into gear and started reconnecting the parts to the whole. And as I lined up the pieces, my jaw nearly dropped with one cold, stark realization. I brought my hand to my mouth, starting to speak, but my voice was vacant. Then I found words again, managing a bare whisper as I turned to Ryan.

"She was pregnant when Stefano pulled the trigger." And the corollary to that hit me like a harsh smack in the back of the head. *Motivation.* "Was that why she did it? Was that her motive?" I shifted my gaze to Marcus. "Did it have something to do with you?"

Marcus held up both hands as if in surrender. "I have no idea. I wasn't even born."

I didn't mean to imply that Marcus was the motivation for the murder, but even so, it had to have played a role in our mother's thinking. She probably wanted the life insurance money so she could run away with her lover and her unborn child.

I spun to face Ryan, who looked like a madman still—like this new wrinkle was rattling him to the core.

"Do you think this had anything to do with it?"

"I think *what the hell*. That's what I think," Ryan said, clenching and unclenching his fists. "I seriously cannot believe that she hid a pregnancy. But then, this is the woman who buried names of her accomplices, along with a goddamn drug-dealing route, in a dog jacket sewing pattern. That woman could hide anything. She's like a squirrel hiding nuts."

"She must have killed it in hide-and-seek," Marcus said softly, and a sliver of a smile formed on his lips. I glanced at Ryan, our eyes locking, sharing the realization that Marcus had just made a joke about our mother. *Our mother.*

All of ours.

One and the same. The green-eyed, husband-murdering, drug-dealing, cheater of a woman who had slept with this kid's father while she'd been married to my dad.

Such a twisted, sordid tale. *Dateline* would have a field day with this new development.

Marcus took a sheet of paper from his jeans pocket and unfolded it. "I brought this. I wasn't sure if you guys would believe me. But here it is," he said, then handed over a birth certificate. With steady hands, I held the paper and read every detail, Ryan by my side, peering at the document too. From the state of Nevada. Marcus Carlton's birth certificate. The mother's name was Dora Prince. The father's was Luke Carlton. The date was three months after our mother became inmate #347-921.

In black and white.

"Have you always known? That she was your mom? Or did Luke try to keep that from you?" I asked as I handed it back and studied Marcus's face, looking for clues, for the family resemblance. Michael, Ryan, and I had plenty of differences, but we all looked like brothers.

Did Marcus fit the mold? He had the same eyes as me. The same square jawline. I saw shades of myself in this boy, and it was odd to be looking at him in this new light.

"He wouldn't have been able to. Even if my dad and stepmom had wanted to hide it, they wouldn't have had much luck. My stepmom is from Vietnam. We look nothing alike."

"Ah, got it," I said, speeding onto the next questions. There were so many they were piling up, but I desperately wanted to make sense of this. "So there was no hiding that you weren't her biological kid. And you knew who your biological mom was, but Luke swore you to secrecy when you were younger?"

Marcus nodded. "Exactly. He didn't want to hide my birth story from me, partly because he needed us to lie low for a while. That's what he told me when I was in grade school. He told me they'd been threatened. That's why he left Las Vegas in the first place with me after I was born. He said once she went to prison, my mom and dad were warned that I'd be hurt. So we had to get out of town." He paused, drawing a breath. "And I guess you guys too."

Ryan flinched. "He said that? That we would all be hurt?"

Marcus held up his hands. "I don't know every detail. But my dad said that it was too dangerous for us to stay in

Vegas so he moved to San Diego with me, and met my stepmom there."

Ryan dropped a hand on my shoulder and exhaled, hard. His words came out dry and crackly. "You know what she said to me the other week? The last time I was there?"

"When she finally confessed to you?"

Ryan nodded. "She said, 'They told me they'd hurt you all. They told me they'd come after my babies if I said a word.' I bet it was TJ and Kenny who said that."

The hair on my arms stood on end as the full meaning registered. "Do you think she meant all of us?" I tipped my chin at Marcus.

But Ryan didn't answer. Marcus did. "That's what she's told me too."

"*She?* You've seen her? You've met her?" Ryan asked, then stopped himself, halting the conversation. "I gotta get Johnny Cash out of the car. Let's go inside."

A few minutes later, I let my older brother, the dog, and my younger brother into my house.

Younger brother.

The fact still didn't compute. "You go see her?" I asked the boy who had once just been another kid at the center trying to *rise above*. Now he was my flesh and blood.

"I have before. A few times. Look, it's not like I have some deep relationship with her," he said, his tone somewhat apologetic. "Obviously she never raised me. I'm closer to my stepmom. But I visited a few times. My dad used to take me when I was a lot younger, and then he dropped me off when I still wanted to see her. He knew it was important for me to go, and I wanted to know who my mother was."

"What was that like? Seeing her?" I asked as I headed to the fridge to grab sodas. It was a natural instinct—invite someone into your house, offer them a beverage. Maybe I needed one normal moment in the midst of this madness.

Marcus bit the corner of his lip, then answered, "She's . . ." He let his voice trail off, searching for words. "She's emotional, and she's not really—"

"She's not all there. You can say it." Ryan heaved a sigh. I handed out the sodas, then clapped my older brother on the back. Ryan had been hit hardest by our mom's incarceration, since he'd held on to the hope that she might be innocent for so much longer than the rest of us had. It was only fitting that he'd be the one to give voice to the descent Dora had taken behind bars.

Ryan cracked open the soda can.

That familiar action jarred me—the three of us drinking sodas at my kitchen table. This was the definition of surreal—our trio parked at the same table where I'd eaten free-range eggs this morning, a slice of avocado on the side. Now, I was chatting with the instant brother who'd fallen from the sky and into my life this afternoon. And yet, he hadn't just appeared out of nowhere. He'd been skirting the perimeter. "Why are you here now, Marcus?" I asked, opting for directness. "Why did you want to let us know who you are?"

Marcus gulped. "I wanted to . . ." He broke off, then dropped his head in his hands.

My instinct to help kicked in. "Hey. What is it?" I asked softly.

"I feel so stupid," he mumbled.

"Don't feel that way, just tell me. Tell us."

Marcus raised his face. Glanced away. Swallowed. Then looked back at us. "I just feel so disconnected sometimes from my family. I love them, but I feel like I'm not a part of them. Like I'm not part of anything." He leveled his gaze with ours. "My dad and I don't always see eye to eye, and my stepmom tries to include me, but she's busy with my little sisters, and I just feel like I was grafted onto their family. Like they were all just stuck with me. They had no choice but to take me." His voice turned colder, but sadder too, as he added, "I was nobody's choice."

My heart ached for the kid. My family had been blasted to pieces, but I'd always felt tethered to my siblings and my grandparents. "Is that why you were following us?"

Marcus nodded, a confession in his dark-brown eyes. "I wanted to see what you guys were like. That probably sounds stupid, but once I moved out of my parents' house this summer, I just couldn't stop thinking about it. I didn't lie to you about why I was at Shannon's. I'm part of the Protectors, and I went to Shannon's street as part of the patrol. But also to keep an eye on her. And since I knew your names, and found out you volunteered at the community center, I started going there to hang out."

My breath caught as I processed this new detail. Marcus *had* been stalking us, but not to cause trouble. Rather to see what the Sloans were like. To gather intel. I had no idea if I would've done anything differently in his shoes. "You knew who I was when you came to my math tutorial?"

"I did," he said with a nod, and a brief smile formed on my face. I couldn't deny that I admired the hell out of the way Marcus said those two words—*I did.* Because he owned it. He owned his actions. He stood by the fact that he'd been spying on us. "I wanted to know if you all seemed . . . well, cool."

I turned to Ryan, whose expression had softened. The initial shock in his blue eyes had been replaced by something else. Concern maybe? That was certainly what I felt. This kid had been left unanchored in a crazy world, born in the strangest of circumstances, told to keep secrets. All he wanted now was a connection.

"Did we? Seem cool?" Ryan asked, a playful note in his voice for the first time since this conversation had started.

Marcus laughed lightly, then gestured to me. "Well, you're the only one I've talked to. And yeah, I think you're cool," he said. "And I think it's cool that I'm good at math, like you are."

"Me too," I said with a smile.

"You need to meet Michael and Shan. They're pretty awesome as well," Ryan added.

"I'd like that."

I wasn't ready to invite the kid over for Christmas dinner, or break out the family photo albums. I wasn't going to take him out for pizza and ice cream yet. But I didn't intend to show him the door either.

I did what I knew was best—I spoke the truth.

"Look," I said, scooting my chair closer to the table. "I don't know what to say. I'm floored. Part of me feels like you were tricking me by talking to me while knowing what you knew." I chose bluntness. My mantra, my mission —no more lies, no more secrets. "But on the other hand, I get it. I probably would have done the same. You had a boatload of stuff to deal with, and now I get why you made that comment in the car this morning about not knowing it was me who was going to be driving you to the test."

"I didn't want you to think I was taking advantage of you. Of the fact that we're . . ." The careful words came out awkwardly, like he was afraid again to say "brothers."

"That we're . . ." I stuck on the word too, then pushed past it. "That we're brothers."

That sounded so immensely weird. Even stranger without Michael and Shannon being there. I'd call them in a few minutes. Then I remembered where I was supposed to be right now. At Elle's match. Looking at the time, I realized it was probably almost over, and frustration coursed through me. I'd call her soon too, and explain why I'd missed the match, and surely she'd understand. Probably be excited, in a way, that one of the boys she watched out for had done something brave.

Because that was what Marcus's appearance here today was—downright brave.

"I'm sorry to just spring it on you. There's not really a handbook for introducing yourself as the long-lost brother. Or a Hallmark card. I was trying to figure out what to do and say, and then you talked to me that day in the hall at the center," he said to me. "That's when I realized I needed to get my act together and just man up and introduce myself. That's what Elle helped me with."

The house went silent. My ears rang with her name, and a chill ran down my spine. "What did you just say?"

"Elle helped me," Marcus repeated, as if this was no big deal.

When it was a big deal. A huge deal.

"Elle? Elle at the center?" I asked, as if there could possibly be another Elle.

Marcus nodded enthusiastically. "I've been talking to her since the beginning. She's been counseling me. She's kind of amazing."

That definitely described her.

Kind of amazing.

But for the first time ever, other words popped into my head. Words I'd never associated with her before. Words I didn't *want* to associate with her.

If I'd felt the slightest bit tricked before, that was nothing on how I felt now.

Elle Mariano had lied.

45

ELLE

My right thumb was trying to secede from my body. It was a lemming, fighting its way off the cliff of my hand.

Because . . . the pain.

The slicing, searing pain ripped through my hand in a tornado of hurt. I gritted my teeth, not wanting to cry. *Don't let the opposing team see you weak.*

Play had halted. My teammates skated over to where I was curled up in a ball on the rink. Janine wrapped an arm around my waist and helped me up.

"C'mon, girl. Let's get you some ice," she said softly, guiding me off the rink.

I whimpered as I skated slowly to the carpeted floor. Camille was there, ready with an ice pack. "Here, let me help you."

With my left hand, I waved Janine back to the floor. "Go. Finish. I'm fine," I said with a wince, as another wave of agony crushed the life out of my hand. My right hip joined in the pity party too, aching from where I'd smashed onto the hardwood of the rink, my hand and hip taking the brunt of the fall. Carefully, I sat on a bench at one of the tables.

The whistle blasted, and my teammates returned to the track, the music blaring again, and the emcee bleating loudly on the overhead PA system. As the game whirled behind me, my sister pressed the ice pack on my traitorous thumb, wrapping it around my hand to the wrist.

I flinched from the cold as the biting chill swept over my hand.

"You're going to be fine. I bet that smarts like hell though," Camille said gently.

"Is it broken?" I croaked out.

"In my humble opinion as a self-appointed orthopedic nurse, I'm going to go out on a limb—sorry, no pun intended—and say nope. But you should get it checked out."

Alex walked over and slid in next to me. "You okay, Mom?"

I lifted my face and smiled faintly at my son. "I'm going to be fine."

He raised an eyebrow then peered at my hand. "You should get it checked out. Like Aunt Camille said."

I shoved off the pain. "I'm okay."

"No. We need to take you in to get it looked at. Make sure it's not anything serious," Alex said, slipping into his role as man of the house. He dipped his hand into the pocket of his cargo shorts. "By the way, your phone went off. I didn't look, but here it is."

He placed it on the table, and the text message icon flashed on the screen.

Several times, indicating several messages. My stomach plummeted when I saw who they were from.

I hurt a thousand times worse as I gingerly unlocked the phone with my left hand and read each one.

46

COLIN

I pictured raging waters sloshing over the front of the kayak as I paddled through a rough spot. I jammed the paddles harder into the water than I needed to, but the current—the tension on the rowing machine—pushed back. I rowed faster, the equipment at the rowing club screeching loudly, as if it was about to snap. Part of me didn't care. Part of me cared deeply. Another part of me was pissed, and the only thing that mattered was the battle I was waging with the machine.

And myself.

Maybe I shouldn't have said those things. Maybe I should have been smarter, kinder, softer.

But at the very least I'd been honest.

That had to count for something, didn't it?

The machine had no answers. As it simulated a river, the rowing machine simply jerked and pulled, and I fought back, wishing I were on the water for real, far away from land and able to totally disconnect.

But it was eleven o'clock at night, and this was the only way to fight the demons that whispered temptation in my ear. I was mad, I was frustrated, I was ashamed, and beneath it all, I was strangely happy too.

For Marcus. For the chance the kid took and the chance I had to get to know him in a new way. For Shan and Michael as well. Ryan and I had taken Marcus to meet them, and it had gone well. But dammit. Today should have been something positive and good. Something that could represent a fresh start.

But the day turned sour when I'd overreacted. I'd been too blunt with Elle, too honest, and I hated thinking how she might feel right now.

I wished I could erase those messages. Wished I could do the day over again.

Now, all I wanted was to spend the night with my onetime loves.

Patrón and pills.

Instead, I rowed. I paddled. I gripped. The sound of the gears slammed in my ears over and over. Soon, soon, it would drown out my horrible longing. It had to.

Oh God, please, it had to.

47

ELLE

My mother dangled the white pill in front of me, waving it back and forth like it was a dinosaur vitamin for a three-year-old. "Just take one."

I batted it away.

"Listen to your mama, who's a nurse. It'll taste so good," my mom said in a singsong voice.

I shook my head. I didn't want to make a bigger deal of my crash than it was. "I don't want it."

My mom shot me a glare as I settled into the couch. "You have a dislocated thumb, and you're in so much pain your sister said you were squealing. Now stop being so pigheaded, miss."

"I was not squealing," I insisted. "And, please. It's a dislocated thumb. *Thumb,*" I said, emphasizing the extreme mildness of my injury. The urgent care doctor had diagnosed me with a simple dislocation. Then he'd clasped my hand in both of his and manipulated the thumb back into place.

Sounded easy. Hurt like a son of a bitch.

Fine. Maybe I *had* squealed then. Possibly I'd shed the tears I hadn't let slide down my cheeks at the rink. Perhaps they'd even served double duty—tears of pain and tears of sadness from Colin's texts.

I'd deserved them.

Still, they'd hurt.

The doctor had placed a metal splint on my thumb and told me I'd be fine in a day or so. "These types of injuries hurt like the dickens when they happen and for the next twenty-four hours, but then it's pretty much over and done. But just in case, I want you to have some of these," he'd said as he wrote out a prescription for pain meds.

I reached for the light blanket on the back of the couch and pulled it over my legs, then shifted to my side and yelped.

"What is it?" my mom asked, her eyes wide, worry written in them.

"My hip. It's not dislocated though. It just hurts, since I landed on it too." I rubbed the spot where I'd fallen. Using my right hand. Which made my thumb throb. That pain radiated through my hand, up my forearm, and straight to my damn shoulder. I winced. "Guess I shouldn't use this stupid thumb to rub my stupid hip."

"Sweetie, just take one. You'll feel better."

"I don't want to," I said. I needed to stay strong. I couldn't let a *simple dislocation* rattle me.

"Mom." I turned my focus to the hallway door. Alex had popped out of his bedroom. "Take the pill. You'll feel better. You were crying all evening."

"I was not," I said with a huff.

My mom heaved a sigh, then shrugged and addressed her next words to Alex. "Nothing we can do about this stubborn lady."

"People. You act like I fell off a cliff. This is nothing. I'll be back in business tomorrow."

"But you're out of roller derby the rest of the season," Alex said, pointing out those doctor's orders too. No contact sports for two weeks. Nothing that could lead to reinjury. The season was over in fourteen days.

"Ugh. Thanks for reminding me. Maybe I should take one now. To numb the pain of missing my games," I said, cracking a small smile.

"Now you're talking," my mom said, and held out the glass of water.

"But just half of one, please. I don't want to be all dopey."

My mom nodded and broke the pill in half, dropping one part back in the bottle and handing the remainder to me, and I swallowed the pill. I only had ten in the prescription, and I'd probably only take this one. I didn't need to spend a sleepless night tossing and turning from the lingering pain.

"Hey. Speaking of missing games, what happened to Colin? I thought he was going to come today, and we were going to hang out," Alex said, as he sat cross-legged on the floor. My chest tightened, and I met his gaze. This was hardly the letdown of a lifetime, or even a big letdown in the scheme of things.

Still, I hated that Colin had canceled the first get-together with my son.

"He couldn't make it. Something came up," I said, both lying and telling the truth.

"Well, that sucks," Alex said, annoyance in his voice. "I was kind of looking forward to all of us hanging out."

"I'm sorry."

"It's not your fault, Mom. It's his. If you say you're going to be somewhere, you should show up."

"I know, sweetie. But something came up for him, and he had to deal with it."

Alex scoffed. "If you say so."

I had to wonder if I sounded the way I had when I'd defended Sam and his unreliable ways, back in the early days.

"She does say so," my mom chimed in, intervening as she shooed Alex back to his bedroom.

All alone on the couch, I reached for my phone and reread the message.

My gut churned once again.

Colin: I believe in honesty, so let me say this. I just met my new brother. You already know that though. And the rational part of me understands that you couldn't say a word. But are you fucking kidding me? There are rules, and then there are rules you bend. You knew this secret about my family and about me. And the entire time I had no idea. When you said you had a headache, it wasn't a headache. It was from knowing you were keeping a secret. It was a lie. I know I should understand that you had no choice, but I don't know how to do that right now. I don't know how I feel about any of this.

Colin: Or how I feel about what's happening with us.

I took a deep breath, sucking it in, letting my chest rise and fall on that last one. It was a jagged little knife, chopping at pieces of my heart.

His words weren't cruel. They weren't mean. They

weren't underhanded digs. That was what made my heart ache even more. He'd spoken the bare truth, and I'd known this could happen—that his feelings for me might alter when he learned I'd kept Marcus's secret.

Still, it hurt so much that this choice might mean the end of the sweetest thing I'd had in ages. I'd been falling so hard for him.

Maybe I should take the other half of the pill, to lessen the pain. I reached for the bottle, but it was so far away on the table. I barely had the energy to fumble for it now.

Soon, my eyes started to flutter closed, and the aching in my thumb subsided. The pain padded away, slinking out of the room, leaving me with only this whitewashing, this smooth, easy feeling in my body.

But before I slipped into slumber, I tapped out a short response with my left hand.

Elle: I'm so sorry. There was nothing I could do.

I hit send then decided I wanted to fall asleep on a happier note, so I skipped over to the Facebook page for the Fishnet Brigade to see if my roller derby friends had posted any photos from the game. I smiled at an image one of the blockers had shared of the team before the match, then at one of me sending Janine around the curve during the game. I posted a smiley face in the comments, then ran my finger over the picture as I yawned, the pill working its magic on my brain as well as my hands.

I clicked back to the page to search for more, when a notification appeared. Someone had replied to my comment, but it was from a weird name I didn't recognize, and the words were an eerie warning.

Be careful who you get involved with.

"What?" I mumbled, but I was already floating on a cloud of comfortably numb, and the mystery slipped away along with my cares.

48

———

COLIN

The phone rang and rang and rang.

But then, if I were her, I probably wouldn't answer either. Tossing the phone onto the counter, I grabbed my cup of coffee and downed a hearty gulp.

Honestly, I shouldn't even be calling her so early. I should let her sleep. She was probably up late last night, anyway, celebrating her team's win. I was proud of her and sad that I'd missed it.

Sadder still over the note I'd sent.

I leaned back against the steel fridge and closed my eyes. What had I been thinking? But that was the problem —I hadn't been thinking. I'd been *feeling* and letting all those stirred-up, messed-up, mixed-up emotions from meeting my long-lost brother rule over me.

I'd simply reacted. Lightning fast, like I did in sports. When I went bungee jumping, I didn't let myself think. I didn't give myself any space to contemplate the decision. I just jumped and free-fell.

That kind of split-second fearlessness came in handy in

my pursuit of adventure sports. But it could be the death knell for a budding relationship.

I cursed at myself as I drank more of the caffeinated brew, then set the nearly drained mug on the counter. I'd already logged some time on the lake this morning, on top of last night's epic two-hour rowing club workout. The bookends to my midnight and dawn had worked—they'd kept me on the straight and narrow. I'd been tempted last night—the pull of the one sure way to drown my sorrows had been potent. But I'd stayed strong, so at least I had that victory.

Now all I wanted was to see Elle and make sense of what had gone down. But it was too early, so I grabbed my keys and sunglasses, left my house, and headed to visit the two people I knew would be up at this hour on a weekend.

I drove over to the Golden Nugget and found my dad's two best friends where they always were on a Saturday morning. Sanders usually joined Donald at his table for a few final rounds with his favorite dealer before Donald's overnight shift ended. They'd cap that off with eggs and bacon, then meet their wives for coffee.

At this hour on a Saturday, Sanders was the only one at Donald's table, so I caught them up on the latest news from the detective about the drug dealing, as well as yesterday's shocker.

"Is that not the craziest thing you've heard?" I asked, as I finished the story and perused my cards.

Donald blew out a long stream of air, finishing it off with a low whistle. "If it's not the craziest, it's damn close. She was a real piece of work, that woman."

I huffed. "Yeah, that's for sure. Did my dad even know about the stuff she was up to?"

Sanders shook his head. "Hell no," he said emphatically. "He knew she was getting into some bad shit and running into trouble with money. But being pregnant? No way. He'd have told us for sure."

"He would?"

Sanders nodded as he studied his cards, exchanging one for a new card. "We were all pretty up-front with each other. He told us some of what was going on at work. Like when there was some trouble at the company for a spell and he was trying to make head or tail of it. Told us, too, what was happening at home with Dora and the fights they had about money. And, of course, stuff about you guys. Teaching Mike to drive and Shan to play pool. Hell, we all heard the story of that hickey you got," he said with a wink, darting out his index finger toward my neck as if I were twelve again.

I chuckled, remembering when I'd made up an elaborate tale to avoid admitting a girl had given me a hickey at a middle school dance. My dad saw straight through it and teased me mercilessly. Evidently, my dad had told his best buddies too. That warmed my heart.

I returned to less amusing topics. "What about the cheating though? Did my dad know about Luke?"

"He was suspicious," Donald said as he doled out two more cards to me.

I arched an eyebrow. "He knew she was fooling around?"

"He didn't have any evidence, but a man just knows these things," Donald said, setting down the deck and parking his hands on the green felt of the table.

Sanders chimed in. "He could tell from her behavior. That's what he told us—that she'd been spending more time out of the house. More time unaccounted for. But, you know, he wasn't going to hire a PI or anything like that, and it was different back then. People didn't have cell phones with cameras, walking around snapping pictures of people getting up to things they shouldn't be. So it was easier for her to get away with it."

My gut churned, and my shoulders tensed with simmering hate. I detested everything my mom had done to my dad. *Every single thing.* "Did he care? Was he bothered? Was he in love with her still?"

Donald tipped his chin at the other man. "What do you think, San? Did Thomas still love Dora?"

Sanders sighed deeply. "Ah, hell. How can I answer that? We weren't fond of her. We didn't like Dora way before any of the real shit went down, because she was fucking around on him. So I don't want my dislike for her to cloud my answer. But I think he cared for her. He was as good to Dora as anyone could be to a woman like that, and he showed her respect because she was the mother of his children. And more than anything, he cared about you kids. You were the center of his world. The four of you— that's what he loved most. Being your dad."

As Sanders picked up his cards, I stared distantly out at the sparse morning sprinkling of gamblers at slots and tables, blinking away the tears that threatened to well up. My father had been gone so long, and while I still thought of him every day, time had a way of soothing the pain. The years made the hurt recede into the horizon.

But losing him would never take away the good things my father had passed on to me—love, respect, and truth. I might have spiraled after my dad's death, but I'd picked myself up since then. I'd apologized for my mistakes. I'd become a better man—the man my father had taught me to be.

And that man needed to see one woman now.

49

ELLE

The blanket fell to the floor.

I rustled myself from the couch, sitting up as I yawned. The light shone brightly through my living room window. I glanced around, getting my bearings, then I spotted a note on the coffee table. From my mom—it was written on a yellow piece of stationery with a cartoonish fox in the corner.

Hey, sweetie, I picked up Alex this morning. You were sound asleep. I'll take him for the day. Get your rest, my love.

I grabbed my phone to check the time. It was after nine. I'd been conked out since before midnight. Those pills must have worked brilliantly. I wiggled my thumb gingerly, and it didn't hurt anymore.

I wished I could say the same about my heart. I'd need super-duper strength pills to numb the pain I felt when I thought of Colin, how angry he was and how he felt so deceived by me. I understood why, and I'd tried to prepare myself for this moment, but it hurt more than I could have imagined.

As I placed my phone on the table, another memory

boomeranged front and center. An odd Facebook comment from last night. Something strangely . . . menacing. I clicked on the app and scanned the post on our team's page. But whatever I'd been remembering was now gone. The post only included comments from my derby teammates, fans, and friends.

Weird. Maybe the pain pill had made me a little loopy.

I padded to the bathroom, brushed my teeth, and took a quick shower. When I was through, I pulled on a pair of shorts and a T-shirt, headed to the kitchen, and punched in the '90s channel on my music app. I hummed along to a Pearl Jam tune as I hunted for eggs and bread in the fridge.

The music was interrupted by a knock on the door.

With one hand gripping the open fridge door, I made a wish, hoping against hope that it would be Colin. A foolish wish.

After his texts, there was no way he'd be here.

I headed to the front door, peered through the peephole, and squeaked when I saw that dark hair, that sandpaper stubble, and those yummy lips. *That man.*

I burst into a grin.

Wait.

Prickles of worry tripped across my skin. What if he was still pissed? What if he'd come here to tell me he never wanted to see me again?

I inhaled deeply, letting the air fill my chest, and gathered my strength. Whether he was mad or not, whether I was hurt or not, we needed to talk. I opened the door, ready to finally explain.

He was faster. He locked eyes with me. "Hey, so I'm an asshole, and I'm so incredibly sorry."

The grin returned to my face, and I shook my head. "No, you're not," I said quickly, needing to reassure him. "Not at all. Do you want to come in?"

He nodded and walked inside. I shut the door behind him, and we stood in my tiny entryway. Though I was happy to see him, my heart still hurt from his messages, and from the weight of the secrets I'd had to keep.

"Colin," I said, starting with my own mea culpa. "You have to know that if there were a way I could have told you, I would have. I desperately wanted to. It was so hard for me not to say anything. I hated keeping it from you. But I couldn't do that to Marcus."

"I know. I swear, I know," he said, relief and frustration in his voice as he dragged one hand through his hair. "And I should have known better. I was so blindsided, and then a million times more shocked to learn he'd confided in you before he told us. But instead of sitting down and talking to you to try to understand the situation, I just blurted out all my feelings. Over text, no less." He stopped to shake his head and take a quiet breath. "I've tried so hard to be truthful and open. After years of keeping secrets and hiding problems, I've worked hard to speak the truth. But I was too honest. I spoke too much and said hurtful things."

"But they were truthful things too."

"At the time. But that doesn't mean they needed to be said. I should have waited to talk to you. Instead of reacting like that. I don't want to be that guy."

"Then don't be that guy," I said matter-of-factly. I understood that he'd been knocked to his knees by news he couldn't have prepared for, but I also wasn't going to be on the receiving end of his frustration. "Be the guy who gives me a chance to explain and work it out. And be the guy who treats me with respect even if you're upset."

"I will. I promise I will," he said, his voice a plea for forgiveness. "That's not how I want to treat you. I was just so stunned by everything that I stopped thinking." He rocked lightly on his heels as Eddie Vedder sang on the stereo in the kitchen. "It was all so out of the blue. Ryan was telling me about his trip, and his dog was jumping in the car, and, Elle . . ." He stopped to look me in the eyes, letting the enormity of the moment register. "Then my half-brother appears, takes off his cape, and says, 'Ta-da!' It was beyond surreal. He talked for a long time, and then he told me he'd spoken to you about it. And boom." He smashed one palm against the other. "It was like slamming into a wall. I just didn't know what to think, and I snapped back at you. I should have taken some time to process the news and filtered myself. Instead, I processed it through you. Over a text message. And I just typed everything that came to mind, rather than talking to you." He downshifted to a gentler tone, meeting my eyes and doing what I'd asked. "So, please talk to me."

At last, I was free of the burden of this secret. "I didn't want to keep it from you. But he asked for my confidence before he told me he was your brother, and I was torn apart when I found out. But it would have been so wrong for me to tell you." I reached for him, running my fingers gently across the tanned skin of his arm, wanting contact.

"Wrong? Elle, that's not what I—" Then he stopped and gestured to my thumb with the splint on it. "What happened to your hand?"

I shrugged it off. "Nothing. I crashed during the match."

He reached for my hand, brought it to his lips, and brushed a kiss onto the small splint. My heart fluttered.

"Are you okay?" His tone was etched with concern.

"I'm fine. Everyone is making a big deal of it. It's a dislocated thumb, and evidently it's relocated now," I said as I wiggled my thumb. "It's not like I broke a tibia crashing off a sheer rock wall or something. But it did hurt like hell yesterday." I smiled. "I'm feeling much better this morning though."

"Can I still hold your hand?" he asked, rearranging our hands to gently slide his fingers through mine, lacing them together. My heart danced a crazy jig. So much for that momentary panic. Now the organ in my chest was engaged in a full-blown tango of joy.

"Yes," I whispered.

He stepped closer, tenderly clasping my hand. "I didn't mean it when I said I don't know how I feel about you. Maybe for a few seconds, or a few minutes, I didn't know which way was up or down. But then when I thought about it, I know exactly how I feel about you."

"And how do you feel?"

50

COLIN

This was the real risk. *Close your eyes, step off the cliff. No guarantee that there's anything to break your fall, but do it anyway.*

"How I feel is this." I took a breath before I spoke. "That I should have come and talked to you. That I wish I'd been there yesterday to help you up when you fell," I said, wrapping my other hand around her trim waist. She fit so well in my arms. "That I wanted to spend time with you and your son."

Her eyes sparkled when I mentioned Alex.

"And I know I need to make it up to him that I didn't show up, as much as I need to make it up to you. Because the two of you are a package deal. You matter so much to me, and I want to do right by your kid."

"You will do right by him. You already are," she said, her voice breaking as she inched closer, melting into me.

"I want so much more than what it's been. I can't pretend I just want *this*," I said, raking my eyes over her from head to toe. "I do want whatever you can give. I do want to have you all night long. But I want the rest of you too." I let go of her waist and placed my palm on her chest. I was guided by the truth of my feelings for her—and the depth of them too. "I'm falling for you."

Instantly, she grasped my hand, tugging it even closer to her chest. "I'm falling for you too, Colin. I was going to tell you the other night at your house," she said, words tumbling free in a mad rush. "I don't want these lines between us anymore. I don't want to just keep seeing you. I want to see what we can become. I told Alex that I'm dating you, and I want you to be in my life."

I nuzzled her neck, layering kisses on her skin, my heart beating hard and fast. "I want that so much, Elle. I want all of you."

"You can have all of me," she whispered, then pressed her lips to my ear, making me shudder and turning me on. "Preferably now. In my bed. You and me."

As much as I wanted to RSVP all the way to that invitation, she was injured.

But there were plenty of ways to make her feel better. "How about I give *you* some TLC?"

She tapped her chin, as if considering it. "Okay, sold."

Scooping her up, I carried her through the living room and down the hall, finding her bedroom easily.

Gently, I stripped her down to her panties, tossing her shorts and tank on the floor.

She froze and held up her index finger. "Wait."

I raised an eyebrow in a question.

"Close your eyes," she told me.

I shrugged happily, figuring whatever was coming next would be worth the surprise. A drawer opened behind me with a squeak, then I counted the seconds as she moved around. Nineteen long ones later, the mattress dipped lightly, and she told me to open my eyes.

Holy fucking fantasy.

The socks.

The roller-skating socks. They were white with purple stripes at the knees, and they were so hot. My dick was operating at a ninety-degree angle now. But this wasn't about me.

It was about her.

I crawled up on the bed, running my hands up her legs, from the socks to her knees to those gorgeous thighs, which led to my favorite place in the universe. I kneeled over her, bending my face to her center. Kissing her belly. Her hips. Inhaling her. Her scent drove me wild. I pressed my lips against the waistband of her panties, then tugged at them with my teeth.

She laughed lightly, but her laughter was swallowed up as I yanked them to her knees, and her hips shot up.

"Colin," she whispered, surprise in her tone. But excitement too, judging from the sexy little murmur she made.

Once I had the underwear to her ankles, I tugged them off.

"Just like I've always wanted," I said, meeting her eyes. Hers were full of lust—a lust that matched mine. "You in just these."

"That's what I like—being your fantasy."

"You're all my fantasies," I said.

Then I spread her open. Traveled up her legs. Kissed the inside of her thighs. Nipped that enticing, tantalizing spot where her legs curved into her slick folds.

I ran my tongue along her wetness, and she rose up, arching into me.

I took my time with her, making her feel so damn good, tasting her, kissing her, savoring her until my beautiful woman came undone on my mouth, her sweetness on my lips, her pleasure flooding my tongue. Her heady taste was all over me as she cried out my name like the chorus of a classic rock anthem.

51

ELLE

I dangled my bare feet in the stream as the water gurgled between my toes.

The sun beat down hellishly, but tall trees with lush green branches shielded us from the bright rays, and a soft breeze circled. We'd walked on one of Colin's favorite trails, which wound its way along a small creek.

"Did that mega intense hike get you all ready for your triathlon?" I teased, nudging him with my elbow as we perched on a rock at the edge of the water.

"Absolutely. Did you know the Badass Triathlon now includes a mile-long nature stroll?"

I pumped a fist. "Excellent. Sounds like my kind of race."

He draped an arm around my shoulders. "Kind of ironic, too, that you're the one with the splint and yet you worry about me doing crazy stuff."

I turned to him, dropped my hand to his leg, and squeezed his strong thigh. "I do worry about you, Colin," I said, meeting his gaze.

He flashed a small smile. "I like that you worry about me."

"I worried about you yesterday too. I worried how you were going to take the news from Marcus," I said softly. "How was it?"

A bird chirped on a nearby branch, and Colin gazed at the rocks on the other side of the creek as he told me about meeting his half-brother, from the utter shock, to the sparks of humor he said he saw in Marcus, to how Michael and Shan had reacted when he'd told them—which was in much the same way he had. "Honestly, I didn't know how Michael would take it, since there's no love lost with him and our mom. I was worried he wouldn't want to have anything to do with Marcus."

"But he didn't react that way?"

"Oh, he was surprised as hell, and had a few choice words to say about Dora Prince. But he's *always* looked out for us younger ones, and I guess Marcus is part of that now. But the whole thing is this big reminder of my mother, and how I barely know who she is. She's like this strange, evil magician presiding over all of us still from behind bars. Or maybe a master puppeteer, and she pulls all the strings whenever she wants," he said, holding up his hands to demonstrate an evil mastermind, adding in a cackle.

"She didn't pull this one," I pointed out. "Marcus came to you on his own."

He huffed. "I know, but she played her part by not saying a word for years." He shook his head in disgust. "How do you keep a kid a secret? Why? I don't get her. I don't know what language she speaks, if she's even human. I seriously don't understand how I'm connected to her. I hate that I've ever had anything in common with her."

He turned to me, the sunlight streaming through the branches and illuminating the deep frustration etched on his handsome face. I ran a hand gently through his hair. "I don't know her at all, but I don't think you're like her. You're such a good person, Colin. You're one of the best people I've ever known."

He cupped my cheek. "Thank you," he said. But he didn't seem to hold on to my words, because his tone turned dark again as he let go of my face and clenched his fist. "Most of the time, I can deal with the stupid decisions I made as a kid, but sometimes I *hate* that I had friends who were connected to the Royal Sinners. I can't believe I associated with them even peripherally."

"And yet you didn't wind up in it. You didn't venture down that path."

"But I was such a mess as a teenager," he said, gritting his teeth.

"Please. It's not like I have some spotless record as a teen. I got knocked up."

"Yeah. But something good came of that. Your kid."

"True. But still, I was pregnant when I graduated from high school. Of course I don't regret it, but my point is, you shouldn't let the past gnaw at you either. You are your present, and what I see in front of me is pretty great." A light breeze swirled the water at our feet as he smiled—a soft, tender smile. "Hate is a hard thing to hold on to. It can eat away at you."

He nodded a few times, like he was letting my remarks sink in. "Do you think that's what's happening to me?"

"I know a lot of it's directed at her, but I think you're mad at yourself too, Colin," I said softly, placing a hand on his arm, tracing his tattoos that I loved. "Because you've struggled with some of the same things your mother struggled with. And I think that's the thing you hate—that you have this one small thing in common with her. Perhaps the person you need to forgive is yourself." Then I softened my voice as I said the thing that I knew would be hardest for him to hear. But the thing that needed to be said. "Maybe to do that, you need to see her."

He sat ramrod straight, as if he'd been jolted with high-voltage electricity. "Are you kidding me?"

"No. I'm not. And I'm just putting it out there. That's the social worker in me. But I think you beat yourself up because you used, and she used. And maybe seeing her once will help you to let go of the hate you feel toward her. To see you're not like her. Because it's really a part of yourself that you're mad at."

He didn't say anything at first, just ran his hand over his chin and exhaled hard as he stared out at the stream. A small bead of worry rolled through me, and I hoped I hadn't crossed a line with my suggestion, but I didn't want to take it back either. I truly wanted him to consider it. "I think seeing her would be less about her and more about you. Almost as a way of making that last amends to yourself." I tapped his chest lightly. "To forgive yourself."

The corner of his lips curved up. "You're too smart for my own good. I'll think about it."

"Good." Warmth spread through me at the fact that he was open to the possibility.

"Is this coming from experience? Did you hate Sam?"

I answered immediately. "No. I felt sorry for him. I was sad for him. I felt completely helpless. But I had to let go of all those feelings. He wasn't a good dad. He wasn't a good man, and there was nothing I could do to change him. I had to stop fighting all the battles with him. I couldn't make him a better father. I couldn't make him stop using."

He nodded sagely. "You can't make anyone hit bottom. They have to find it on their own. And man, am I glad I found mine. Even if it took collapsing in a race to do it," he said with a wry note in his voice. "Because I've come far since then, and it all led me to you."

52

COLIN

Forgiveness was granted in all of a minute by the fourteen-year-old.

"He's your brother?" Alex's jaw dropped, and then he asked me for every last detail.

I gladly shared the story with Elle's son over pizza at Gigi's Pizzeria that night. Alex shook his head in amazement in between bites of cheese pie. "I guess I can let it slide this time that you missed my mom's match. That's a good enough reason. Even though there's no next time—she's out for the season."

"You know what that means?" I asked, as the waitress cleared the table. "When the Fishnet Brigade wins big, we need to plan an awesome celebration for her and all she did to get the team there."

"Totally."

Elle didn't say much. She simply smiled, and nothing could have made me happier than seeing her relaxed and comfortable at dinner with me and the most important person in the world to her. We'd come so far. We'd made it past so much already. I'd never expected to knock down her walls so soon—or at all. But it had happened, and here we were, making our way through together.

When the check came, Elle reached for it, but I grabbed it sooner and paid. And as we left the pizzeria, I tossed out a question to Alex. "Ever been to the Zombie Apocalypse store?"

"No," he said, his eyes wide and curious. "What's that?"

"Exactly what it sounds like. It's over in Chinatown. It's a small shop where you can work on your skills in preparation to go to battle with the undead. It's tongue-in-cheek, lots of novelty items, but it's a lot of fun."

"Mom, can we go?" Alex asked, looking like a dog asking for a bone.

"Only if we can go now," Elle answered.

The three of us spent the next hour in the odd little store, where Alex plied the store manager for tips on how to stay ahead of the brain-eaters.

It was as perfect a night as one could be, and I wanted to remember it as the start of a whole new chapter with the woman I adored.

53

—————

ELLE

After Alex crashed and I got ready for bed, I sent Colin a good night text.

Elle: Today was perfect. Thank you.

His reply landed in seconds.

Colin: It was. Let's do it again soon. All of it.

I was closing out of the text app when a new message appeared. But it wasn't from Colin. It was from an unknown number.

Hey, pretty lady. Don't you be messing around with that new guy. WJ

54

RYAN

I turned off the engine in my truck, hopped out, and headed inside the convenience store off the highway. I grabbed a bottle of iced tea, walked to the counter, then nodded to the cashier. *My little brother.*

"That'll be one dollar and twenty-one cents."

"No family discount?" I joked.

Marcus smiled and shook his head. "Sorry, man."

The convenience store was empty, so I rested my hip against the counter, opened the bottle, and took a gulp. I tapped the plastic. "Can I treat you? It's hot as hell outside."

"Sure."

I returned to the cold shelves, grabbed another bottle, paid for it too, then handed it to the guy who I used to think was stalking my family. Now I was getting to know the kid. We weren't instant buddies, and I hadn't signed the two of us up for kumbaya-with-your-long-lost-bro classes. But I *did* want to get to know Marcus, so I was trying to do it in a natural way. I'd taken him to lunch yesterday, the day after we'd met, and Marcus had told me he worked at this store to save money for community college, and that he was living with friends.

Which made me wonder if the kid was on the outs with his dad.

His dad was another reason I was here today.

"Listen, Marcus," I said, as a car pulled up to a gas pump in the lot. "I want to see your dad. I need to talk to Luke because I really want to get some info about the affair and about the pregnancy, and see if that played into why our mom killed my dad." Those words—they tasted like dirt. For so long I'd believed my mom might be innocent, but I'd been coming to terms and to peace with her guilt. Still, I was determined to help solve the case and do everything I could to help find the other men involved.

Or at least to learn what had motivated my mother. The more information I gleaned, the greater the chance the cops had of nailing the other guys. John said he was still gathering evidence, but TJ and Kenny Nelson hadn't been found yet, and by all accounts, those two had left a trail of destruction behind them over the years. My chest burned with rage over the fact that two killers were walking free.

If it were up to me, I'd have knocked on Luke's door already and demanded some answers from the man who'd screwed my mother behind my father's back, then hid the kid he'd had with her. I'd done it once, but I couldn't do that now. It wouldn't be fair to Marcus.

"You want to talk to him?" Marcus repeated.

"I have before, yes. And I want to talk to him again. I want to see what he knows. But to do that," I said, gesturing from the kid back to myself, "I'd have to let him know I know about you."

Marcus shook his head. Adamantly. "No. Please no."

I tilted my head, my radar going off, detecting fear in

Marcus's eyes. "Why? He told you about your mom. You said it wasn't a secret."

"I know. But he doesn't know I talked to you guys."

"Are you going to tell him?"

"He would freak."

"Are you sure?" I was asking for myself, but for Marcus too. I didn't want to see this kid heading down the path of secrets like I had.

His eyes shifted around, a worried look in them. "I just don't think he'd be happy about it. I didn't tell him I was going to meet you guys. I haven't seen him much since I moved out."

"Why not?"

Marcus shoved a hand through his hair. "We don't always see eye to eye. If he knows I'm talking to you, he's going to worry about Stefano's friends. About Kenny and TJ. He's going to think they'll come after my sisters and my mom."

That was understandable, but I had to help him face it head-on. "But is that a real threat? If it is, maybe we need to deal with it, rather than ignore it," I said in a calm voice. "I can help you with that, you know. That's the business I'm in."

Marcus leaned forward and pressed his palms against the counter. "See, I have no idea. All I know is he's terrified still of what went down back then. I heard him talking to my stepmom when I was younger, telling her those guys threatened him—that if he said anything, they'd go after him. He made them seem like the guy from *Saw* or Leatherface from *The Texas Chainsaw Massacre*. Hell, the other day some dude with a goatee came in here chomping on potato chips, complaining about his phone, and generally kind of being creepy, and for a split second, I started thinking he was one of them."

"Why? What was he doing?" I asked, my hackles rising.

"Because he was . . ." Marcus started, then shook his head. "I don't know. He just seemed like the type of guy who'd stir shit up. That's all."

"Okay, I hear you. He set off your radar, and you have to listen to that. Now that you're connected to us, and that's started to come out, you've got to be careful, Marcus. We can talk about a security detail for you too, if you want, but you really should talk to the detective."

"I will. Soon. I was supposed to, but had to cancel because I got called into work, and then my car was in the shop. I know I need to see him."

"I can help arrange it if you need me to. Are you worried your dad doesn't want you to talk to him?"

"I don't know," Marcus said, barely audible.

I had no choice but to relent. I didn't know Luke Carlton well enough to understand his father-son relationship with Marcus—hell, this was all brand-new to me. But I'd have to work with this wrinkle, not against it.

"Hey, do you want to come over for dinner sometime?" I asked, my voice gravelly now. It was an awkward request, but Sophie had insisted I ask, so I was doing it.

Marcus's eyes lit up. "That'd be cool."

"I'll make sure to invite the whole crew. Michael, Shan, Brent. We can have Colin and Elle. And Alex too, if you'd like."

"I would," he said with a smile.

I had the sense that Marcus had been missing something his whole life, and it wasn't his biological mother. It was a connection to the rest of his family. And that was easy enough for me to give.

55

MARCUS

After Ryan left, I dropped my forehead to the register. My heart beat furiously, as if I'd been sprinting. My hands were clammy. That was what talking about my dad did to me lately.

Freaked me the hell out. Damn near set off an anxiety attack.

I couldn't tell my dad that I'd found the Sloans. I couldn't take that chance yet. I'd already taken a big enough risk meeting them. But knowing they existed had gnawed at me for years, and I'd longed to know them, especially since I'd been growing apart with my dad. For reasons I wasn't entirely sure I could give voice to.

My phone buzzed and I looked up. My stepmom had texted.

Angie: How did you do on your math test? Any results yet? Fingers crossed.

My heartbeat turned more regular as I wrote back.

Marcus: Got 'em earlier today. Aced it!

Angie: Proud of you!!! Way to go! Sundaes at Baskin Robbins to celebrate with the girls?

Marcus: Ice cream is always a yes.

Her excitement reminded me that I had to think of her and my sisters too. It had been one thing for me to reach out to my family on my mother's side, but I did still have a connection to my dad's family, no matter how strained things sometimes got with him.

I couldn't arrange a meeting with Ryan and my father right now. Things were too new, and too tense. My dad didn't want to revisit the past. Besides, there were too many people who wanted a piece of my dad, like Stefano's friends. My father had taught me to fear them. To keep quiet. They were rogue, uncontrollable men. So for now, I had to keep my two lives separate.

The bell rang, and I raised my head. A hot blonde wearing tight shorts wandered in. She bought a cherry slushy and started drinking it as I rang her up. Her pretty lips on the straw made me stop thinking all about my family.

56

ELLE

Monday morning after I took Alex to school—waiting in my car until I saw him walk through the front doors and safely inside—I called Colin and told him about the creepy text I received from WJ Saturday night.

"Come to my office. Let me see the text," he said.

Twenty minutes later, he was studying the message at his desk.

Hey, pretty lady. Don't you be messing around with that new guy. WJ

"It doesn't even have my name on it. Is there any chance it was just an error? Maybe it was meant for someone else?" I suggested, as I clasped on to the hope that I wasn't the target of some strange stalker, calling me a pretty lady and warning me to stay away from my new man.

"That would be great if it was just a mistake," he said, but his tone was completely pragmatic and I could tell he didn't think "Oops, that was meant for someone else" was a likely scenario.

Or spam.

"I got a strange Facebook comment too," I said, then

told him about the hazy memory from the other night, including how odd the name was on the post. "It was gone as quickly as it was posted."

"Who was it from?"

"I can't remember. I was loopy on pain meds. But it wasn't a real name. It was, like, some weirdly menacing roller derby name, but for a guy."

He nodded and listened intently, my phone in his hand. He'd shifted into all-business Colin, and I sensed this was the newest challenge he was about to take on. He opened a browser window on his computer, and tapped the number into a reverse phone search. It showed up as *unavailable*. "Pretty sure this text came from a burner phone. If I looked up your number, it would show the wireless carrier it's registered to. A burner phone isn't registered, so it's hard to trace. Let me see what I can do though." He set down the phone, cupped my cheeks, and met my gaze once more. "I promise, Elle. I'm going to fix this for you."

I didn't know how he could, but I loved that he wanted to. That he pulled me close and brushed his lips on my forehead. That he wanted to take care of me. No one had taken care of me in years. I wrapped my arms around him and breathed him in—his clean, freshly showered morning scent. I stayed like that for several minutes, there at his office, curled up with him. This was where I wanted to be when times were good, and where I wanted to be when times were tough.

He felt like a new beginning. Like my truest second chance.

The second chance I was finally letting myself have.

* * *

The next day, Colin stopped by the center to tell me he'd tried a number of leading-edge technologies, including the most advanced IP tracker, to identify where the text had come from. None had revealed the sender's info.

"Do you think it's about us? The note?" I asked him, worry in my tone. That was all I could figure. That someone was trying to stop me from seeing him. "Do you think it's from your ex? The one who didn't want you doing the triathlon?"

He shook his head. "No. I don't think so. I haven't heard from her in a year. That's so over it's beyond over."

Fear tripped through me. "Then who do you think is sending these to me?"

"I don't know. But I'm not going to stop until I find out."

57

COLIN

All the damn technology in the world at my fingertips and I couldn't crack how to trace this goddamn burner phone. We didn't know where the phone had come from and hadn't been able to triangulate any calls from it, and there was no way to trace it from the message Elle had received.

"Tell me, Larsen. Tell me when you get a pitch for a company that has this tech, and we're getting in on the seed funding round," I said, frustration thick in my voice as I sifted through app stores, past pitches from scrappy start-ups and app makers, and all the presentations I'd ever heard on new cell phone technology, with Larsen by my side hunting too.

Were the drug dealers who used these phones really so far ahead that they'd found the one fail-safe method of covering their tracks?

"I'm on it," Larsen said with a crisp nod.

"Nothing's working. My brothers don't even have tools for this, and that's the business they're in. Security."

"Isn't that the point though? Not to go all internet privacy on you, but isn't that why burner phones exist?

Because people feel like they have no privacy. Facebook won't even tell you who sends you creepy messages because of privacy guidelines."

I sat up straight. "What did you just say?" The cogs whirred in my head.

"Facebook won't even tell you who sends you creepy messages because of privacy guidelines?" Larsen repeated tentatively, furrowing his brow.

An idea hit me—it was out of left field, but sometimes the best ideas were born there. I latched on to something Detective John Winston had said. *The gang culture, oddly enough, loves social media. They post pictures of themselves online, on Instagram and Facebook, holding wads of bills from their drug sales or showing off electronics they stole.*

"You're brilliant," I said, then flipped open my laptop, logged into Facebook, and started hunting. There were many ways to solve a problem. You could tackle it point by point, or you could triangulate it.

I'd had no success tracing the number, so rather than go from number to name, I'd have to amass a list of possible names and see what matched. I rolled up the cuffs on my shirt—*nothing ventured, nothing gained*—and spent the next few hours digging into Facebook and Instagram for images of the Royal Sinners.

Don't mess with the Royal Sinners.

That was what they said about themselves.

Those were the words used in Elle's messages.

Don't you be messing around . . .

Whoever WJ was, he had effectively identified himself as a gang member in the text. Gang members had nicknames—*weirdly menacing ones.* WJ wanted to own his intimidation, and I was determined to find him.

I had something these gang guys didn't have.

Ingenuity. Resourcefulness. And one hell of a brain. I

knew how to use my head to solve a problem. As I hunted, I unearthed a braggart's den. I found a treasure trove of images, just as John had said we would. Young guys holding wads of cash. Guys aiming guns at the camera. Others pointing to the ink on their arms. *Protect Our Own.*

I captured screenshots. I saved images. I took notes. I checked geotags on Instagram. I studied the pins on the images.

I did it again the next day.

And the next.

And the next.

I didn't have an answer, or a name, or a number. But I had a database now. Soon, WJ would tag something. That was what these guys did. Then I'd zero in on him.

58

ELLE

Two Elles.

Over the next few days, I returned to my split self. Only this time I was Happy-Go-Lucky Elle, and I was Sleeping-with-One-Eye-Open Elle.

My schedule was packed with work, and pickups, and spending time with my two guys. It was stuffed with Colin playing a few rounds of *State of Decay* with Alex, and then basketball with Rex, Tyler, Marcus, and Alex at the center. Tomorrow was jam-packed too—during the day I had a board meeting with the center's directors over the remodeling progress, and at night Ryan was proposing to Sophie. He'd planned a surprise family celebration for Sophie afterward.

Life was almost too good to be true.

Almost.

Because there, in the background, slinking over my shoulder was my phone stalker. *WJ.*

I hadn't said a word about it to my son. I didn't want him to worry, especially since I'd promised to always protect him. But I desperately needed to talk to someone.

"It's been several days since the text message. Maybe it's all over," I said to my sister at the Skyway rink on Thursday evening.

"Let's hope so. Did you get a new cell phone like I told you to?"

"What's the point?" I asked as Camille straightened up napkins and straws at the snack counter. "My number is on the center's website. Anyone can get it."

Camille gave me a pointed look. "Maybe it shouldn't be so easy to reach you."

I drummed my nails against the counter. "I want the boys to be able to reach me. That's the point of doing what I do. To be accessible. To be a resource for them. I can't shut myself off from the world."

"Just be careful. Because someone clearly doesn't like your boyfriend if they're sending you messages not to mess around with him."

I sighed heavily and twisted my hair into a makeshift ponytail, wondering who that could be.

* * *

Twenty minutes later, I picked up Alex from Janine's house.

I chatted briefly with Janine on the porch then headed to the car, waving goodbye. "Good luck this weekend. I'll be there cheering you on, though it'll pain me not to skate," I said.

"It'll pain me more not to have my favorite blocker," Janine said with a pout.

"Are you going to come with me to the final match this weekend?" I asked Alex once we were inside the car.

"Can I stay home and hang out by myself?"

I flinched at the idea, gripping the steering wheel. "No. I want you to come with me."

"But why? You're not even skating. I just want to hang at home. Play Xbox and stuff."

"We'll have fun. We'll get pizza at the rink," I said through pursed lips. I didn't tell him the truth—that I could barely stomach letting him out of my sight.

He groaned.

"Alex, don't do that," I said, as I changed lanes.

"I just don't feel like going. Can't I just chill? What if Rex and Tyler come over?"

But before I could say no one more time, my phone buzzed in the console.

"Want me to see if that's Colin?" Alex asked, grabbing the phone.

"I'll look at it later," I said hastily, as the truck in front of me slowed. I didn't want Alex seeing any messages from Colin, though we hadn't exchanged many dirty ones lately. Still, my phone was private. It was mine.

"*Mom.*"

I hadn't heard that tone in years.

His voice was laced with fear.

I snapped my gaze to him, and my son was staring at the screen, jaw agape.

Pure, primal terror burst through me, like a dam breaking. "What is it?"

But I knew.

It could only be one thing.

"Who sent you this?" he asked, his voice thin as a thread, cold as winter.

I yanked the wheel right and pulled into the lot at a Burger King. Slamming the car into park, I grabbed the phone from him.

The hairs on the back of my neck rose.

Pretty ladies should be smarter about who they get INVOLVED with.

The phone slid from my hand, clattering to the console.

"What is that?" Alex asked again.

I inhaled deeply, then did my best to channel a calmness I didn't feel. "I've been getting some strange messages."

He shook his head adamantly then stabbed his finger against the screen. "This isn't strange, Mom. It's creepy. It's stalkerish. Who is sending you these?"

"I don't know," I said, my hold on a cool, collected tone faltering.

"Someone who doesn't want you to be with Colin." His voice rose with every word.

I bit my lip and managed a small nod. "It seems that way."

His eyes widened as big as the moon. "Mom! I like Colin. He's a cool guy. But seriously, this is freaking me out."

It was freaking me out too. More than I could ever have imagined. But I couldn't let on. I had to stay strong for Alex. I had to be titanium.

"Colin is working on it," I said, taking my time with each word. "He's working on figuring it out, and we'll make it stop."

"'*We*'?" he asked, arching an angry eyebrow. "Who's 'we'? You and Colin? Or you and me? Or you and—"

"I've got this. I've got this under control. You don't need to worry about it."

"Just like when you had things under control with Dad?"

I held up my index finger. "That is not fair. And this is not the same."

"You're right," he said, spitting out the words. "It's not the same. Because he's not Dad. He's just a guy."

"*Alex*," I said.

He stopped talking, crossed his arms, and slumped down in the seat.

"Let me get you home and make dinner," I said, as calmly as I possibly could.

I stuffed my phone into my purse in the back seat, as if that would erase the message. But the text was still there, like a shadow that lurked by my side. Colin had thought a Royal Sinner was sending these to me, and I was sure now that he was right. I was sure, too, that someone in the Royal Sinners didn't want Colin in my life.

And now my son maybe felt the same way.

* * *

He didn't talk to me at dinner. All he said was "Thanks." Then he got up from the table, showered, and went to bed.

"Night."

Barely a word.

Just like *that* year.

The year he didn't talk.

The year he was nearly destroyed by his father's death.

I sank down on my couch and ran my hand over the back of my neck. My sparrows. My guide to finding my way home. My son was my home, and I'd helped him find his way back to me after he'd lost his father. I'd do it again and again and again. I reached for a framed picture of him on the coffee table—his fourth-grade school photo, with his goofy, toothy grin. A small smile surfaced as I ran my finger over it. A tear threatened my eyes, but I refused to allow it to appear. I would not wallow. I would not weaken.

I had one goal in life and it was to take care of my son, no matter what.

But Colin meant more to me already than I could have dreamed. He'd told me he had some leads and was tracking them down, and I was grateful for that. Damn grateful. But I was torn.

Ironic, because I thought it would be *my* choices that brought me here.

Instead, it was the past.

The one Colin had zero control over.

Through no fault of his own, that past had resurfaced to the present. The past where a gangland shooter killed his father, and the present where a member of that same street gang was harassing me.

All because I was in love with him.

Holy hell.

In love.

I was in love with him.

How the hell was I going to do the right thing? And what was the right thing to do?

59

COLIN

I wished I could be there with her. Holding her till she fell asleep. Kissing her forehead as her eyelids fluttered closed. Brushing loose strands of hair away from her face.

Instead, from the wooden swing on the back deck of my house, I zoomed in on the screenshot Elle had sent me a few hours ago. The one of her latest text. A night breeze tripped through the trees as I studied the message. I stared so long I let my vision go blurry. The message turned hazy around the edges of the words, and the letters seemed to float off the screen.

Pretty. Ladies. Smarter.

Then one word, in all caps, slammed into me.

INVOLVED.

I tapped the community center's web address into a search bar. Quickly, I found Elle's bio, where it said she prided herself on being *involved* with the local community.

In my head, I replayed the messages.

Be careful who you get involved with.

Hey, pretty lady. Don't you be messing around with that new guy.

Pretty ladies should be smarter about who they get INVOLVED with.

All from *WJ.*

The blurry haze evaporated. The clouds burned away, and the sky was clear. I'd figured a gang member was somehow targeting her, because she was involved with a man whose family had been torn to pieces by a gang. Someone like Kenny or TJ Nelson, who didn't want the case reopened. Someone who was trying to intimidate my family through the woman in my life.

But that theory didn't entirely add up.

I called Ryan. My brother answered on the first ring. "What's up? It's late. You okay?"

"Yeah. You answered quickly. What are you up to?"

"Sophie and I just finished a game of pool," he said, and if there was ever a code for banging, that was it. But now was not the time for razzing my brother.

"You told me something the other day, about visiting Marcus at the convenience store," I said, reminding Ryan of a conversation we'd had earlier in the week. It hadn't seemed like much at the time, but now I was examining every possible connection. "He mentioned a guy who'd come in?"

"He did. Said he got some weird vibe from him. Thought he reeked of Royal Sinners. Marcus said the guy had a goatee and was bitching about his phone."

"And that made him think the guy was a Sinner?"

"It was more a gut reaction to him, I think. And Marcus said his dad has always been worried about those guys coming after them."

I snapped my fingers. That was it. What if the warnings Elle had received weren't about me, but about Marcus?

Elle wasn't only involved with me. Elle was involved with the local community. Elle was involved in helping the kids at the center. Elle had been deeply involved with helping Marcus. And Marcus's father had been worried about gang members targeting his family. Were they targeting Marcus through Elle?

In the morning, I called Marcus and asked him for help.

"Tell me everything about the guy who came by your store the other day," I said, and my younger brother described the guy in detail, right down to the fingernails on his hands.

* * *

After I finished a training swim at lunch, my phone buzzed on my way out of the gym. I'd set up an alert for any new photos from the Instagram and Facebook profiles I'd marked as likely belonging to the Royal Sinners. The account that had pinged was called *Don't Mess With*, and it often featured snapshots of stolen goods.

As I walked across the parking lot to my car, I scrolled through the new set of photos.

Boatloads of electronics. Laptops, tablets, some phones.

In some of the pictures, a guy pointed at his stash, his fingers in the shape of guns. The guy's face wasn't in any of the pictures, but I punched the air when I read the caption.

Looks like Wicked Jack is gonna make a couple of cool Gs on this haul. Burner phones are the shizz, but electronics are the biz. $$$$$$

"Wicked Jack," I said out loud. "That's WJ."

Anger rolled through me, and I slammed the door of my car. Who the hell was this guy harassing Elle because of Marcus? What did Marcus have to do with the Royal Sinners? Was it because he was in the Protectors? I couldn't imagine gang members caring that much about a guardian angels–style group of volunteers, especially teenagers. The Royal Sinners trafficked in guns, drugs, and stolen goods, so why would a group of unarmed vigilantes bother them? And why would they care that Elle was talking to Marcus?

Outrage filled my chest, but I forced myself to let it go, and set to work.

The thing about gang guys was they didn't always realize that some types of technology were highly traceable, like pictures on the internet. They might have mastered the burner phone and made its anonymity their ally. But Instagram? That social media platform was like a dog with a microchip. And street gangs tagged. They left their mark. They bragged.

In a few minutes, I had a location. As I looked at the picture one more time, something else clicked.

"Wicked Jack's" fingernail was black-and-blue.

It matched the description of Marcus's convenience store visitor.

60

———

ELLE

As I dressed for Ryan and Sophie's proposal celebration, slipping into my dress and fastening a necklace, my nerves were frayed and worn thin. I ran a brush through my long hair, tugging, pulling, and yanking. Punishing it as a distraction from my worries and fears. I tossed the hairbrush in a basket on the bathroom counter, left my apartment, and took my son to my mother's house. "Have fun with Grandma."

Alex shrugged. "Okay."

There it was again. The dead voice. The empty tone.

I wrapped my arms around him and gave him a hug. "I love you. We will figure this out. I promise."

"Okay." It was warmer this time, tinged with hope. He managed to quirk his lips up in a small smile, and I held on to that smile. Clutched it close to my heart. Then I followed him to the door, where the person who'd been on my side my whole damn life waited.

My mom.

"I need to talk to you alone," I whispered.

"Of course, sweetie," she said, stepping outside on the porch with me and closing the door behind Alex as he went inside. She reached over, tucking a strand of my hair over my ear.

Being my mom.

My rock.

I swallowed past the lump in my throat.

"What is it?" she asked.

"I'm torn. So torn right now, and I don't know what to do," I said, my voice wobbling.

She squeezed my arm. "Okay. Let me help you figure it out."

So I told her.

Laid it all out for the woman who was my mother, my friend, my person.

But as I shared the story of my worries, my son, and my new love, I realized something entirely new.

She wasn't my *only* person.

Colin was too now. He'd become that for me.

And I wasn't alone, shouldering my family.

I wasn't the sole person looking out for my son, protecting him.

He had so many people.

But he definitely had three—me, my mom, and now Colin.

And I didn't have to carry all this weight myself.

Maybe I realized it at the same time she did too.

"I'm happy for you, honey. After everything you went through with Sam, you deserve a real partner, someone to go through all of this with, hand in hand," she said, then laid out her thoughts for moving forward, sharing her advice.

I nodded and smiled. "Thanks, Mom."

She brought me in for a hug. "Now go have fun tonight." She tipped her forehead to the house. "I've got this. I've got your back."

That felt damn good.

To have that faith in others.

61

COLIN

The second the call came from Marcus, I pounced on it.

"Talk to me," I said, then glanced at the time on my wrist. I needed to leave the office now to make it to Ryan and Sophie's event.

"I went in early for my shift, and I found the video from last week," Marcus said. "I just played it on the work computer in the back office and shot a video of it with my cell. You should have it any minute. I emailed it."

"Let me see if it's here." I switched to my email program on my laptop, clicked on the new message, and hit play. The video was in black and white, and the conversation was barely audible.

"Do you know who he is? You think this is the guy who's sending harassing notes to Elle?" Marcus asked.

"I don't know for sure," I said, then zoomed in on the guy's hands. I grinned. Like I'd won the lottery. Lo and behold, there it was. The bruised fingernail. A chill ran down my spine. "It has to be the same guy. The caption on the Instagram photo, the same stubbed fingernail, plus the location. I just don't know his name." I crooked my head against the phone as I grabbed a screenshot and dropped it into a reverse image search. "But I'm going to call the detective after I plug this into a—"

My heart stopped beating. My blood froze. That last name. It echoed in my nightmares.

"You still there?" Marcus asked.

"Yes," I whispered, my voice a hiss.

"What is it? Who is it? What did you find out?" He sounded as if he were dangling out of a window, white-knuckling the sill.

I recognize the emotion because it mirrored mine.

The photo had taken me to a Facebook page for Jerry Stefano's teenage son. The photos matched the ones I'd found on Instagram.

"Lee Stefano. The shooter's son. And it looks like he's following in his father's footsteps. He calls himself Wicked Jack, and he's in the Royal Sinners."

62

MINDY

New York–New York. One of my favorite spots in this city I loved.

I was early to the party, because that was my MO. No need to be late, ever. I never was.

I reached the bar, scanned behind the counter, then spun around and surveyed the place once more. Some days, I was looking for particular people.

Most of the time, I just looked for anything that felt off. Instinct.

I'd always had it. It was why I worked in security.

Tonight I was off though. So I ordered a pink cosmopolitan and took a delicious sip.

"Since when do you drink girly drinks?"

I smiled at the sound of Brent's voice. "Hey, friend," I said, turning around to give my buddy a hug. "It's my guilty pleasure. Don't tell a soul." I pressed a finger to my lips.

"I won't tell anyone either."

That voice. Whoa.

Deep and raspy.

I turned around to see someone else had joined us.

Dark-blond hair, piercing blue eyes, square jaw.

Brent nodded to the man. "John Winston, meet Mindy Gamble."

"And clearly you can't live anyplace but Vegas with that last name," he said as he extended a hand.

"Nope. With my last name, I'm not permitted to leave the city limits."

He smiled a crooked grin as we shook. "Pleasure to meet you, Mindy Gamble."

Briefly, I considered a cheesy line like *The pleasure is all mine.* But instead, since I knew who he was, I said, "I've heard a lot about you. I hope you get those fuckers."

He grinned. "That's the goal. That's always the goal."

"If I can do anything to help, let me know."

Brent squeezed my shoulder. "This woman has her ear to the ground. Nothing gets past Mindy."

John arched a brow. "Is that so?"

I shrugged, giving him a playful grin. "I do my best."

"Then we should talk."

I patted the stool next to mine, and he took a seat.

Brent wiggled his brows and stage-whispered, "And that's my cue to go."

I rolled my eyes at him.

John Winston might be one of the sexiest men I'd ever seen, but I wasn't gunning for romance, or even a hot night.

Nope.

But I would be happy to talk business, since that's what I depended on these days.

Brent took off, and John and I chatted. I told him I had sources on the street, people I'd talked to over the years.

"Listen," he said, scratching his jaw. "There are some guys we're looking for. They've been out of town though. If they come back and you hear anything, I'd appreciate a call."

"I hope to be giving you one, then."

63

ELLE

Sophie's hand was adorned with the most gorgeous diamond I had ever seen. Brilliant and vintage cut, it was 100 percent Sophie. I held my friend's left hand and couldn't stop oohing and aahing at the beautiful bling. Nor could Shannon.

We all gathered around the blue plush lounge chairs in one of the bars at New York–New York, having just surprised Sophie with the proposal celebration Ryan had put together for her. I focused on the diamond and on Sophie's happiness, letting it distract me from the uncertainty plaguing my own life.

I wanted to soak up the romance. I wanted to savor all my friend's happiness. Sniff it like a fine perfume I could enjoy and hope to bask in myself.

"Tell us everything. Did he actually take out the ring at the top of the roller-coaster too?" I asked.

Sophie shook her head, her pretty platinum-blonde curls bouncing. She looked windswept, and radiant too. Not to mention like a total knockout in her pinup-girl dress with a peach pattern on it. "As soon as we reached the top, that very second when the car just sort of hovers there on the track and you're about to scream your lungs out, he shouted, 'Sophie, will you marry me?'"

Shannon clasped her hand to her mouth, then dropped it just as quickly. "That is so perfect."

Mindy grinned broadly. "I love it. That's fantastic."

"And what did you say?" I asked, making a rolling gesture with my hands, eager for Sophie to tell the rest of the tale. A Bruce Springsteen tune played in the background at the bar, where the men toasted to Ryan. Colin, Michael, and Sophie's brother, John were all there. "Well, obviously you said yes," I quickly supplied. "But how? Tell us, tell us."

"I shouted, '*Yes!*' It was that simple," Sophie said, and her joy was infectious. I beamed as I listened. I couldn't stop smiling.

Ryan leaned in, draped an arm around Sophie, and raised his finger in the air. "Actually, to be precise, she said, 'Oh my God, yes, yes, yes!'"

Sophie swatted him on the elbow. "*Ryan Sloan.*"

"*Sophie Sloan,*" he countered.

He tugged her in for a kiss, and I clapped loudly and cheered them on.

Then I felt a soft flutter. Colin brushed his lips over my ear. "You look beautiful tonight," he whispered. "And I'll be right back. I need to talk to John. But I have good news."

I flashed him a smile. "Can't wait," I said, my eyes following him briefly as he walked into the casino with Sophie's brother. I hoped the good news was that he'd cracked the case and that my stalker would be arrested. Colin had been hard at work on it, but other than check-ins, we hadn't had much time to really connect this week. And that was something I really needed tonight.

"Tell us the rest," I demanded when Sophie and Ryan managed to pry their lips off each other.

"I need every single detail of how my brother finally got down on one knee," Shannon added.

As Sophie laced her fingers together and continued telling the story, my phone started buzzing in my purse. I excused myself and stepped away to answer the call.

It was Marcus.

"Elle," he said, and his tone had shifted. Gone was the nervous young teen; in its place was a young man.

"What is it?"

"I'm worried about you. I think I put you in harm's way. Helping me. I think that's why you got those messages."

"Marcus," I said softly. I hated that he was taking on this burden.

"No, it's my fault, but I want you to know I'm going to do everything I can to help solve the case. And Elle," he said, a strength in his tone that sounded brand-new. "I think I can."

"You can?" I asked tentatively.

"Yes. I can't say much more, but there are things I'm putting together, figuring out. And I'm going to do everything in my power to make this right. You made a difference for me. You made a huge difference. You gave me the courage to get to know my family. And there's something I can do for you, and for my brothers and my sister."

"Marcus, what is it?" I asked, worried.

"It's good, Elle. I promise."

"Are you sure?" I pressed.

"Remember what you taught me? Rise above." He took a deep, fueling breath. "I'm going to do it."

And I got it. I knew. He was becoming a man. He was stepping into his future.

"I'm behind you," I said, voice breaking.

"Thank you."

When the call ended, I leaned against the wall, reflecting back over what he said.

The steps he was taking.

The changes he was making.

I was changing too. A few weeks ago, hell, maybe even a few days ago, I might have shut down. Might have gone into self-protective mode.

But I could be protective and still live my life.

I had a plan for my son, a plan for my family, and a plan to spend some time with my man.

I drew a breath and returned to the party.

64

COLIN

As John and I threaded our way through the slot machines, I glanced back at the bar and spotted Elle holding Sophie's hands and beaming. Man, was there anything better than a proposal to send the woman you were crazy for into romantic overdrive? I couldn't wait to have a minute alone with her tonight. We hadn't been together all week, and I wanted to feel her in my arms. To hold her, touch her, taste her. To tell her how I felt, tell her I wasn't just falling.

I'd fallen.

But this had to be done first.

The problem wasn't fully solved yet.

That was where John came in.

We continued past the Willy Wonka slots, where the chocolatier presided over the Oompa Loompas, and reached a quiet hallway near the restrooms.

"I've got some info for you," I said, then told him everything about the texts, the convenience store visitor, the Instagram pictures, and the name.

"Thank you. This is helpful. We'll take care of it."

But I wasn't done. It was my turn to ask questions. "Is

Stefano's son part of the case? Why would he have something against Marcus and be trying to get to him through Elle?"

John blew out a long stream of air. "Lee Stefano *is* one of the reasons there is an investigation. When he started falling into gang activity, we were tipped off about what he was up to, and started looking into the possibility that his father had accomplices in the Sinners. Lee might have a bone to pick with Marcus."

"But Lee's dad is in prison, so what would he have against Marcus or Elle now?"

"That's what we're working on. My belief is that Kenny and TJ Nelson were supposed to look out for Lee Stefano and keep him out of trouble. They did for a while, but then they stopped trying to keep him away from the gang and brought him into it instead. He's one of them now, and I'm willing to bet that Lee is doing his part to look out for the men he thinks of now as his brothers—Kenny and TJ."

I knit my brow. "How is he looking out for them? Especially since they're on the run."

"That's exactly why Lee's looking out for them. So we don't get to them. This is Lee protecting them, and they don't like that Marcus is talking to you. I have some leads I'm chasing down, but my gut is telling me that these guys figure the more Marcus talks to your family, the more they're at risk of being caught."

"Do you think Marcus knows something about the case?"

John paused and clenched his jaw, his eyes hardening. "I have my suspicions."

"Jesus Christ," I muttered in utter frustration. "This is like an onion. Peel off one layer and there's another one underneath."

"Believe you me, I know. But we're getting closer to the

key suspects, and now it looks like Lee Stefano just put a sign on his back that says *arrest me for harassing, stalking, and grand larceny*. After all, electronics aren't cheap," he said with a wry grin. "And on that note, I need to cut out. I've got some arrests to make, God willing."

I said goodbye to the detective, then returned to the restaurant to find my woman and tell her the good news.

65

MICHAEL

I knocked back a beer at the poker table, settling in for a game as I surveyed the happy couplings of my brothers and sister. The party was winding down, and Ryan came over to sit down next to me for a round of cards.

"So, you're up next. And I'm not talking about cards," Ryan said, gesturing meaningfully back toward the group.

"What do you mean?" I waved a hand dismissively. "I'm single as the day is long."

Ryan laughed. "Yes, except for that little problem of Annalise. We haven't forgotten about her."

That name. That beautiful, tempting, taunting name. The one who'd haunted my dreams. "There's no problem there," I said.

"You're still hung up on her, aren't you?"

I scoffed, dismissing the idea that I was mooning over a girl. "Hung up on her? I don't think so."

Ryan cracked up and pointed at me. "That's a good one. How long did you practice to make that 'I don't think so' sound convincing?"

"I have no idea what you're talking about," I said as the

dealer showed his hand. His beat mine. The house scooped up all the chips.

"You know exactly what I'm talking about. You should just look her up. Find her."

"Yeah? That's your advice? This from the guy who's so deep in happily ever after he can't even see straight?"

Ryan nodded vigorously. "Exactly. I want you to have that too. You'll always wonder 'what if.' Better to try than to keep asking. Better to find your what-if woman than to wonder if she's asking the same questions."

It must be obvious she'd been on my mind, even though I hadn't seen her in years. Not since I'd bumped into her at an airport in France, and we'd had an hour together on a layover. I didn't think I'd hear from her again, and then she'd reached out to me a day ago.

But I pushed her out of my mind now as Mindy walked toward us—I'd asked her to join me for cards at the end of the party. I wanted to talk to her about something my dad had said way back when, about some trouble at his company. I wanted to see if it added up to anything. She waved when she spotted me, and I tipped my chin and patted the stool next to me.

I hoped I'd have more luck solving my dad's reopened case than I was having with relationships, and one woman from my past in particular.

When Colin found me after his talk with John, we both had so much to say. But he insisted I go first.

I told him my plan, what I'd been processing since talking to my mom earlier, hoping he'd feel good about it too. "What do you think?"

"I think it sounds like a great way to spend a Saturday morning."

I beamed, grateful that he was on board.

He ran a hand along my arm. "And now I have a great plan for Friday night," he said, and the naughty glint in his eyes told me all I needed to know.

We rushed back to my place, and along the way, he filled me in on his conversation with John. I felt a huge surge of relief, but there'd be more time for talking later. After all the stress of the last week, and high on endorphins from the party, I wanted to lose myself in him for a little while.

"Just you and me now," I said, taking his hand as I led him to my bedroom.

"That's the way I like it," he said.

I turned on some music, and he pulled me against him, kissing me and stripping me at the same time.

I did the same to him.

We were both pent-up, more than ready.

And he was a man on a mission. He moved to his back and brought me on top of him, so I was straddling him.

As he reached for my wrists and looped them around his neck, I felt only possibility. This week had felt like danger, I was ready.

And, oh hell, so was he. His cock was a thing of beauty —hard, hot, and heavy in my hand as I lowered myself onto him. Sensations rolled through my body. That delicious stretching. The intense depth. The way he moved. His eyes were dark, and I swore I could see all his desire written in them. His potent lust for me. I was sure two people had never wanted each other more.

Here he was in my home. Fucking me. Taking me. Owning me. Giving me more pleasure than I'd ever experienced, more passion than I'd ever known.

Every single cell in my body was comprised of ecstasy, because he'd done it again. He'd fucked me to the edge of reason. He'd ushered me to the far reaches of erotic joy, and I was breaking apart like a rainstorm, a gorgeous, brilliant summer rainstorm, as I came with no signs of stopping. My climax had no end in sight. It washed over me, it pulled me under, and it consumed me.

My whole body was an orgasm. There was nothing else but this endless rush of pleasure blasting through me and taking me captive.

I moaned and groaned and cried out, and I couldn't stop, because nothing had ever felt so good. And then my words became nonsense, just the echo of the intensity raging in my body.

Soon he tossed me on my back, wrapped my legs

around his waist, and fucked me until his own oblivion smashed into him.

This was what I'd needed tonight.

More of him.

More of us.

More of this deep, tender connection that was taking over my whole damn heart.

ELLE

The next morning, as we'd planned, Colin and I went to pick up Alex at my mom's. We wanted to talk to him together, about the scare this week with the threatening text messages, about the progress made on identifying who they were from, and about the future. Our future.

That was the plan. That was what my mom had helped me figure out and what Colin and I had decided together.

And as I left her house, she mouthed, "You've got this."

I crossed my fingers, whispering, "I hope so."

Then we returned to our apartment.

"Look at me," I said to my son, taking the lead once we'd all settled in our living room.

He listened. "Yes?"

I took his hand in mine. "Life is hard," I said, my voice confident. "Life is full of challenges. And we are going to face them together. We have made it through hell and back. We aren't going to back down. We aren't going to run. We will be smart and courageous. We will stand up and do the right thing."

This was me setting a goddamn example. Because I'd learned something from the way my son's father died.

I was titanium.

But that didn't mean I had to be ice.

I was fire and love and strength.

I was courage and patience and guts.

I was a mother, a woman, a lover.

A social worker, and a person who faced her fears. Who confronted them. Who zip-lined through them.

Alex said nothing at first, then squeezed my hand back. "I know. We will. And I'm sorry," he said softly, looking between Colin and me. "I got scared."

"It's okay to be scared. I get scared. But you need to know that whatever scares you, whatever worries you, we can talk it through. We can figure it out. Whatever challenges come our way, we'll tackle them together. You have me, and you have Colin," I said, turning to Colin.

He nodded solemnly. "You do, Alex. I'm here for you, for you and your mom, always."

Alex smiled at him. "I'm glad. Because I have an awesome mom, and I want her to be happy. And I know you make her happy," he said, his voice choked with emotion.

"I'm so happy," I said, absorbing the moment, then shifting gears. "And those messages? That stalker? He was sending me messages because of my work. Because of my job. Because I am trying to help kids make brave choices. Not because of Colin. But we do need to look out for others. We need to keep an eye on Marcus. I don't know what's going on, but he needs our support right now."

"I like Marcus. He's one of the good ones."

I ruffled his hair. "He is, and we will. And so are you. And so am I. And so is Colin. I love you. And I will look out for you always."

"I love you too, Mom. And I need you to know – it wasn't the zombies and the games that helped me before. It was you."

My throat tightened, and tears sprang in my eyes. "You're my strong boy."

"And you're my strong mom. And I'll look out for you too," he said confidently, like the grown man he was becoming. And in this moment, I was so grateful. Grateful for the son I had, and how far he'd come. Grateful for the man by my side. And grateful that the three of us were forging this bond. Almost like a family.

68

COLIN

More than anything, I felt honored to be part of this conversation with Elle and her son. That I was included, entrusted, in their lives like this made me want to be a better man, made me want to be a good example for Alex too.

And now that we'd cleared this hurdle, and I officially had the stamp of approval from the son of the woman I was in love with, I couldn't wait to tell her. So when Alex had gone to his room to play video games, I turned to Elle, cupped her cheeks, held her gaze, and said, "I'm so in love with you."

Then I kissed her.

So much was still up in the air.

I didn't know when the case would close.

I didn't know what would happen to Lee Stefano or my mother or anyone.

All I knew was this woman had my heart in her hands, and I would fight for her. Like she would fight for me.

"And I'm in love with you," she said. "I'm done living out of fear. I trust you, and I want you to be a part of our lives. I want to be with you and love you and protect my son, and I'm a good enough mom and a smart enough woman to do all of it."

I ran a hand through her hair. "And that's another reason why I love you. You're so damn strong and tough, you know what you want, and you love hard and fiercely."

"That's how I want to love you, Colin Sloan," she said, and we kissed again.

It felt like a promise.

Like we were sealing a vow to each other.

It said we were in this together.

No matter what.

And when we were done, we knocked on Alex's door, and the three of us killed zombies, cheered each other on, and faced our fears.

Well, zombies are terrifying and always will be.

69

COLIN

When I woke up at dawn on Sunday morning, the sun streaming through the open window in my house, I didn't embark on my usual routine. The mountains called to me, but I ignored them. The lake wanted my company, but it would survive without me today. No gym, no workout, and no quiet contemplation.

There was one thing I had to do, so I lobbed a call to my youngest sibling and suggested a road trip.

Marcus was game. "I'll be ready in twenty minutes."

I suspected this was why Marcus had wanted to get to know my siblings. Not necessarily for a trip like this, but to be *invited*. To be included.

Two hours and one hundred miles later, we were drinking slushies and arguing over whether rock music was better than hip-hop. Marcus kept trying to take control of the radio, tuning in to stations I didn't want to listen to. I gave Marcus a hard time because that was in the how-to-be-a-brother handbook, and the hazing made the kid laugh.

At the next gas station, we added Doritos to the haul. I

ripped open the bag. "I think this might make my system go into shock. It's the first true junk food I've had in ages."

Marcus scoffed. "Dude. You drink soda all the time. Your body's not a temple twenty-four seven."

"Touché. I just can't give up the hard stuff, I guess. Me and Diet Coke—we're like this," I said, twisting my index and middle finger together. "Diet Coke has gotten me through many moments of temptation."

"Then you need to keep worshipping the almighty beverage," he said.

We returned to my car and plowed through Doritos, Peanut M&Ms, and more Diet Coke as we drove.

By one p.m., we pulled into the lot at Hawthorne. I froze momentarily at the gate as I showed my ID. It was as if all my systems simply stopped functioning for a few seconds. Not because I was nervous. Not because I was scared.

I didn't feel either of those emotions.

Instead, astonishment gripped me.

I was amazed that the woman who had given birth to me had lived nearly eighteen years behind this fence, past that barbed wire, beyond the concrete walls.

Ryan had told me that today was a visiting day, but Dora Prince wasn't expecting us. Didn't matter. I wasn't here for her, though, or for the investigation. I didn't come to question her, or obtain evidence. I had nothing to ask her. That wasn't my job. That wasn't my role.

I was here for the healing.

As much as I'd tried to dismiss Elle's suggestion, it had hovered at the front of my brain for the last week. To keep moving forward in my life, I had another step to take.

Recovery was a daily practice. It didn't end. I would always be unfinished, but this was part of coming to peace with my unfinished self.

Before we entered the visiting room, I turned to Marcus and said, "Bet you didn't think you'd be here with me visiting our mom today, did you?"

Marcus shook his head. "Nope. But is it weird to say I'm glad we're here?"

I managed a small smile. "It's not. Let's go see her."

"Let's do it," Marcus echoed as we entered the cold concrete visiting room.

A minute later, a woman in orange walked through the door, a corrections officer at her side.

I felt nothing, and I felt everything.

She was the woman who'd raised me for thirteen years, and she was the woman I'd hated for eighteen years. She was the mother and the murderer. She was everything I never wanted to be, and then I'd become like her in ways I never wanted.

She was a prisoner, and she was a human being. One who still felt emotions, because oceans poured from her eyes, and they were tears of joy, as if all she'd ever wanted was to see her kids.

Despite all my efforts to remain stoic, a lump rose in my throat.

"My babies," she said, crossing the distance in a nanosecond and wrapping her two youngest kids in the strangest hug I had ever experienced. That was no small feat for her to hug two grown men, considering we both towered over her tiny frame. "My babies, my babies, my babies," she sobbed.

She couldn't stop weeping, or saying our names.

Eventually, the corrections officer made her let go. The front of my shirt was wet from her tears.

"Colin," she said with a crazed kind of joy as she looked at me. Then she shifted her gaze. "Marcus."

"Hi," Marcus said, and his voice seemed horribly dry as he added, "Mom."

I couldn't bring myself to call her that. But I had something else to say to her. I clapped Marcus on the shoulder and met my mother's eyes.

"You don't have to worry about Marcus anymore, because he has brothers and a sister who will look out for him. He has a good family on the outside. And I want you to know we're going to do everything we can for him. He's part of us." I swallowed and raised my chin up high, girding myself for the hardest part of the visit. For the reason I drove to the prison for the first time in years.

A piece of my heart had been metal, an alloy of shame and guilt. With words like a scalpel, I cut it from my body. "Because I'm a good man," I said, letting go of the hate, letting it crumble to the ground. It couldn't weigh me down any longer. "I had a good father, and you have good kids. All of them."

Then, because it was the compassionate thing to do, I sat down with her and spent the next hour listening to her talk.

On the ride home, just as Marcus and I stopped for a bite to eat, John Winston called.

DORA

My dream.

My kids.

They were here, and to see them together was a riot to my senses. A carnival of lights and sounds. Two of them together. This was Christmas and my birthday all at once.

I couldn't stop looking at them, couldn't stop memorizing the features of their faces. It had been so long. The one I'd had to protect all those years ago when he was growing inside me. Marcus, my youngest. My surprise secret baby.

And Colin. Oh, my sweet Colin. I hadn't seen him in years. So handsome. So smart. So much like his father.

My shoulders shook, and I choked up. How so very similar he was to his dad.

As I talked to them about my shows, and the other girls in here, and the books I'd read in the prison library in the last few weeks—*500 Spanish Verbs*, a James Patterson book, a biography of Martin Luther King Jr., Anne Frank's book —all I could think was at least someone I trusted was looking out for my youngest.

It was Luke's job.

Maybe he was. Or maybe he wasn't. I didn't know. He didn't come. Once upon a time, he had. He'd made promises to me. But then, he'd stopped showing up. And I had no idea what had happened to him, till I found out this summer that he'd gone and married someone else several years ago. He'd told me he'd wait for me, till I was free.

But clearly he'd lied about that.

What else had he lied about?

Maybe someone would figure that out.

Enough about him. Enough about men. They were nothing but trouble.

My boys though?

They hadn't forgotten me.

Today I felt like the luckiest woman in the world to see them both.

The hour went by too quickly.

In the blink of an eye, it was gone.

No.

Dammit, no.

This wasn't fair. I wanted to rewind time. I wanted my hour back. I wanted it to last all day and into the next and the next and then more and more and more.

But they stood, they started walking, making their way to the door. I grabbed them both. One more hug. One more moment. Just to feel them in my arms.

I shook as I hugged them, my chest rattling with the wish to keep them close, but then, that was impossible.

Time once more slipped away as they left.

My heart screamed to see them retreat, to watch them fade. I watched till they were gone. And then I watched longer just in case.

But the time was over, and Clara set her hand on my shoulder. "Back to the Ritz, Prince," she said.

She walked me back down the concrete hall, down, down, down.

"They came to see me," I said, and I heard the wonder in my voice.

"They did."

"They're good boys."

"Seems that way."

I stopped and looked at her, the woman who was in charge of my comings and goings. "They are good, Clara. They're good," I said, insistent.

She nodded. "Yeah."

I tapped my chest, a tangle of emotions swirling inside. "What about me? What does that say about me?"

She sighed, tightening her hold on my shoulder. "You're here for murder, Dora. You're here for life."

Life.

She said it heavily, like a stone, and it was. It was the weight of all my choices.

"But they came to see me," I said, clinging to that fact.

Facts mattered.

"Take solace in that. As you seek your redemption, take solace in that."

"Isn't it too late for that?" I asked.

We reached my cell. She met my eyes. Talked to me like I was a person. Not an animal. "I pray every night for you, for all the women here, that you find your redemption behind these bars. That you become a better person in this place. Let your kids help you do that."

My throat squeezed, like hands were gripping it. Tight and cruel.

But true.

It was all too true.

Then she handed me a book. "For the next book club. Keep reading, Prince. Keep going."

I took it, clutched it.
Read it that night.

71

LEE STEFANO

Business was good. Business was damn good today. This was a stellar kind of afternoon.

I'd already netted a cool G and then made sure I had plenty to pay my guys too. They deserved it. TJ and Kenny taught me everything, and I was damn grateful for them. My brothers in arms. My brothers in sin.

As I pocketed the last wad of cash and started packing up, my phone buzzed. I grabbed it, slid my thumb across the screen, and answered. Kenny. He was like the father I didn't know.

"Yo, what's up man?"

He wasted no time, diving right into it. "You better get out of there. Word on the street is that they're onto you."

I tensed, flicking my gaze from left to right on the street corner I was working today. I saw no boys in blue, but Kenny's warning could only mean one thing. "Thanks, brother. It means the world to me that you look out for me."

"Always."

He always had—ever since my dad was tossed into the

joint, we'd looked out for each other. My dad had protected him, swallowed his name and TJ's, kept their secrets locked up tight.

As it should be. *Protect our own.* I patted my ink as I shouldered my bag.

I'd protect mine too.

Take care of my guys. That meant I needed to jet.

I turned around, coming face to face with a guy with dark-blond hair, blue eyes, and a satisfied smile on his face.

My eyes widened, and a wave of fear crashed over me.

He could only be a cop.

"Lee Stefano, it's great to see you. You're under arrest for stalking, harassment, and grand larceny."

I spun, ready to take off, to run like hell, but he had me.

The cop fucking had me.

Then a thrilling realization hit me as he read me my rights. A rush of satisfaction burst inside.

He was going to toss me in jail. And once I was there, I would earn my Sinner stripes. Time behind bars. It would show everyone how tough I was, how strong I was, and that I was just like my father.

He'd done much worse. But still, I was following in the footsteps of the family business.

This would prove to the Sinners that I was one of them.

72

ELLE

My heart still raced furiously. That had been a hell of a game of laser tag. It was made all the better by Colin's news.

I hung up and turned to my son as we walked toward the rental counter to return the laser tag equipment. "My text message stalker was arrested this morning."

Alex punched the air. "Yes! That is awesome."

"The cops got him on grand larceny too. He stole tons of electronics. Laptops, iPhones, tablets."

Alex scoffed. "Androids are way better than iPhones. Better games on them," he said, and I smiled because we were doing this. We were living life.

We were talking and playing and being strong. I'd found the internal resources to deal with the highs and lows of life, without turning off my heart.

"Anyway, he's in jail now. Colin just talked to the detective who's been working on his father's case," I said, before we reached the counter.

Alex stopped in his tracks. "I have a question. You said in the car the other day when you were talking about the messages that Colin was 'working on it.' I was freaked out at the time, but now I'm curious. What did you mean?" he asked, his voice softer now. He hadn't let me explain the other day; he hadn't wanted to listen. He wanted to now.

"He took it upon himself to find out who the guy was. He studied the texts, and he researched a number of possibilities as to who was sending them, and he used every tool at his disposal. Instagram, Facebook, and then good old-fashioned elbow grease. He pulled together clues from things people had said, from pictures he had seen, and when Lee Stefano posted again, Colin was ready, and he was able to track him down and give the information to the police."

Alex whistled in admiration. "That's impressive. That's some serious detective work."

"It is," I said, a burst of pride surging inside me over what Colin had done and for my son's understanding.

"That's pretty cool too," Alex said, like an admission.

I furrowed my brow. "What's cool?"

"That Colin did that for you. That he didn't stop until he'd solved the problem. Dad was never like that. He didn't solve problems. He only caused them."

I looped an arm around him, my heart lighting up. "Colin didn't just do it for me. Or for us. He did it because it was the right thing to do. He's that kind of a guy."

"He is. He's good to me. I'm good to him. He's good to us."

That was the truth, the whole truth, and nothing but the truth of my heart.

73

JOHN

I removed my shades when I spotted the young man waiting at a picnic table in the park. Though it was a Monday morning, the park was quiet, and the picnic tables were far enough away from the playground for a private conversation. Marcus had said he didn't want to meet at his apartment or at the store where he worked, and not anyplace where someone might see him. I'd chosen a park thirty minutes outside of Vegas.

The teen sat on the table itself, head down, tapping away on his phone. When I reached him, I saw he was swiping pages in an e-book app.

"Thanks for meeting me," I said.

"Thanks for meeting me here."

I took a seat next to him on top of the green slatted wood of the table.

"So you arrested Lee Stefano yesterday?"

I nodded. "We found him at one of his regular blocks. Part of his territory for selling stolen goods. Same place that was tagged in the photos," I said. It was almost as if the thief wanted to be taken in. Or, more likely, that he wanted his "Sinner Stripes," as they were called. Stefano's son wanted to be able to say he'd served time, like his dad. Now that I had him in custody, I was hoping Lee would talk. Would tell me more about TJ and Kenny. Where to find them. I wanted nothing more than to see those two men behind bars for the rest of their lives, and Stefano's son could be the linchpin to making that happen. Lee's mother, Bianca, was the one who'd tipped us off in the first place that there might have been others who'd played a part in the murder of Thomas Paige nearly two decades ago.

That was TJ and Kenny's first conspiracy to commit murder.

Didn't seem to have been their last.

My blood boiled over the evidence I'd amassed linking those two men to other crimes, and more unsolved murders. By all accounts, TJ Nelson had embraced his job as the broker of Stefano's hits, working with other gunmen over the years that followed, taking his role as the planner and plotter to a new level. He was the man pulling the strings on hits for the Sinners, and Kenny was his right-hand guy. I was determined to find them, especially since I'd learned that TJ had had words with Thomas Paige several weeks before the man was killed. I was talking to other witnesses later today who knew more about that encounter, and I hoped to hell I'd be able to link all the details together and track down the Nelson cousins.

They were tough to nab. Harder to find. They'd earned some kind of protection from their brothers in the gang. Some of that protection had come in the form of Lee Stefano trying to keep Marcus quiet by intimidating the social worker he'd been confiding in. I wasn't 100 percent sure why those men wanted Marcus's mouth zipped, but I had a few good leads. Marcus was untouchable; they'd never hurt him. But they needed him to keep their secrets quiet, so they'd tried to shut him down.

But I needed Marcus to talk. Because I was damn sure Marcus knew more than he'd told me when we met a week ago. And I was determined too to understand why Marcus was an untouchable.

"Is Lee going to leave Elle alone now?" Marcus asked.

Maybe the threat to someone he cared about would push him into talking finally. "Yes, we've got him. And I think we can get him to give up some info on Kenny and TJ."

"What about my stepmom though? Will they leave Angie alone?"

I arched an eyebrow. This was news to me. "Someone's sending her harassing messages too?"

Marcus nodded, his young eyes etched with worry. "I saw her and my little sisters a few days ago, at Baskin Robbins. I overheard her talking on the phone. I think she's worried that those guys are coming after her."

"To make sure your dad stays quiet about all that he knows about the murder of Thomas Paige?" I asked, hoping Marcus would finally give me an answer.

Ever since I had uncovered the details of Dora Prince's drug trade—that the woman was a dealer, Stefano was her supplier, and she sold to the Nelson cousins and many, many others—I was sure that her ex-lover had intel about the business she'd been in. Luke claimed he met Dora at Narcotics Anonymous, but I wasn't convinced that's how the affair began. Nor did I buy that Luke's hands were clean. Because as I saw it, Dora Prince planned the murder of her husband to get his life insurance money so she could run away with her kids and her lover.

Luke had to know *something* about the murder. Especially given the leads I was chasing down about him.

If someone was trying to shake down Marcus's stepmom now, well, that only bolstered my belief that Luke was involved.

And Marcus might know.

He was here. He was trying. He just needed to feel safe.

"I can protect you," I said calmly. "I can protect her. That's what I do."

Marcus hung his head, exhaled, then lifted his face and met my eyes. He started talking, and holy hell-of-a-secret, this was the mother lode. This was the golden goose of information.

74

COLIN

Rex rappelled down the rock, landing gently on his feet.

He raised his arms in the air. "Just call me Spidey Investor Intern."

"That's your official new name," I said, high-fiving him.

After I showed him the basics, he climbed about ten feet, his first time ever.

"When can we go again?" he asked.

I beamed. "I knew you'd love it."

As we loaded the climbing gear into the trunk of my car, we made plans to go again. Rex had started interning with me, doing basic tasks at the office while he went to community college. He was *dee-lighted,* as he put it, to earn some cash.

And he was damn good and reliable. No surprise there. Looking out for his little brother made him a stand-up guy who showed up for his commitments.

We got in the car to head back to town.

"So, how's your lady? When are you going to ask her to marry you?"

A laugh burst from me. "We just became official and now you want me to get down on one knee?"

"You love her, man, don't you?"

"I do."

"Then what's the holdup?'

"Listen, there's no doubt I want to be with her."

"Aren't you the guy who takes risks all the time?"

I laughed at his persistence, at his big personality. At all his Rex-ness. "I do believe in risks. And here's the thing. When I ask Elle, because I *will* ask her, I want it to be the right time." I checked the time as we slowed at a light. "Right now, I just want to be in her life, and I am. And that makes me happy."

He punched my shoulder. "You're the man. But when you do ask her, you better invite me to the wedding because I want to wear a tux."

"I promise."

I had all the faith in the world that I'd be able to keep that promise, in all its shapes and colors.

For now, though, I dropped off Rex and headed to the skating rink to see my woman.

She was mine. We were together. That was all that mattered.

75

ELLE

I longed to be the one sending Janine racing around the curve. I craved the rush of the wheels, the speed of the chase, the vibrations of the music in my bones. Instead, I cupped my hands around my mouth and shouted my encouragement from the half-wall at the edge of the rink.

"*C'mon!*"

"*Block her!*"

"*Go, Cool Hand Bette!*"

I screamed and cheered the loudest from the sidelines, rooting on the Fishnet Brigade. The league championship was underway, and victory was in our grasp. Just a few more points. Just a few more minutes.

"Bet you twenty bucks they win, even without their best player."

That voice. It sent goosebumps over my skin. It lit up my chest. It warmed my soul.

I turned around. My heart skipped, and my skin sizzled. And I beamed as I patted the seat next to mine. "Join me," I said.

"Don't mind if I do."

He sat next to me, dropped a kiss to my cheek, and took my hand. Everything felt so right. So true. The two of us together, in the open, living life.

"I bet they win too," I said, and my heart beat fiercely against my ribs just from being near him.

"You know," he said, taking his time with the words as he inched closer, "if they do, we should celebrate."

Celebrate.

That's what we said the night we almost kissed at The Venetian. That night had been our start. It had sent us hurtling down this twisting, turning path to deeper friendship, to lust, to love.

"We should. But no almost kisses this time," I said playfully as I slid an arm around his waist. "Because I'm ready for everything."

He leaned in, dipped his face to mine, and pressed a kiss to my lips.

A few seconds later, someone groaned. "Am I going to have to see that all the time?"

I snapped open my eyes to see Alex. "Um. Not all the time?"

He waved a hand. "Don't worry. I've battled zombies. I can handle this. But maybe some more money for games, please."

I smiled, happy to give him that, happy he was doing just fine.

After I handed Alex the money, Colin and I watched the rest of the match together, cheering loudest when my team won.

Then he dipped his hand into the pocket of his shorts. "A gift for you." He dangled a long pair of socks in front of me. They were red with Vs of illustrated birds on them.

"They're perfect," I said, and grabbed them. "Where did you get them?"

"My soon-to-be sister-in-law knows how to find *anything* on the Strip. And she found a store for me that sells all kinds of socks."

I clutched them to my chest. "I love socks, and I love you."

He quirked up his lips. "And I love you in your sexy socks."

As I looked around, I saw I had everything in one place. I wasn't two Elles. I wasn't separating my heart from my head. I was living my whole life—a woman, a social worker, a sister, a daughter, a lover, a mother.

A person, whole and happy and completely fulfilled.

76

COLIN

The disco lights swirled in crazy-eight circles, and Elle raced in a circle around the rink, sexy as always, wearing her tight T-shirt, short skirt, and red socks. Bon Jovi blasted out of the sound system.

"Catch me if you can."

There was no way I was backing down from that challenge. I pushed harder and faster on my wheels, and soon enough I caught up with her, grabbing her waist and pulling her to the side of the rink.

Breathless, she laughed in my arms as "You Give Love a Bad Name" echoed around us.

"Hey, you're not even supposed to be skating for another week," I admonished her.

"No," she said, correcting me as she shook her head. "The doctor said *no contact sports*. Skating itself is fine."

"*Contact sports*," I said. "We've violated that doctor's order already."

She laughed. We had the rink to ourselves. Alex had gone home with Camille, and Camille had given Elle the key, so we were all alone, the game over and everyone cleared out.

After a few more circles, we slowed to a stop at the side, and I brought her close. I threaded my fingers through her hair and kissed her—a hot, wet kiss that had her shuddering in my arm. She moaned as I deepened the kiss until our mouths tangled together and became nothing but a fevered, hungry prelude to hard sex.

She looped her arms around my neck, pulling back to look at me with love in her eyes. "I always hoped," she whispered.

"Always hoped what?"

"That we'd find a way," she said, and exhilaration tore through me. It sped through my body in a mad rush of longing. Longing that had been fulfilled with her. I wanted to be her home.

"I'll always find my way to you."

She was the only kind of intoxication I wanted anymore. I planned to stay hooked on her for all time.

She was the risk. She was the reward.

The next morning, we went kayaking again. In a tandem boat. We paddled around the lake, enjoying the clear blue sky of an early morning on the outskirts of Vegas.

When we were done, she thanked me again for taking her, then ran a hand over my hip, tracing the outline of my phoenix tattoo. "For new beginnings," she said. "And I had an idea about new beginnings. I was going to ask if you'd be interested in starting a climbing or kayaking group for the boys at the center. They never get to go, and I bet some would like to."

"I would love to," I said, and that felt fitting too as our lives intertwined even more.

77

KENNY

Boom.

I was on fucking fire.

I slammed my ride into reverse and gunned the gas. I cranked up the tunes, blasting my victory music. I smacked my palm against my guy's as we took off from the scene of the crime. We'd pulled off another one. And it energized me, lit me up from head to toe.

Like fireworks.

This time it was robbery, and we had fat wads of cash to show what we'd pulled off.

I dropped off my partner in crime, slammed a palm against the dashboard, and then did my favorite thing in the world—snorted a line.

Right off the dashboard as the music blared, thrumming through my body. And now I was amped up.

As I headed toward the Strip, I dialed TJ's number, giving him the report on what we'd pulled off tonight. A simple robbery, but nothing was simple about the dough. TJ knew who to target. He knew who brought in bank, and when he sent me on a job, they were big ones. I'd earned it, and after a few weeks of lying low, getting out of town, I was back and better than ever.

"It is good to be back in town. Good to be on the motherfucking job again," I said. "You're the man. The best goddamn getaway driver there is," he said.

I thumped my chest. "You know it. For eighteen years. No one is better. No one in the whole damn world."

He laughed. "Eighteen spotless years, cuz. Now don't fuck it up."

I scoffed. "How would I fuck it up? We're invincible."

That's exactly what I was, and tonight was my kind of night. What better time to hit the tables? I headed to the Wynn, tossed my keys to the valet, and strutted inside, knowing I would be taking the house tonight. Bet it all on me. I was gold. I had the Midas touch. I'd pulled off so many jobs as the getaway driver.

Ever since my first one eighteen years ago.

And I've gotten away with that. TJ and me—we were motherfucking scot-free.

No one could touch us.

Inside the casino, I scanned the tables, jazzed up.

I hadn't been at this hotel in a couple of years. I hadn't been in town in a few months. We usually did jobs out of town, and this was my first day back. Perfect night to celebrate with some blackjack. I peeled off some of the dough that was mine, exchanged it for chips, and parked myself on a stool.

"I'm here to clean up," I declared.

The dealer barely cracked a smile.

That was cool. I didn't need him on my side. I didn't need anyone. I was Kenny Nelson, the invincible Royal Sinner.

The king of scot-free living.

Oh yeah.

This was all I needed.

I played a few hands, winning big.

I did a dance in my chair, holding up my drink. "Oh yeah, bring it on. I'm gonna beat the house tonight."

The next round, I had a perfect winning combination, when I felt a hand on my shoulder.

78

JOHN

When Mindy's call came, I was ready. Because I'd been ready. We'd been poised for this opportunity since the case reopened. Since we'd gotten the first tip from Jerry Stefano's one-time girlfriend. It was all a matter of amassing the evidence, finding the accomplices, and then making the arrests.

Kenny and TJ had been out of town, but we'd heard they were back.

And now, holy hell, he was here. Fortunately, I was as close as anyone else because I was in the Wynn, where Sophie had corralled me into a shopping trip, a tux fitting for her pending nuptials. I glanced in the mirror while checking out my reflection, when my phone rang.

"Kenny Nelson is here. Playing blackjack," Mindy said, then added that her security cameras had spotted him thanks to facial recognition.

God bless technology.

"I'll be right there."

I hung up, and Sophie's eyes widened. "I don't know

what it is, but whatever it is, I can tell you need to go right now."

And I did.

I took off, heading in the direction of the blackjack table still in my tux, knowing that my sister would sort out the tux issue with the store. I weaved through the casino, focused, purposeful.

Heading straight to the table Mindy mentioned. My partner would be here soon for backup, but as Kenny came into my line of sight, an astonishing sense of calm pervaded me. Everything in me was patient, focused. That was how it was in these moments. I never panicked, I never freaked out. It was as if my body was designed to go calm, to go steady at times like this.

When I saw him at the table, my jaw clenched briefly as I thought of all he had done.

All he had hurt.

All he had killed, in his own way.

And here he was, showboating over winning in blackjack.

Somehow that felt like an affront to everything I loved about this city. But there's a saying about winning.

I was five feet behind him, four, three, two, one.

Calm. I was solid and calm and so damn pleased when I dropped my hand on his shoulder.

Kenny turned around, eyes bugged out.

"Win some, lose some. Kenny Nelson, you're under arrest."

EPILOGUE

Colin

Hot. Sweaty. Exhausted. Aching.

And elated.

Add in thrilled, as the finish line came into view one hot Saturday afternoon at the end of August and I saw where Elle waved and cheered me on from the sidelines of the Badass Triathlon. I was overjoyed as I put one foot in front of the other, ceaselessly running until I nearly collapsed in her arms.

Nearly. But didn't.

I finished this one the way I wanted to, and even though every muscle screamed and my throat cried out for water, I was flying high. So high, I lifted her up in my arms. She wrapped her legs around my waist and kissed me.

"You did it!"

"I did it."

There was no medal. There was no prize. There was no

ranking. There was only this—the satisfaction of a job well done and the love of a good woman.

That was everything, and I wanted to share it with my family the next day. The crew joined me for a celebratory dinner at my house—Brent and Shannon, Ryan and Sophie, Elle and Alex, Michael and our grandparents, as well as Marcus, Rex, and Tyler. Those boys seemed to travel in a pack, and I was glad my younger brother had such good friends—friends who were also good guys.

Marcus had more than that. He had his new family too, and he'd been spending more time here at my house, crashing from time to time at night when he had class the next morning, since his school was nearby and had started a week ago. But he hadn't seemed liked himself lately. Not since we'd visited our mom in Hawthorne a couple of weeks ago. He'd seemed remote, nervous even, spending more time clutching his phone as if he was waiting for a dreaded call to arrive.

I had asked a few times about his mood, and if he wanted to talk. Marcus always shook his head and said no. I tried again that evening after everyone left and the two of us were straightening up in the kitchen.

"What's going on? College harder than you thought?"

"No. It's fine," Marcus said as he loaded a plate in the dishwasher.

"Is it work?"

His phone rang. With the speed of a cheetah, Marcus whipped his cell from his back pocket. He glanced at the screen and answered immediately. I didn't even see the name or the number.

"Hey."

A pause. I tried to tune in to the conversation, though I knew I shouldn't. Still, I was damn curious, especially since the caller sounded a hell of a lot like Detective John Winston.

"Holy shit. That's amazing," Marcus said, and the sullenness vanished. It was replaced by something that looked and sounded like jubilation. Marcus ran a hand through his hair and exhaled like he'd been holding a thousand breaths. "Tonight? You arrested him tonight?"

I straightened, set down the dishtowel, and mouthed, *Who?* Anticipation barreled through me as I zeroed in on Marcus.

"Yes. I can talk. I'm at Colin's house." Marcus covered the phone and said, "Can John come over?"

"Um. Yeah. Obviously," I said, then made a rolling gesture with my hands. *Hurry up and tell me.*

When Marcus hung up, I parked my hands on my hips. "What's going on? Who was arrested?"

"Kenny Nelson."

I punched the air. "Yes. Fuck yes!"

"The cops have him in custody now," Marcus added, and he'd become the very embodiment of relief. Then his expression shifted once more. "But it's not over. TJ Nelson is still at large."

"They'll find him too," I said as excitement consumed me. This was huge. This was a big break, and I couldn't wait to tell my brothers and sister and grandparents . . .

Wait.

"Why did John call you? Why is he coming over here?" I asked, curiosity taking over. Something didn't add up. Some piece was missing.

EPILOGUE

Marcus

All my practice in courage had led me to this.

To say the hard things.

Do the hard things.

And it was finally time to tell my . . . my brother.

I loved that word. *Brother.* Loved what it meant. Loved what it had given me.

Trust. Hope. Most of all, faith in myself.

I raised my chin and pulled the string on the ball of yarn that would unravel my biggest secret. "I've been helping the detective for a few weeks now. Helping him with the case."

Colin was poised like a leopard. "How?"

Tension radiated across my body as I gave voice to the depths of it. "My father."

Colin's jaw ticked in question. "What about him?"

I unraveled the next thread. "He was involved."

Colin never broke his gaze, staring intently at me, desperation in his tone. "How? How was he involved?"

I swallowed, and words rained forth. All the terrible truths I'd started to suspect over the last year. Things I didn't want to be true. But in the last few weeks, I put all those details together. Added them up. Figured them out.

And now all the awful secrets I'd learned tumbled forth. "There are things I know about my dad. He *is* a piano teacher. But he's much more. So are the Royal Sinners. They're a street gang, but they're powerful. They have friends in high places. And my dad is one of them. He's so far inside that hardly anyone knows who he really is, or that he's starting to lose control of some of his men. Like Kenny and TJ."

Colin blinked, then asked in a rough voice, "Your dad works with those guys?"

I squared my shoulders, drew a deep breath, and answered with the cold, bitter truth about my family.

"He doesn't just work with them. They answer to him. My father is the head of the Royal Sinners."

THE END

Ready for the stunning conclusion of the SINFUL MEN series? All secrets will be revealed in MY SINFUL LOVE, available fore FREE IN KU!

BE A LOVELY

Want to be the first to know of sales, new releases, special deals and giveaways? Sign up for my newsletter today!

Want to be part of a fun, feel-good place to talk about books and romance, and get sneak peeks of covers and advance copies of my books? Be a Lovely!

I've written more than 100 books! **All of these titles below are FREE in Kindle Unlimited!**

The Love and Hockey Series

The Boyfriend Goal

A roommates-to-lovers, teammate's little sister hockey romance!

The Romance Line

An enemies-to-lovers, player and the publicist, forbidden romance!

The Proposal Play

A brother's best friend/marriage of convenience romance!

The Girlfriend Zone

A coach's daughter romance!

The Overtime Kiss!

A single dad/nanny romance!

The Flirting Game!

A neighbors to lovers, fake dating romance!

Hockey Ever After

Just Breaking the Rules!

A brother's best friend/workplace/one who got away romance!

Just Playing for Keeps!

A grumpy sunshine, fake dating romance!

Holiday Romances

Merry Little Kissmas

Fake dating my brother's best friend at Christmas!

<u>My Favorite Holidate</u>

Fake dating the billionaire boss at Christmas!

Darling Springs

It Seemed Like a Good Idea!

An only one-bed-in-the-room, forbidden, small town bodyguard romance!

I've Got a Crush On You!

A grumpy sunshine, workplace romance where the boss has a secret identity!

The My Hockey Romance Series

Hockey, spice, shenanigans and cute dogs in this series of standalones! Because when you get screwed over, make it a double or even a triple!

Karma is two hockey boyfriends and sometimes three!

Double Pucked

A sexy, outrageous MFM hockey romantic comedy!

Puck Yes

A fake marriage, spicy MFM hockey rom com!

Thoroughly Pucked!

A brother's best friends +runaway bride, spicy MFM hockey rom com!

Well and Truly Pucked

A friends-to-lovers forced proximity why-choose hockey rom com!

The Virgin Society Series

Meet the Virgin Society – great friends who'd do anything for each other. Indulge in these forbidden, emotionally-charged, and wildly sexy age-gap romances!

The RSVP

The Tryst

The Tease

The Dating Games Series

A fun, sexy romantic comedy series about friends in the city and their dating mishaps!

The Virgin Next Door

Two A Day

The Good Guy Challenge

How To Date Series (New and ongoing)

Friends who are like family. Chances to learn how to date again. Standalone romantic comedies full of love, sex and meet-cute shenanigans.

My So-Called Love Life

Plays Well With Others

The Almost Romantic

The Accidental Dating Experiment

A romantic comedy adventure standalone

A Real Good Bad Thing

Boyfriend Material

Four fabulous heroines. Four outrageous proposals. Four chances at love in this sexy rom-com series!

Asking For a Friend

Sex and Other Shiny Objects

One Night Stand-In

Overnight Service

Big Rock Series

My #1 New York Times Bestselling sexy as sin, irreverent, male-POV romantic comedy!

Big Rock

Mister O

Well Hung

Full Package

Joy Ride

Hard Wood

Happy Endings Series

Romance starts with a bang in this series of standalones following a group of friends seeking and avoiding love!

Come Again

Shut Up and Kiss Me

Kismet

My Single-Versary

Ballers And Babes

Sexy sports romance standalones guaranteed to make you hot!

Most Valuable Playboy

Most Likely to Score

A Wild Card Kiss

Rules of Love Series

Athlete, virgins and weddings!

The Virgin Rule Book

The Virgin Game Plan

The Virgin Replay

The Virgin Scorecard

The Extravagant Series

Bodyguards, billionaires and hoteliers in this sexy, high-stakes
series of standalones!

One Night Only

One Exquisite Touch

My One-Week Husband

The Guys Who Got Away Series

Friends in New York City and California fall in love in this fun
and hot rom-com series!

Birthday Suit

Dear Sexy Ex-Boyfriend

The What If Guy

Thanks for Last Night

The Dream Guy Next Door

Always Satisfied Series

A group of friends in New York City find love and laughter in
this series of sexy standalones!

Satisfaction Guaranteed

Never Have I Ever

Instant Gratification

PS It's Always Been You

The Gift Series

An after dark series of standalones! Explore your fantasies!

The Engagement Gift

The Virgin Gift

The Decadent Gift

The Heartbreakers Series

Three brothers. Three rockers. Three standalone sexy romantic comedies.

Once Upon a Real Good Time

Once Upon a Sure Thing

Once Upon a Wild Fling

Sinful Men

A high-stakes, high-octane, sexy-as-sin romantic suspense series!

My Sinful Nights

My Sinful Desire

My Sinful Longing

My Sinful Love

My Sinful Temptation

From Paris With Love

Swoony, sweeping romances set in Paris!

Wanderlust

Part-Time Lover

One Love Series

A group of friends in New York falls in love one by one in this sexy rom-com series!

The Sexy One

The Hot One

The Knocked Up Plan

Come As You Are

Lucky In Love Series

A small town romance full of heat and blue collar heroes and sexy heroines!

Best Laid Plans

The Feel Good Factor

Nobody Does It Better

Unzipped

No Regrets

An angsty, sexy, emotional, new adult trilogy about one young couple fighting to break free of their pasts!

The Start of Us

The Thrill of It

Every Second With You

The Caught Up in Love Series

A group of friends finds love!

The Pretending Plot

The Dating Proposal

The Second Chance Plan

The Private Rehearsal

Seductive Nights Series

A high heat series full of danger and spice!

Night After Night

After This Night

One More Night

A Wildly Seductive Night

Joy Delivered Duet

A high-heat, wickedly sexy series of standalones that will set your sheets on fire!

Nights With Him

Forbidden Nights

Unbreak My Heart

A standalone second chance emotional roller coaster of a
romance

The Muse

A magical realism romance set in Paris

**Good Love Series of sexy rom-coms co-written with Lili
Valente!**

I also write MM romance under the name L. Blakely!

Hopelessly Bromantic Duet (MM)

Roomies to lovers to enemies to fake boyfriends

Hopelessly Bromantic

Here Comes My Man

Men of Summer Series (MM)

Two baseball players on the same team fall in love in a forbidden
romance spanning five epic years

Scoring With Him

Winning With Him

All In With Him

MM Standalone Novels

A Guy Walks Into My Bar

The Bromance Zone

One Time Only

The Best Men (Co-written with Sarina Bowen)

Winner Takes All Series (MM)

A series of emotionally-charged and irresistibly sexy standalone MM sports romances!

The Boyfriend Comeback

Turn Me On

A Very Filthy Game

Limited Edition Husband

Manhandled

If you want a personalized recommendation, email me at laurenblakelybooks@gmail.com!

CONTACT

I love hearing from readers! You can find me on Twitter at LaurenBlakely3, Instagram at LaurenBlakelyBooks, Facebook at LaurenBlakelyBooks, or online at LaurenBlakely.com. You can also email me at laurenblakelybooks@gmail.com